# The Case Files of Crimestopper

# JACK EDDY

*From the Notes of Police Reporter*
## BRAM GEARY

## Volume 2

By Dick Stodghill

JLT-CHARATAN PUBLICATIONS

ISBN: 978-0-6151-9687-9
JLT-CHARATAN PUBLICATIONS

For Jackie – my companion, my helpmate, my wife

All stories in this collection were originally published in the following issues of **Alfred Hitchcock Mystery Magazine:**

A Policy For Murder  (June 1994)
Death On the Devil Strip  (November 1994)
Nightmare On North Hill  (March 1997)
The Phantom Of Johnnycake Lock  (December 1997)
Mayhem On Market Street  (March 2002)
Switchback  (November 2002)
The Survivor Of the Storms  (October 2007)
Panic On Portage Path  (January/February 2008)

# CONTENTS

# MRS. BAUER'S BOARDINGHOUSE
## 38 DUDLEY STREET

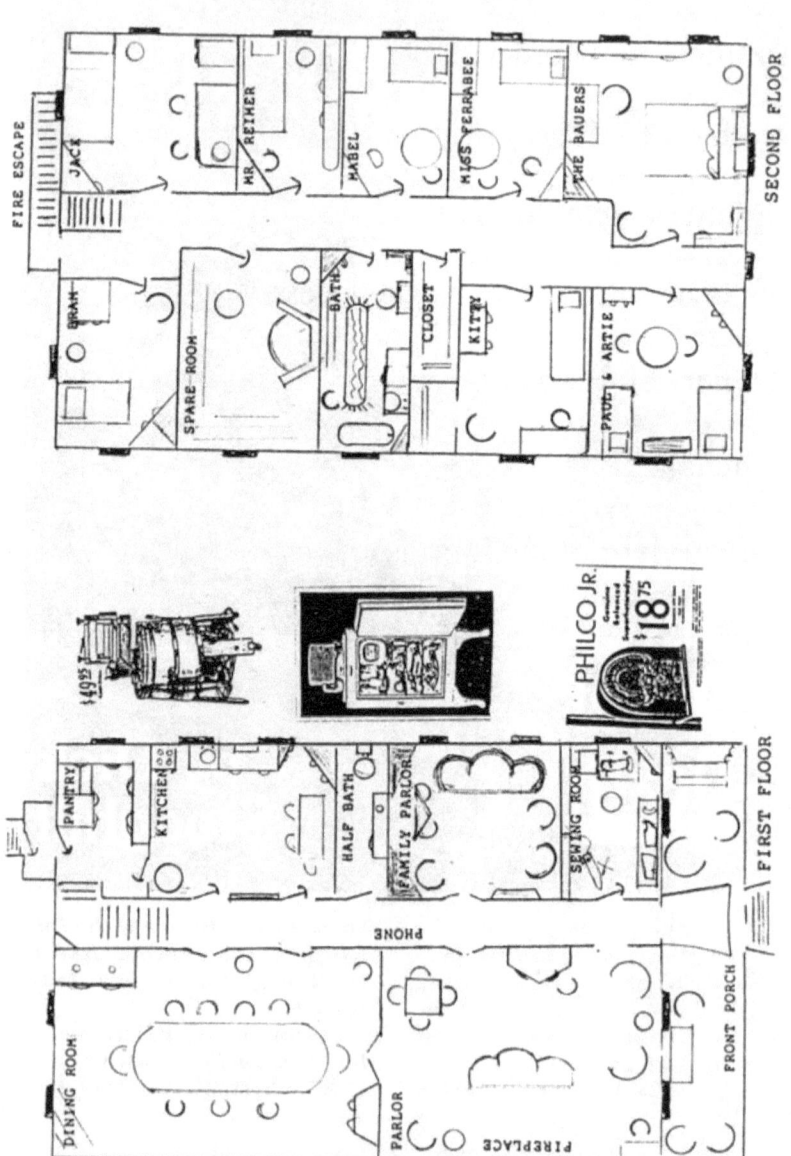

# INTRODUCTION

Like the eight stories in Volume 1, these are set in Akron, Ohio in the late 1930s. They continue with Jack's adventures, Bram's sometimes troubled career and his on and off romance with Sue Baney.

As is true of many fictional characters, Jack Eddy came to life as a composite of several people. The first was another make-believe person named Jack Ford, the central figure of a 23-part BBC series entitled "When the Boat Comes In." A recently discharged British soldier of the First World War, he was tough, brash and ambitious, a man driven to succeed. He was handicapped, however, by three other characteristics: compassion, honor and loyalty. People lacking those latter traits provide the competition in the upward struggle and therefore have the advantage over the Jack Fords.

As an investigator for Pinkerton's National Detective Agency I worked with a man who was a real-life Sam Spade. Reckless and daring, he was a true adventurer who could think on his feet and change personalities in the blink of an eye better than anyone I have known. A little of him crept into the makeup of Jack Eddy.

The third person that influenced the protagonist taking shape in my mind was Eddie Wolfe, my platoon sergeant for much of the time I was in combat with the 4th Infantry Division during World War II. Along with being compassionate, loyal and honorable, he was the bravest man I have encountered. He frequently placed himself in jeopardy so that someone else was not. When men of higher rank were floundering, he took charge and no one seemed to resent it. He was a great man.

When it was time to choose a name for the protagonist of this series, both Jack Ford and Eddie Wolfe came to mind. So there it was: Jack Eddy.

Bram Geary, the police reporter who wrote of Jack Eddy's adventures, began as just another narrator, then gradually took on a personality and characteristics of his own.

9

Several of the stories are rooted in actual events, but with much different outcomes.   A few are loosely based on experiences I had with Pinkerton's.   Others started with nothing more than a title or a beginning in mind and then went wherever Jack and Bram decided to take them.

The Akron streets traveled by Jack Eddy and his sidekick have changed in many ways, not at all in others.   The big Wingfoot sign still towers above the Goodyear complex on Market Street but Plant One is gone and little remains of the once-thriving East Akron business district.   Ptomaine Tommie's vanished long ago, as did the Lenox Café, but you still can eat a fine meal at the New Era.

The house at 38 Dudley Street where I lived as a boy was big, but not as big as Mrs. Bauer's boardinghouse.   Now only a vacant lot remains.   Neither Jack nor Bram would recognize downtown Akron, although Bram's old *Times-Press* workplace has become the home of the *Beacon Journal* while the Metropolitan Building, Jack Eddy's hangout, survives under a different name.

The atmosphere and attitudes of the late years of the Great Depression are portrayed as I remember them. Aside from Jack's adventures, the news stories mentioned actually took place. For the majority of Americans life was far better than it had been during the bitter years of 1930 through 1932.   The election of Franklin D. Roosevelt brought hope and a belief that conditions would improve. They did, but gradually.   Even so, Communist Party headquarters was located at the main intersection in downtown Akron.   When men grow desperate and their families are hungry they will listen to any words that offer the possibility of putting food on the table. – DS

# A POLICY FOR MURDER

After a busy morning on the police beat and a greasy sandwich at the Buckeye Lunch, I was watching the passing parade on Main Street when a dandy straight from the pages of *Esquire* came sauntering by. His gray borsalino was set at a rakish tilt, the shine on his Florsheim wing-tips dazzled the eyes. A red carnation graced the lapel of his blue serge suit, and his neatly trimmed mustache would have looked at home on the upper lip of actor William Powell.

A dude of the first order, a type rarely encountered in the stout and hardy Industrial Valley. With studied casualness he flipped his cigarette toward the curb and turned in at the Mayflower, Akron's finest hotel.

Sartorially speaking, the man was everything I was not. Sometime soon I would have to visit a shoe shine stand, then have my pants pressed. In truth they were more in need of cleaning than a hot iron, thanks to the snow and slush of an uncommonly cold December. Now with the temperature up to forty it seemed spring-like until the jingling of a Salvation Army bell in front of Polsky's department store served as a reminder that winter was in its infancy.

I forgot the weather and the dapper stranger when Jack Eddy came bounding across State Street against the light. After sidestepping one car and deftly dodging another, he gave a one-finger salute to the driver of a boxy relic from the 1920s when its horn blared "guh-doo-gah."

As he hurried past I called, "Hey, fella, gotta match?"

He didn't break stride or even glance my way. I swung into step beside him and said, "Where's the fire?"

"Robbery at a jewelry store, buddy. Just came over the teletype from the JPA."

Jack Eddy, an assistant manager at the Akron branch of Wellington's National Detective Agency that winter of 1937-

38, had told me months earlier that the agency was on contract with the Jewelers Protective Association to investigate all jewel robberies in the country. Even the G-men consulted Wellington's extensive files on jewel thieves.

"You're late," I said. "The cops beat you by a few hours." I mimicked the downtown newsboys: "R-e-e-ad all about it in the *Times-Press*." Then normally again: "My story's in the first edition."

"No need to read about it, friend. "The JPA report was all I needed to know it's another Anderson Spangler job."

"Anderson Spangler? Sounds like a stock broker or vice president at Firestone, not an outlaw."

"Don't let the monicker fool you, buddy. Spangler's the sharpest case man in the country. He knows a good stone from a bad one, but that's only the half of it. What sets him apart is the ability to judge distance down to the fraction of an inch. When it comes to working through an alarm system network, nobody can touch him." He took a photo from a jacket pocket and handed it to me. "That's the bugger."

I glanced at the picture, then pulled up short. "Hold on, Jack, you're headed the wrong way. I saw this guy go into the Mayflower not five minutes ago."

"Not a chance, sport. Spangler never shows his face within a hundred miles of a job once it's set up. And always has a few unimpeachable witnesses to back up his alibi."

"Don't tell *me,* Jack. That's the guy as sure as you're born."

He saw I was serious. For a long moment he stood tugging on an ear, then started back toward the hotel. "Won't hurt to check, I guess, but I still say you're whistling Dixie."

Jack Eddy came to a halt just inside the door. Anderson Spangler was seated in a lobby armchair reading an early edition of the *Beacon Journal*, the other paper in town. After pushing his work-a-day black fedora far back on his head Jack murmured, "If I wasn't seeing it with my own eyes, I wouldn't believe it." He gave me a light poke on the arm. "I owe you one, buddy."

Jack straightened his hat and adjusted his necktie before walking over to where the out-of-town dandy was seated.

Sensing his presence, Spangler glanced up from his paper, did a double take, then sprang up from the overstuffed chair, right hand extended, a big smile on his face. "Jack Eddy! What brings you to this burg, my friend?"

"I've been here since last spring, Andy, and I'll bet you've known that all along."

A pained expression came over Spangler's face. "Now, Jack, you know I don't like being called Andy. Are you saying you're not in Indianapolis anymore? But you're still with Wellington's, of course?"

"Come off it, Andy. You know I wouldn't leave the agency, and you probably knew I was being transferred before I got the word myself."

"Jack, Jack, Jack. You give me far too much credit, but then you always have."

"The man isn't alive who could give you too much credit, pal. But what's with you these days, staying in town while a job's being pulled?"

"A job? You've lost me, Jack."

Their thrust-and-parry word game continued a while before Jack got around to introducing me to Spangler. We sized each other up while shaking hands. There was something in his pale gray eyes that told me he wasn't just another man with the taste and money for fancy clothes. Smooth as silk on the outside, hard as nails underneath. Again William Powell came to mind, this time playing the role of Nick Charles in *The Thin Man*.

I tagged along when Jack Eddy set out again for the jewelry store. When Jack flashed Spangler's photo the employees recognized him immediately. He had been in several times and a few days earlier had purchased an expensive diamond stickpin.

The thieves had bypassed one display case completely, taken only a few items from another, several more from a third. It was no smash-and-grab job.

With the help of an alarm system schematic given him by the manager, Jack showed me things I had missed on my earlier visit. He pointed out how carefully the holes had been cut in the glass of each showcase, coming close to and yet missing the all-but-invisible wires that would have triggered an alarm. And how in getting to the cases the thieves had worked their way through a maze of wiring concealed under a blue carpet that had since been rolled back.

Even more impressive was the hole bored in the wall from the store next door. The thieves had entered a rear door of the adjacent room, first disabling a simple alarm. Once inside they had gone to work on the wall that to me appeared much like any other. In reality it was laced with wires that looked a lot like strips of narrow electrical tape. The hole, about twenty inches square, was in the one wire-free place at a convenient height for squeezing through. Anywhere else, or by miscalculating an inch in any direction, and a squad of policemen would have awaited them in the jewelry store. One thing was obvious: all fat men could be crossed off the list of suspects.

"Does Spangler have X-ray eyes or what?" I asked. "How could he do it?"

"Maybe with a copy of this," said Jack, drumming a finger on the schematic. "Maybe not. I don't know how the guy works but I'd give my right arm to learn his secret."

I went back to the showcases. "It gets me how little they took. Once you're inside a place, why not just load up with all you can carry away?"

"Because Spangler doesn't do business with any ten-cents-on-the-dollar fence. If that were the case, buddy, we'd have nailed him and his boys long ago. He's interested only in the best stones, ones that can be re-cut or reset without being identifiable. He'd ignore the Hope diamond unless he was certain it could be reworked in a way that no one would be the wiser."

"No more than they took, is it worth all the trouble?"

Jack gave a terse laugh. "Believe me, friend, it is. But it takes a certain type of man, not your everyday thief. Fortunately Spangler is the only one of them around right now. And you can bet he was choosy in picking his crewmen and didn't leave anything to chance in training them."

"If Spangler's as good as you say, how did you find out he even exists?"

"He made a mistake on his first job a dozen years ago in Indianapolis. He was sixteen at the time."

"Kind of young for a master criminal, isn't it?"

"Spangler was born with more know-how than most thieves acquire in a lifetime. He had it all figured out by his junior year at Shortridge High."

"So what was that one mistake?"

"Took more than he should have, then went to a ten-cents-on-the-dollar fence. Live and learn, buddy."

After supper at the boardinghouse on Dudley Street that was home to both of us, Jack Eddy crossed the hall from his room and rapped on the door of mine. He shook his head when I said, "Getting anywhere on the jewel robbery?"

I was spiffing up for a date with Sue Baney. Jack sat on the edge of the bed and watched as I knotted my necktie. The tail was too long so I had to undo it and start over. Jack laughed when a third attempt proved necessary. He said, "I can't figure it out, friend."

"I've been trying to use the crease from the last time as a guide but it won't come out right."

"I'm not talking about that remnant from a horse blanket you call a necktie. Anderson Spangler, I can't figure why he stayed in town while his crew pulled the heist. By the way, at the time he was in an all-night poker game at the Portage Hotel with a real estate broker, a city councilman, and a big shot at General Tire. His hanging around doesn't add up unless he picked a store in Akron just to get my goat."

"That would be a sap's play, Jack. You're flattering yourself thinking it's a personal thing between the two of you. In a risky situation there's only thing that would make a man step out of character and that's a woman."

He was shaking his head. "What makes this different is I've been on Spangler's tail for years."

"And he always stuck to his routine. Why change now?"

Lost in thought, Jack didn't reply. When I was ready to leave he got up, grinning, and gave me a one-knuckle punch on the arm, the kind that stings like a shot from a dull needle. "Maybe I'm slipping, buddy. I've got an operative on him at the Mayflower, so we should know before long if you're right about it being a dame. If you are, lunch is on me tomorrow."

I was so confident I could already taste the spaghetti at the Walsh Brothers' place downtown.


It had been a great evening until we stopped for sodas at Kesselring's far out on Triplett Boulevard near the airport. When we went outside again, my '32 Chevy wouldn't start. There was nothing to do but call a cab, drop Sue Baney at her apartment and continue home.

While paying the cabbie I saw Jack Eddy peering out the oval window of the front door. "Now what?" he said, smirking. "Don't tell me, let me guess. Your clunker gasped its last breath and you were somewhere on the outskirts of town at the time, right?"

"And you find that amusing, do you?"

"Buddy, I've been telling you for months to junk that rust bucket. Now maybe you'll listen."

He led the way to the parlor where at first glance pudgy Mabel Klosterman, the only one who hadn't gone up to bed, appeared to be reading *The Ladies' Home Journal*. Behind it I saw she was holding Jack Woodford's latest sexy novel. The excitement of it was making her squirm around on her chair.

Jack handed me the back section of the *Times-Press*, then turned to the used car ads in the *Beacon Journal*. I didn't find much of interest but looked up when he began chuckling. "Here's one for you. A 1931 Essex, thirty-nine bucks."

"Very funny. Not much available in my price range."

"In your price range you should be looking under bicycles."

"You're a riot tonight, Jack. A real riot." After scanning a few more ads I tossed the paper aside. "Did you hear from the man keeping an eye on Spangler?"

"Yeah, and for once you were on the beam. He went stepping out with a broad, a cute piece of fluff according to the op. They were back at the hotel dancing when I hung up the phone about the time your cab pulled up front."

The telephone was in the hallway near the front door, which explained why he was standing there as if he were the housemother awaiting my arrival. Oh well, I told myself, the evening wasn't a complete washout. I might not have transportation in the morning, but I'd have spaghetti for lunch.


A wrecker had towed my car to City Chevrolet, a large dealership on Market Street a few blocks east of downtown. After work I braved a biting west wind and walked there to see how things stood. A mechanic had already given it a quick look so I said, "Whaddya think, can it be fixed?"

He gave me a baleful stare. "Anything can be fixed, ace, but if this was a horse I'd shoot it."

The estimate was eighteen dollars to get the weary old buggy running again. For seventy-five they could put it in halfway decent shape, but no promises would come with the job.

I went outside and wandered around among the used cars, ducking behind one whenever a salesman came into view. A 1936 Ford Tudor looked good but was a little steep at three fifty-nine. I admired a nifty '35 Terraplane priced at two seventy-nine, then stopped for a while at a ,32 deluxe coach much like my own car. Instead of being gray with the paint worn down to the primer, this one was a sparkling ebony black. At a hundred seventy-nine dollars the price seemed right.

Uncertain about what to do, I walked back to Main Street, hoping to bum a ride home with Jack Eddy. What little was left of the afternoon was ominously dark even for December. Headlights were coming on, lights from store windows cast oblong patterns on the sidewalk. Snow began falling before I reached the shelter of the Metropolitan Building.

While Jack wound up his day reading reports filed by Wellington operatives, I relaxed in a corner of his private office. We both looked up when the woman who doubled as receptionist and secretary cleared her throat at the doorway. "A Mr. Anderson Spangler is here to see you, Mr. Eddy."

I laid aside the Wellington magazine, a house organ printed on slick paper and distributed to the thirty-three agency offices around the country. A soldier on horseback adorned the cover. Above him in old-English type was a motto: WELLINGTON'S – WHERE WRONG-DOING MEETS ITS WATERLOO. Despite that affront to the senses, the stories inside were interesting. The latest issue contained a piece I had done on a Jack Eddy caper along with the usual fare on modern crime-fighting techniques, accounts of recent events, and adventure tales of Wellington agents pursuing Black Bart, the James Gang, and other desperadoes in the Old West.

"Think he's come to confess?" I said jokingly.

"Sure, buddy. And that was a pig that just flew past the window."

Spangler walked briskly into the room, hat in hand like one businessman calling on another. Same business, different approach. Jack motioned him to a chair. "What's on your mind, Andy?"

Spangler winced but allowed Jack's deliberate use of the nickname to pass without comment. After a period of silently eyeing each other Jack said, "Rather talk in private?"

With a laconic smile Spangler looked toward my corner of the room. "Not unless your friend writes up the stories he hears in your office." I stole a glance at the magazine I had just laid aside.

"Okay, so spill it."

For a moment Spangler toyed with his pencil-line mustache. "There's a girl I met here in Akron, Jack. She's in a spot of trouble, and I'd like you to see if you can get her out of it."

"Forget it, Andy. The agency isn't taking you on as a client."

"Not me, Jack, Beverly Keeler. She's a sweet kid, you'll see, and innocent as a newborn babe. She's got money to cover your fee, so I'll be completely out of the picture. That's straight, word of honor."

Rather than laughing, Jack tilted back in his chair and ran slim fingers through sandy brown hair that at twenty-six was already growing thin on top. Its sparseness went well with his angular features. When he leaned forward again, his elbows were on the desk, chin resting on folded hands. "Okay, shoot. But no guarantees, understand?"

"Sure, Jack, I know how it goes. It's like this, a while back Bev worked for a lawyer, a Stefan Damokura. Legal secretary, girl of all trades, know what I mean? So twenty grand that was supposed to have been in an escrow account at the bank disappears, and he accuses Bev. Now I ask you, Jack, would anybody pull a stunt like that, then stick around waiting to be collared?

"Anyway, the only other one in the office was a kid fresh out of law school just learning the racket. Now he's the key witness, the one who makes it something more than Damokura's word against Bev's. Even that way the court would probably believe the lawyer, but this kid Kenneth DeRidder wraps it up like a Hershey's kiss."

Jack took a crooked cigarette from a crumpled pack of Pall Malls, checked to see it wasn't broken, then lit it and blew a perfect smoke ring. "So what makes you think I could do anything to help her? What've you got in mind, Andy?"

"Nothing, Jack, and that's the truth, so help me. It's out of my line, but I figure if anyone can get to the bottom of things it's you. So will you talk to her?"

Jack wasn't quick with a reply, so Spangler said, "Look, what's to lose? Have her come in, and if you buy what she says, see what you can do. If you don't, toss her out the door. But that won't happen, take my word for it."

Jack Eddy hesitated a moment longer before giving a shrug of acceptance. "Maybe I'm nuts, but okay, send her in. One thing, if I do take the case, the first time I even suspect you're entering into it someway I'll go to the judge and lay the whole thing out for him. Got that, Andy?"

Spangler arose, a wry smile on his face. " If I didn't figure that's the way you'd play it, Jack, I'd be talking to somebody else. A fair shake for the kid, that's all I want."

When he was gone Jack sat tapping a pencil against his desk for a minute or so, then turned to me. "Whaddya think, buddy?"

"I think you said one thing that makes sense."

"What was that?"

19

"Maybe you're nuts."

Everyone offered conflicting advice about my car. The most succinct came from my boss, city editor Ben Goldsmith: "Get the old jalopy fixed, Geary, and now! I can't have my police reporter riding around town on buses."

Before dinner at the boardinghouse I discussed the situation with Mr. Reimer, the retired druggist. "Be very cautious, Abraham," he said. "We're in a recession, you know, and a great many economists think it will get worse in the months ahead."

That sort of talk always made me wonder when the Depression had ended and the recession had begun. The difference escaped me, as it did the laid-off rubber workers who gathered in small groups on Akron street corners and discussed matters beyond the ken of any economist in a warm and cozy office. It wasn't as bad as 1932, but that oft-mentioned corner that prosperity was just around had proved to be a long one.

Kitty Bauer, the vivacious daughter of the landlord, came flouncing into the parlor. "Are you still talking about cars?" she said. "For heaven's sake, Bram, buy a new one. Something ritzy to impress Sue Baney."

Her father, who so far had escaped the latest round of layoffs at Goodyear, looked up from his newspaper. "Humph! That boy has as much business buyin' a new car as I have buyin' a house out on West Hill so I could hobnob with the Firestones and the Seiberlings." He shifted his frown to me. "Act like you got some sense, young fella, and get yourself a nice Ford about two or maybe three years old."

Bus Bauer drove a twelve-year-old Oakland but swore by anything Henry Ford produced. It was hard to figure; Bus was a diehard union man and Henry wasn't known as a booster of collective bargaining.

Thoughts of cars were forgotten when Mrs. Bauer called, "Supper's on the table!" We were no more than seated in the dining room when the phone rang. Bus Bauer mumbled an oath while getting up to answer it, returned quickly and without any pretence of patience said, "Might've known it'd be for Jack Eddy. Sounds like your office again. After this you can answer the damn thing yourself."

Jack winked at me while pushing back from the table. He did it again when he got back, this time at Kitty. When the platter of beef and noodles was empty and we'd polished off a bowl of custard, he took me aside. "Beverly Keeler's at the agency waiting to see me. Want to ride along?"

Without a car I had nothing better to do. I shot the breeze in the outer office with Cal Andres, the op pulling night desk duty, while Jack talked to his prospective client.

When they came out together after half an hour, I blinked a couple of times and sat gaping. Beverly Keeler was a knockout. About five-two, Sue Baney's size, but slimmer. Her hair was a darker shade of brown than Jack's, and her hazel eyes flecked with green were the warmest I had ever seen. Her shy little smile would have melted any man's heart.

I couldn't take my eyes off her while Jack was introducing us and saying something about going around the corner for coffee. Only when he said, "I'll finish the paperwork and catch up with you in a few minutes," did I realize he meant for me to escort Beverly on my own.

There were scattered patches of ice on the sidewalk, and her high heels weren't meant for it. We had taken only a few steps when she slipped and I grabbed her around the waist to keep her from falling. After that she kept her arm linked with mine until we reached the New Deal Lunch on the southwest corner of Market and High.

When we were seated across from each other, I said, "So Jack's taking on your case?"

"Do you know about it?"

"A little. I was there when Spangler talked to him this afternoon. Is this Damokura pulling a frame up?"

"I guess so. It was such a surprise ... well, it hit me so hard I haven't known what to think. Anders says Mr. Eddy is the best in the business. Is that true?"

"The best I've run across. If anybody can help you, he's the one. You call Spangler Anders, do you?"

"All his friends call him Anders."

21

"Know what line of work he's in?"

"He's a retail consultant."

I choked on my coffee, but it wasn't my place to set her straight. It was a good ruse for someone in need of explaining a job without regular hours that still managed to provide a bulging wallet. You might say Spangler showed jewelry stores how to move their best merchandise overnight.

Jack Eddy arrived sooner than I'd hoped. After that he did the talking. When called for, Bev supplied answers. Every so often she'd glance my way, smiling a little but not flirting. She was just being kind, seeing I was smitten. Anyone could have seen it. If Sue Baney had been there I'd have had ten years of explaining ahead of me.

Jack, ignoring my loud yawn and weary sigh, drove south on Brown Street rather than heading home. Kenneth DeRidder's small apartment was above a corner store. He admitted us reluctantly. Law books and legal pads covered with scribbling lay on an old library table that occupied most of the living room.

Horn-rimmed glasses enhanced DeRidder's studious appearance. His hair was tousled, he had a prominent Adam's apple and dark circles under his eyes. His necktie was still in place but loosened. The ambitious type, I surmised, who worked day and night. A more refined version of Jack Eddy.

Jack didn't waste time on social amenities. "I think your boss set Beverly Keeler up for a hard fall."

DeRidder raised a skeptical eyebrow. "Steve? Why would he do that?"

"For the money, why else? I don't know the details yet, but I'm digging them out. In the meantime, if you're smart you'll do some checking on your own. How will it look if you testify against her and it turns out she was framed? Think anyone'll believe you weren't in on it?"

DeRidder tossed his pencil aside, shaking his head. "I can't go along with you. It's pure speculation on your part, and you're hardly an impartial party." He spoke with conviction but didn't appear all that certain of himself.

"Think about it, sport," said Jack. "If I'm right and you're wrong, it'll make a lousy start for your career. Better do a little nosing around down at the office before you get on a witness stand."

DeRidder's expression led me to believe he would give serious thought to the advice.


Shortly after first edition deadline Jack Eddy came striding into the city room. After greeting the big shots, taking particular care to cozy up to Ben Goldsmith, he settled on a corner of my desk and said, "Damokura plays the ponies in a big way, buddy. What does that tell you about the twenty grand missing from that escrow account?"

"Not much. Plenty of people bet the horses without dipping into someone else's money."

He laughed scoffingly. "You'd follow it up, friend. You know you would. I've got an appointment to see him in fifteen minutes, and I want you along."

"Oh swell, Jack. This is going to be another of those confrontations, isn't it? The kind where you go into your Jimmy Cagney act and start off by calling the other guy a dirty rat."

He gestured noncommittally. "I can be nice as the next guy, buddy, when it seems like a smart move."

True, I had seen him play at being subtle. His stock in trade, though, was shaking a man out of his routine, stripping him of his security, then watching to see what he did. Jack Eddy thrived on unpleasant encounters. I didn't. Still, it would be interesting to observe Damokura's reaction, so I followed him out the door. As usual I was ready to play the foil for Jack in hopes that it would lead to a story.

No one would have mistaken Stefan Damokura's office in the Delaware Building on South Main for one of Akron's leading law firms. No walnut paneling, no thick carpet, no soft lights, no cute receptionist. Two scuffed wooden desks, neither occupied at the moment, were crowded into an outer room. The door to Damokura's slightly larger space was ajar.

He looked up but didn't stand. "C'mon back," he called, then motioned us to cane-bottomed chairs that had started life in someone's dining room.

I had seen Damokura around City Hall and the Summit County Courthouse. He was the sort of lawyer who always seemed to have a scruffy character in tow and talked boisterously to make sure no one missed seeing him. He looked about forty but could have been younger. It was hard to judge because of the flab and heavy jowls that go with starchy meals and too many hours on a barstool. His complexion was pasty, his black hair as greasy as an empty plate after a burger and fries at Ptomaine Tommie's.

"You're Eddy, right?" he said to Jack. "What's the newsie doing here?" Apparently he had seen me around, too.

"Any objection?" said Jack. "Haven't got anything to hide, have you?"

"That's not the point. I don't talk for publication."

Jack feigned surprise. "Is that right? You could have fooled me, pal. Back at the agency I've got a stack of clippings where you had plenty to say. Most of it about Beverly Keeler forgetting to go to the bank with twenty thousand bucks."

Damokura gestured deprecatingly. "The dame stole me blind."

"Funny thing about those clippings, there wasn't a word about the streak of bad luck you've had with the ponies."

"Now just a minute. If you think —"

"No, sport, you've got it wrong. You're the one who needs to do the thinking. I talked to your boy DeRidder, the naive kid you bluffed into believing Keeler did all your banking. Pretty clever the way you had her running down there every day with some piddling amount to deposit."

"You know a better way? Stick it in a desk drawer, maybe?"

"You were setting her up, Damokura. An hour later you were probably drawing the dough out again. Now you're counting on the kid backing up your story in court. Being a shyster yourself, you should know her lawyer will rip him to pieces on the stand. Sure, he saw her make all those trips to the bank, but I'll bet he won't testify he specifically recalls that twenty grand going along with her on one of them."

"That's slander, Eddy. And if your boy here prints a word of it, it's libel. If you think I'm sitting still while some two-bit private dick casts aspersions –"

Jack's laughter cut him short. "Knock it off with the hard-guy routine. You think I don't know how much you've lost at the track?   Or that I'm dumb enough to believe this hole-in-the-wall operation rakes in enough to cover it? Without the kid playing stooge for you, it's going to be an interesting day in court."

Jack had gotten up while he was talking. "C'mon, Bram, let's get outa here. This set-up smells so bad I need a little fresh air."

Damokura was on his feet, too. "The Wellington Agency will be hearing from me," he said, but it was all bluster. There was fear in his eyes, not indignation.

When we were in the corridor waiting for the elevator, I said, "One of these days you're going to use that routine on the wrong person."

Jack was grinning. "I pick my times, buddy. Damokura's shaking in his shoes, and you know it. For the rest of the day Cliff Austin and Cal Andres will stick to him like flypaper. Maybe we'll find out who he pals around with."

"You've got solid information that Damokura was a big loser on the horses?"

"Enough to get started on. I've got a man digging up the details, and what I want you to do is talk to your friend Ruscinski, see if he can tell you anything."

"Look, Jack, I'm not one your ops. The last time I saw Dan Ruscinski I could tell he's getting sick of my face."

Jack laughed again and went into a boxer's crouch, feinting and then punching me just above the belt buckle. A little harder than necessary, I thought. "Come on, buddy," he said. "A face like yours, who could get sick of it?  I noticed Beverly Keeler didn't last night."

I hated it when he said things that made me blush.

Dan Ruscinski had been a classmate of mine at old Kent School on South Arlington. He grew up on Chittenden Street where boys learned to use their fists early on in life. Dan had a drunk for a father and a shopworn mother who sometimes entertained the older boys after school. Dan's higher education came at the reformatory in Mansfield; then he did-post-graduate work at the Ohio State Penitentiary. He learned his lessons well and now lived better than anyone I knew without gainful employment. Aside from Anderson Spangler, of course.

I found him in the usual place, a Howard Street bar misnamed The Lighthouse. Several characters you wouldn't want to meet in a dark corner of a parking lot were with him at a table near the back of the long, dimly-lit room.

A nod of Dan's head sent the others off to stools at the bar. When they were gone he gave me a smile that would have chilled an icicle. He motioned to a chair, then slid his own so close that we were shoulder to shoulder. "Back again, huh, Bram? Keep this up and you might wreck my good reputation. Some o' the boys get nervous when a reporter's around. Too tight with the bulls, know what I mean?"

"It's important, Dan. A lawyer named Damokura, I understand he puts a lot down on the nags and may have gotten in trouble with somebody. Heard anything about it?"

For a second or two Dan studied me with unblinking eyes of blue so pale they seemed transparent. Then he got up, pulling me with him. Making a show of clapping me on the back and then laying an arm across my shoulders, he led me to where the unwholesome trio was seated at the bar.

"Boys," he said, "I wan'cha to meet Bram Geary, an old pal o' mine from back in school. Used to buddy around together out in East Akron. You know what the big lug done? Dropped by to wish me a Merry Christmas and gimme a present."

From one of his pockets he had produced a new fountain pen in a box, an expensive Waterman with a marbled finish. I was certain the office supply store down the street was short one item supposedly in inventory.

Not that I do a whole lotta writin'," he said, "but I really appreciate it, Bram. Now look, stop back sometime when you ain't in a big hurry, and we'll hoist a few and hash over old times, right?"

As he talked I found myself being ushered out the front door. I stood for a moment on the sidewalk, dazed by my sudden exit. Then everything became clear as I walked south past the Quaker Oats plant that made the Mill Street area of downtown Akron smell lie a bowl of cereal. In his own way Dan had steered the two of us through rough waters.

Any answer to the question I asked would involve people best left alone. Poking into their affairs could be risky, perhaps fatal. By keeping my visit too short for conversation and contriving a reason for it, Dan had accomplished two things, fixed me up with an alibi for being there and covered his own backside. He assumed, correctly I hoped, that I had enough sense to recognize the oblique warning.


Universal Ford on Wooster Avenue was advertising used cars at a penny per pound. That was as interesting as most things in the paper. The Christmas doldrums had set in, and real news was scarce. We were running filler stories such as the one saying co-eds at Akron U were up in arms because Emily Post had written that it was okay for females to foot the bill on dates. Sounded like a reasonable idea to me.

The final edition had a story telling of the liner President Hoover running aground on a small island near China. Considering what had happened to the man it was named for, that gave the wags something to crack wise about.

The Japanese expressed "profound regrets for a terrible mistake" after sinking an American gunboat and two Standard Oil ships in the Yangtsze River.

Someone had added things up and found that Akron ranked twelfth among U.S. cities in industrial production. Comforting news for those laid off from the rubber shops.

Exciting stuff it wasn't. I turned to the comic page to see how Dick Tracy was doing in his pursuit of The Blank. Before I found out, the phone rang and Jack Eddy said, "Guess who our friend Damokura went to see after our visit?"

"Mayor Schroy? Coach Porosky out at Buchtel High?"

"Knock off the cracks, friend. Vic Reiner, know him?"

"The name's vaguely familiar."

"He's Jerry Lynch's number one torpedo," Jack said impatiently. "A reporter should know things like that."

I didn't know Lynch, either, but kept it to myself. I knew of him, however. Just about everyone in Akron did. Lynch ran the numbers bank on the near south side, a part of town laced with factories and hovels occupied by people who could use a few extra bucks. Lucrative territory for a numbers runner. He also had men making book on horses in the factories and some of the neighborhood hangouts.

It was said that Jerry Lynch was a fine tenor and therefore a popular figure at the Hibernians and a few bars where the Irish got together. Some of those who appreciated his voice were the same ones who kept his operation running smoothly, meaning they got to listen at times when he wasn't in a singing mood and his Irish eyes weren't smiling.

"It figures," I said, then told Jack about my brief encounter with Dan Ruscinski. Jerry Lynch qualified as one of the men in town whose business wasn't up for scrutiny by those who enjoyed good health and preferred keeping it that way. If Stefan Damokura had placed some bad bets with one of Lynch's boys, he wouldn't have wanted to welsh.

"Better steer clear of that bunch," I warned. Jack hadn't laughed at my attempt to be funny, but he did then. He hung up without comment. Still laughing.


With Christmas putting the skids under real news, the following day dragged on interminably. Jack Eddy called to say the personnel at the jewelry store had been checked out and seemed above reproach. If one of them had passed a schematic of the alarm system to Anderson Spangler, the act had been masterfully concealed. The records of the company that had installed the system were guarded like Fort Knox. The investigation was as dead as my old Chevy.

The report of a murder on the far south side of town near Firestone Park came too late for anything more than a page one brief in the final edition. "The body of a man shot at close

28

range was discovered this afternoon in a Brown Street apartment ..." I called in the report from the police station, then rode to the scene with detectives.

My stomach did a flip-flop when we pulled up in front of a familiar building, the grocery with Kenneth DeRidder's apartment above. The youthful lawyer was seated face down at the big table with the law books and legal pads, encrusted now with dried blood. The bullet that killed him had been fired much earlier, probably the night before.

I turned away, nauseated. After telling the detectives what little I knew about the victim, I went outside and gulped fresh air, then from a booth on the corner phoned the Wellington Agency. Jack Eddy wasn't there. I boarded a Brown Street bus headed downtown.

Rather than returning to the *Times-Press* building I transferred to another malodorous orange bus that took me to City Chevrolet. An hour later I drove home in my new car, the ebony black 1932 Chevy sedan that was much like my old one. They had allowed me twenty dollars on a trade-in, and I had wangled nineteen more off the price so it set me back a hundred and forty. I put fifty down and would owe ten a month for a year.

As I was parking in front of the boardinghouse, Jack Eddy pulled his big Auburn into the space behind. He was out ahead of me, frowning a little as he looked over my purchase. "What did you do, buddy, have the old heap painted?"

"This is a different car, Jack," I said indignantly. "My old one was a standard model, this is a deluxe coach."

"Well excuse me, friend. Mind pointing out the difference, aside from the paint job?"

I stalked off without replying.

Jack Eddy followed me into the house, grinning as he settled in the parlor with the home edition of the *Times-Press*. Mr. Reimer came in and carefully eased down on the opposite end of the couch on which I was sitting. "Have an interesting day at work, Abraham?" he asked.

"Not until a couple of hours ago."

"Oh? What happened then?"

"A murder out on the south end of town. A lawyer named Kenneth DeRidder."

Jack Eddy lowered his paper. "What was that? Is this one of your jokes?"

"No joke. I tried calling you but you were out."

Jack startled Mr. Reimer by bringing his fist down hard on the arm of his chair. "This is a fine kettle of fish!"

One thing about Jack Eddy, he had an unlimited supply of timeworn phrases at his command. As he jumped up and went to the phone, I wondered if his way of speaking fit in with his burning ambition. He was determined to rise to the top at all costs, but would his glib tongue and flippant manner favorably impress the big brass at Wellington's New York headquarters? Perhaps. As Jack might put it, to men in their line of work, actions would speak louder than words.

After a supper of Mrs. Bauer's superb corned beef hash I drove Jack Eddy downtown. Not before everyone went outside and pretended to admire my new car. Everyone aside from Bus Bauer, who grunted contemptuously and said, "Another Chevy!" before going back in the house. You didn't have to have much upstairs to see the others were unimpressed. Only Mr. Reimer seemed sincere in saying I had made a wise choice.

"Well, buddy," said Jack as we neared the police station, "I'll say this much, it runs better than your old clunker. Sounds better too."

I was hoping it would be a quick trip so I could pick up Sue Baney and take a spin around town. That didn't seem promising when we were told that Plato Largis, the detective in charge of the murder investigation, had returned to the scene of the crime. Then it began snowing again as we drove south on Brown Street.

We fast-talked our way past a young cop at the door of the apartment. Plato Largis grimaced when he saw us coming. "Not you two again. He took a cigar from his shirt pocket, an El Verso so dark it looked like a fat stick of licorice, but thought better of the idea and put it back again. "Be a sport, Eddy," he said, "and tell me you're not tied in some way with this case. Just once I'd like to wrap up a job without laying eyes on you."

Jack gave him a smart-guy grin. "Wouldn't want you getting complacent, Plato. This DeRidder kid was supposed to testify for a client of mine, so I'm curious when somebody slaps a seal on his lips."

"Beverly Keeler's your client?"

"You called it, pal."

"That young lady may need all the help she can get."

"I want to be there when you talk to her."

"You know something funny, Eddy? I had you down in my book as a shamus, not a lawyer. When did you pass the bar?"

"Come off it, Plato. She's been set up from the word go, so I want to be dealt in on the game."

A cat-that-swallowed-the-canary smile came over Largis's face. "Even if I operated that way, you're about an hour too late. The coroner's preliminary report says DeRidder died sometime between midnight and three in the morning. Beverley Keeler claims she went to bed a little after eleven. Alone."

"So did I," said Jack. "Does that make me a suspect?"

"Probably not, unless I find out DeRidder was scheduled to testify for you, too."


Aside from background information on the victim there was nothing new on the murder in the morning. Kenneth DeRidder had grown up in Cadiz, a small town among the coal fields that had been Clark Gable's home before coming to Akron for a job in the rubber shops. DeRidder would have been a kid in knee pants at the time Gable set out to see what lay beyond the hills and hollows of east central Ohio. The young lawyer had followed a different route to Akron and met a different fate when he arrived. After four years at Muskingum College came a couple in law school at The Ohio State University. All a waste as it turned out.

Jack Eddy phoned while I was in the middle of a different story with first-edition deadline approaching. "Guess where Damokura was when DeRidder got it?" he said.

"I'm on deadline, Jack."

"Can you believe another of those all-night poker games? He and Spangler have more in common than I realized. This one was at the Anthony Wayne Hotel with a judge, a deputy prosecutor and some big jamoke from your own newspaper. Started about eight and didn't break up until dawn."

Ben Goldsmith's eyes were on me so I kept typing. Even so he left the city desk and came over to stand with one hand on the sheet of paper in my Remington. I'm about to wrap it up, Ben," I said.

Jack took the hint. "Lunch at Tommie's?"

I said, "Okay," and dropped the earpiece on its hook. Goldsmith pulled the copy paper from my typewriter and I inserted a fresh sheet. He took hold of the top corner of that one and said, "Four minutes, Geary."

While easing down onto the stool next to Jack at Ptomaine Tommie's I said, "You think that because of Damokura Jerry Lynch had a hand in DeRidder's murder?"

"You can bank on it, buddy. Lynch wouldn't have pulled it off himself. It's stuff like that he's got Victor Reiner around for. Along with running Lynch's policy bank, Reiner handles most of the strong-arm stuff."

"I can't figure the angle."

"The kid had to have come up with something solid that would have cleared Beverly Keeler and dumped the theft back in Damokura's lap. What else could it have been?"

"Then it was talking to you that got him killed."

"Don't bray like a jackass, friend. Stand back and let the hoods have their way, is that what you're saying?"

"I guess not, but none of it's clear to me, Jack."

"Damokura's all mouth, you saw that. Nothing behind it. Give Plato Largis and his boys an hour to work him over and you'd hear him singing all the way to Youngstown. Lynch was making sure Largis doesn't get that hour."

"Why not silence Damokura instead of DeRidder if he knows something that could hurt Lynch's operation?"

"Dead men don't pay debts, buddy. That twenty grand was probably just a down payment. Damokura's a compulsive gambler so he's a long-term client in Lynch's eyes, a steady source of income. Along with that he probably makes a good mouthpiece when one of Lynch's boys needs one."

"All this is supposition on your part, right?"

"At the moment, maybe. I'll have the pieces put together in a day or two."

"Aren't you the guy who told me to always approach a story with an open mind?"

"This is a case, buddy, not a story. It must have been Goldsmith who said it. Either way it's good advice, but that doesn't mean you don't use the little gray cells."

"Been reading Agatha Christie again, haven't you?"

"Only when I run out of Cain and Gardner. Why?"

"No reason, Jack. Just forget it."

My wallet being somewhat on the thin side, I checked to see what was playing at the second-run theaters. Sue Baney was fussing with a saucy little hat she felt wasn't fixed at the most becoming angle. I looked up from the paper and said, "'Forty Naughty Girls' at the Rialto sounds pretty good."

"You can forget that one, Bram."

"Okay, how about 'Marihuana' at the State? It says 'a lovely girl made hard and brittle by a weed with roots in hell.' Whaddya think?"

"I think you're trying to make me mad. I told you the other night I want to see the Ted Lewis band, remember?"

I did, but was hoping she wouldn't. The stage production plus movie at the Keith-Albee Palace was the most expensive show in town. "Aw, Sue," I said, "Ted Lewis has the corniest act going. He makes Lombardo and Sammy Kaye sound like real swingers. Besides, the movie sounds lousy."

Sue's hat was finally right, but the ends of her mouth had turned down. "Oh, Bram, I really want to."

I felt like shouting "*No!*" when Ted Lewis strolled out on stage, the old top hat that was his trademark cocked over one eye, and cried, "Is everybody happy?" But the show turned out to be great, and there were a few good jazz men in the band, which came as a pleasant surprise. I had forgotten what the evening was costing me by the time we got to the capper,

Lewis climbing a stairway with a lone spotlight on him, top hat in hand while he half sang and half talked his way through "Me and My Shadow."

For me, though, the high point had come earlier in the show. As Ted Lewis sang "When My Baby Smiles at Me" Sue Baney squeezed my hand and gave me one or her pixyish smiles.

Enough silver remained in my pocket for hamburgers at the Kewpee Hotel, which was a lunchroom, not a place to spend the night. As we passed the Metropolitan Building I glanced up and saw a light in Jack Eddy's office. He was burning the midnight oil.

Jack was on my mind as we ate. Sue snapped me out of my reverie by using a red-painted fingernail to beat a rhythmic tattoo on the tabletop. She was frowning when I looked up. "You know, Bram, it would be nice if when we're together you didn't completely forget I'm around."

"Sorry, Sue. I was thinking about Jack Eddy's case."

"I might have known. Maybe the two of you should go steady. What's he working on that's so intriguing?"

"It's all very complicated. You'd never understand."

"No, of course not. A mere female, what chance would I have?"

"I didn't mean it that way. What I'm trying to say is – aw, let's talk about something else."

Her smile lacked its usual warmth. "What you're trying to say is that you haven't the foggiest idea what's going on but you don't want to come right out and admit it. So tell me the story. Maybe I'll fool you and understand perfectly."

"If you're really interested. What happened is a man Jack's been trying to nail for years comes to Akron and sets up a jewel robbery. While he's in town he meets a girl and gets swept off his feet. It turns out she's charged with stealing funds from an escrow account the lawyer she used to work for was supposed to have set up for a real estate deal. The money disappeared before it got to the bank. The key witness against her is a young guy just out of law school working at the firm. Are you with me so far?"

"Bram, there's nothing even remotely complicated about it up to this point."

"Well keep your pants ... uh, what I mean is just wait a minute and it will be. This jewel thief Spangler is so head over heels about the girl that he turns to the best man around to help her out, his old antagonist Jack Eddy. Jack agrees to take the case as long as Spangler stays completely out of it. That's because he's trying to hang the jewel robbery on Spangler, see?"

"Of course I see. Get on with the story, just be more careful about the expressions you use."

"Okay, now here's where it gets wild. Somebody knocks off DeRidder, the young lawyer, so there goes the key witness against the girl. That —"

"Does this girl have a name? Or as Jack Eddy would put it is she just 'that broad'?"

"Sure she has a name, Beverly Keeler."

"Is she pretty?"

"She's okay, I guess, but kind of skinny. Anyway, she's the chief suspect in the murder, being the only one to gain by it. Now Jack has that to worry about."

"Then he thinks she's innocent?"

"He's sure of it."

Sue frowned a little. "Bram, you've taken a simple set of circumstances and played around with them in your mind until you have no idea what's going on."

"Look, smarty pants, how'd you like to be in Jack's position? On one hand he's trying to slap a man in jail and on the other he's trying to keep the guy's girl out of jail. You can see he's in a real dilemma, can't you?"

"Yes, and I love it. And I wish you'd get your mind off what I may or may not be wearing."

I knew my cheeks were fiery, but Sue was smiling so my heart began beating too fast. I pretended not to have heard her last sentence and said, "Sue, have you forgotten how Jack got you out of a real jam last summer?"

"No, and I haven't forgotten how many of them he's gotten you into since then. That's your fault, really, except that Jack knows how gullible you are and takes advantage of it, which makes him responsible."

"Gullible? I have a job to do, you know. Thanks to Jack Eddy I've come up with some great stories. That's all that counts, isn't it?"

She took my left hand in both of hers and squeezed it. "Oh, Bram, you're priceless. You really are."

I was a little put out and thought about pulling my hand free, but Sue Baney was smiling again and began stroking my arm. I just let things go on that way.


I was comfortably adrift in that nether world that precedes sleep when the brainchild of P.W. Litchfield, the president of Goodyear, jarred me awake again. As a young executive many years earlier Litchfield had clock towers built at every plant so the employees would never lose sight of the importance of time. The original at Plant One stood a hundred yards from the boardinghouse on Dudley Street. It sounded four melodic notes on the quarter hour, eight on the half and so on until it reached sixteen. Then came sonorous bongs to make everyone in the neighborhood aware of the hour.

During the day and evening the chimes were one small part of life in East Akron, no more noticeable than the noise of traffic on Market Street, the smell of rubber in the air, the black grit crunching underfoot. Not so at midnight. When the dozen strokes of the big clapper shattered the calm I never failed to remember that all was quiet and serene at The Anchorage, Litchfield's estate far out on Merriman Road.

As usual, I counted every note. Then as silence fell again came soft footsteps on the stairs and the opening of Jack Eddy's door across the hall. I slipped on a robe and went over. While unbuttoning his shirt Jack managed a weary grin. " What's new, buddy?"

"That's what I was going to ask you."

"Hard to say. One thing, Jerry Lynch is having problems with his numbers bank. I'm not sure how it fits in or even if it does."

"How'd you find out?"

36

"Cal Andres buddied up to one of Lynch's ticket sellers. Stood for a few rounds, you know the routine. Lynch isn't getting wiped out, but for a couple of months he's been paying off on more one- and two-buck tickets than the percentages call for. It's eating up his profit, but what's really got him in a stew is that someone may be setting him up for a knockout score."

"I've never paid much attention to the numbers racket, don't really know how it works."

"It can vary a little from place to place but Lynch's bank is pretty much standard. Like I told you, Victor Reiner handles the day-to-day operation. You can buy tickets in five denominations from ten cents to two dollars. The average factory Joe plays for a dime or a quarter, someone with a heftier income, or a guy who's a confirmed gambler, goes for a buck or two a day.

"So you pay the seller, then write your three-digit number on a dated and numbered ticket. He gives you the original and turns the carbon in to Reiner before the stock market closes. You can check the winner in a late edition, the last number on the closing figures of industrials, railroads, and utilities in that order."

He took a December tenth issue of the *Times-Press* from his bedside table and turned to the business section. "Here," he said, pointing to columns of figures in agate type, "the winner is 278. For anyone who played it, the payoff is five hundred to one, but the odds against you are twice that."

"A sucker's game."

"Sure, but you've got a lot of pigeons out there ready to fly."

"How could anyone beat the system?"

"There are ways, friend. The only one I've run across personally is fixing the numbers. Say a rival bank wants to put Lynch out of business and take over his territory. They get to somebody in the composing room at your paper, have him alter the numbers on a given day. Then they spread the word ahead of time so there's a heavy play on that number and a killer payoff. That might work some places, but you couldn't pull it off in northeast Ohio. Too many newspapers."

"Looks to me like you're wasting your time, Jack. How could Lynch's problems have anything to do with Beverly Keeler or Anderson Spangler?"

"Right now I'm not sure. Give me a little time and maybe I'll figure a tie-in. To Keeler, I mean, not Spangler. It's just a hunch, but I seem to smell Damokura in this."

Despite the holiday slump, Goldsmith kept after me for stories. The police were spinning their wheels on the DeRidder murder, Jack Eddy seemed to be stalled on dead center. Auto accidents on slick streets provided my only material of consequence. Six had died in crashes the previous day, leading Mayor Lee D. Schroy to say that given an additional hundred policemen he would cut the toll in half in 1938. Political puffery, but it kept Goldsmith off my back for one day.

Desperate for a story with some meat to it, I decided to do a little nosing around on my own. As often as not that meant making a fool of myself.

Jerry Lynch's legitimate business, his front, was the Emerald Laundry and Dry Cleaning. His white trucks decorated with shamrocks were a familiar sight all over town. The plant was in an old building on Bartges Street near the Ohio & Erie Canal south of the Goodrich complex.

Brief snow squalls interspersed with periods of pale sunlight kept a person guessing as I parked half a block away. With my newer but dirtier suit tucked under one arm, I walked to the sign of the shamrock. The customer service area was sticky with heat coming from the plant at the rear. After a middle-aged woman who looked as though she had lost the knack of smiling filled out a work order and handed me the claim ticket I said, "Is Jerry around?"

"Mr. Lynch? Could be back in his office, I guess. He doesn't check in and out with me, you know."

Without waiting for an okay I walked around the counter and through a door into a steam bath. Sweaty young women, uniformly pale and haggard, were busy at a variety of jobs, none of them pleasant. On the left, middle-aged men in shirtsleeves were doing bookwork in cubicles enclosed by glass

38

that did little to keep out the heat. The place would be a real joy in July.

I asked one of the men where I might find Lynch. Without looking up from his ledger he nodded toward a stairway at the rear. They say heat rises, but the second floor was twenty degrees cooler than the first. After passing three closed doors I came to one that wasn't. Beyond it was a carpeted office where a man sat with one hip on the corner of a mahogany desk. Another stood staring out a window with a view of the bustling, dreary corner of Bartges and Main. When I said, "Mr. Lynch?" he turned, giving me a quick once-over before saying, "Who're you?"

"Bram Geary, *Times-Press.*"

A look of disbelief came over Lynch's round, ruddy face. "A newsie? A newsie poking his nose in here?"

I grinned sheepishly. "It's our slow time of year, so I was thinking of maybe doing a series on a few local businesses. You know, those that everybody's familiar with. You can't be on any street in town for ten minutes without spotting one of your trucks."

Lynch hesitated, then broke out in a smile. "Sounds like a good idea, kid. Wha'ja say your name is again?"

I repeated it, and he said, "Yeah, I've seen your byline. Usually write crime stuff, don'cha?"

"When there's any of it to write. December is pretty quiet."

"Okay, so whaddya want to know?"

The man by the desk cleared his throat and said, "Business is fine, Jerry. I don't think we need any newspaper publicity."

Lynch gestured toward him. " My associate, Victor Reiner. Look, Vic, I don't see how it can hurt."

Aside from his eyes, Reiner could have been any Akron businessman. He wore a blue pin-striped suit and gray spats, the first pair I had seen in several years. He was about six feet tall, three inches shorter than me, which wasn't as big as I had him pictured. His neatly-trimmed blonde hair was held down by a product that gave it the look of being shellacked in place. But the eyes, empty of all feeling, belonged on the face of a leopard.

He left his perch and walked to the door. "It's your decision, Jerry. I think you're making a mistake."

When he was gone, Lynch gave a little shrug, smiling wryly. "Vic's a worrier," he said, motioning me to a chair. He went to a cabinet and produced a bottle of Irish whiskey. "How about somethin' to cut the dust while we talk?"

Half an hour later I sat drumming my fingers against the steering wheel. Now what was I going to do? If I didn't write a story about Emerald Laundry, I could be in trouble with the Lynch mob. If I did, the *Times-Press* business writer, Ted Leipsic, would have fits because I had crossed his beat. Worse than that, Goldsmith might think I didn't have enough to do and find some additional duties for me.

"I didn't figure you for pulling a dumb stunt like that, buddy," said Jack Eddy after a supper of knockwurst and baked beans at the boardinghouse. "What did you hope to gain by talking to Jerry Lynch?"

"Stir things up a little, maybe. If it turns out you're right, I want to be familiar with his operation."

"Well, it's your funeral." He went to the rack in the hallway and took down his hat and overcoat. "C'mon, we've got a date with Stefan Damokura."

"We do?"

"He's waiting at the agency right now."

"You're kidding."

"When do I kid about business? Austin and Andres brought him in half an-hour ago."

"Brought him in? My God, Jack, you didn't strong-arm a lawyer, did you?"

He grinned while tossing my coat to me. "Persuaded, friend."

Damokura was in Jack's private office. Cal Andres, leaning casually back on his chair, was keeping him company. The fat lawyer was irate on the surface, shaky beneath the skin. "This'll cost you, Eddy," he blustered. "Kidnapping a man off the street'll put you behind bars."

Jack draped his suit coat over the back of a chair, loosened his necktie, and rolled up his sleeves. "Maybe we can share a cell, Steve. A kidnapper and a killer."

"If you're talking about DeRidder, I'm alibied."

"Setting it up for somebody else makes you as guilty as the triggerman, pal. A shyster like you knows that."

"Look, Eddy –"

"No, chief, you look. You couldn't wait to get to Vic Reiner after I talked to you the other day. Then the kid did some digging like I told you he would. He confronted you, you yelled for Reiner again, and we all know the rest of the story. What you didn't know was we had men shagging you every step of the way."

Jack went to his desk and sat down. After lighting a cigarette he leaned toward Damokura and in a friendlier tone said, "Here's the set-up, Steve. All I'm interested in is getting my client off the hook. You tell the prosecutor it was a mistake on your part, Beverly Keeler had nothing to do with that missing twenty grand, and then you're on your own."

Damokura wiped his face with a dirty handkerchief. "And if I don't?"

"I turn our file over to Plato Largis." Jack laid his hand on the phone. "As you know, Plato has his little ways of getting people to come across with the truth."

Damokura waved his hand at the phone. "Hold on a minute. Look, maybe I've made some mistakes in my life, but I'm not a killer. Vic Reiner's a hard man, I knew that, but I swear to God I didn't think he'd kill the kid. Scare him, sure, after he nosed around and found out what we were doing, but I didn't figure on anything more than that."

"Tell me about it, Steve. What exactly did DeRidder find out you and Reiner were doing?"

"Getting ready to take Jerry Lynch's operation for a ride. I thought you said you knew."

"I do, but I want to hear it in your own words." Jack looked at me and winked. It was all bluff, he didn't know beans.

Damokura wiped his face again. "It wasn't my idea, it was Vic's all the way. When I got in too deep, he made me set the Keeler dame up as the patsy, then I turned the money over to

Lynch to cover my losses. The next day Reiner came around with this scheme to clean up on the numbers. He didn't give me any choice but to go along. I mean he had me over a barrel."

"Keep going, Steve. Explain this scheme to me."

"Look, Eddy, you know what Vic'll do if I open my mouth."

"You've already opened it, sport, but have it your own way." Jack reached for the phone, and again Damokura waved him off.

"Okay, okay. Vic has a hold over someone in the printing business and he had duplicate rolls of tickets made up. I had some people I know, real down-and-outers, make one- and two-buck plays, then Vic wrote the winning number on the duplicate tickets and turned them in to himself after destroying the originals. Nothing big, just greasing the wheels to break Lynch with a big score. Then he'd take over the operation without getting Lynch's Irish buddies up in the air. The way he had it figured, Lynch would never be the wiser."

"Lynch isn't that big a dummy. You were being set up to take the fall all by yourself. When was this supposed to take place?"

"Next week. Look, Eddy, are you satisfied now?"

"I've been satisfied from the start, providing you make that call to the prosecutor and put Beverly Keeler in the clear." Jack pushed the phone toward Damokura.

"Now? Look, I gotta think this over."

"Fine. You've got thirty seconds, then I call Largis."


Beverly Keeler joined us at the same table in the New Deal Lunch. I held a chair for her, but she only had eyes for Jack Eddy. She was tied in knots, five feet of anxiety. "What is it?" she asked. "Has something more gone wrong?"

Jack was grinning. "Relax, kiddo. Damokura phoned the prosecutor half an hour ago saying it was all a mistake on his part and you're in the clear. He's at headquarters right now making a written statement to that effect."

Beverly leaned back, exhaling as the color returned to her cheeks. "That's wonderful. It's going to take me a while to realize it's really over. I can't thank you enough."

She turned to me, laying her hand on mine and squeezing a little. "And you too, Bram. I'll never forget it."

I hadn't done a thing, of course. There was no way I would have said that even if I hadn't been so choked up I was afraid to trust my voice. Later, as she was leaving, she gave Jack a peck on the cheek. Then she did the same with me, but lightly on the lips.

When she was gone Jack burst out laughing. "You big lug, pop your eyeballs back in your head and take a gander at the expression on your face. If only Sue Baney could see you now."

"You're not funny, Jack."

"I was never more serious in my life, buddy."

After beckoning to the waiter for more coffee he said, "Be careful what you write this time, friend."

Never before had he told me to keep anything under my hat. "I have to write the story, Jack. The whole story."

"You have to write that Damokura cleared Keeler. He's not telling the cops anything about Reiner, so what will you hang the rest of it on? If you say you heard about the numbers scam or DeRidder's murder at the Wellington Agency I'll have to deny it, you know that."

"But —"

"No buts about it, buddy."

"You mean you're going to let Victor Reiner get away with murder just because it's not your case anymore?"

"I didn't say that. We'll sit back a couple of days and see what develops. If nothing does, then I'll put a bug in Plato Largis's ear. I don't think that'll be necessary."

Once again Jack Eddy was right. An hour after the *Times-Press* was on the street the following afternoon a client visiting Damokura's office found the shady lawyer slumped over his desk just as DeRidder had been slumped over the table at his apartment.

I was at the police station when the report came in and was close on Plato Largis's heels when he arrived at the scene.

From a booth downstairs I phoned Jack Eddy. "You'd better get down here fast and tell Largis what Damokura said about Victor Reiner."

After a short pause Jack said, "Hold your horses, buddy. Does Largis know you called me?"

"No."

"Then I've got a better idea. Be on the sidewalk out front in ten minutes, and I'll pick you up."

Before I could argue the point, he had hung up. By the time his Auburn pulled to the curb I thought I had it figured out for myself. The prospect didn't please me.

As he circled the block and headed south I said, "This is crazy, Jack. Let Plato handle it."

"I intend to – in time."

"What are you planning, another gunfight at the O.K. Corral with you playing Wyatt Earp? If so, count me out."

"You think we're going to pay a call on Vic Reiner?"

"Aren't we?"

"That's looney, friend. We're on our way to see Jerry Lynch."

"And Reiner'll be there."

"He's busy collecting the day's loot from his ticket sellers. I checked after you called. Lynch is alone and expecting us."

Jack Eddy did the talking, Jerry Lynch the listening. He didn't even inquire about my story on Emerald Laundry. Of Jack he asked a single question: " When are you telling this to the cops?"

Jack glanced at his watch. "I've got a couple of things to wind up before quitting time, so I guess it'll be morning."

"Fine," said Lynch. As I closed the door behind us he was reaching for the telephone.


Ben Goldsmith was excited over my story. This time it was the entire story, or at least most of it. Goldsmith gloated when he saw the *Beacon Journal*'s and found it lacked the details in mine. The fact that Victor Reiner hadn't been picked up for questioning made it all the better in his eyes. More suspenseful, he said, and good for another story.

He grew increasingly impatient, though, as the days slipped by without the police finding Reiner. They say a reporter is only as good as his last story, and Goldsmith soon tired of reading those of mine saying the manhunt was continuing."

" People are getting sick of this stuff," he said after skimming over my latest before tossing it aside. "I want something fresh."

Look, Ben, I write the stories, I don't make them. That was the thought in my mind. I kept it to myself, naturally.

In desperation I went back to see Jerry Lynch. His numbers bank, closed the day Reiner vanished, was still shut down. It would remain that way until things cooled off.

When I asked about Reiner, he gave me the answer I expected: a blank look, a meaningful shrug with arms thrust out, palms upward. Again he didn't ask about the story on Emerald Laundry, but as I had my hand on the doorknob to leave he said, "Do much swimming, kid?"

I turned my head and found him smirking. "Some," I said.

"Come summer, stay away from Summit Beach. They say the lake's polluted."

"Do?" said Jack Eddy. "What can you do? Lynch was having you on. I don't doubt for a minute that Reiner is wearing cement shoes and keeping company with the fishes, but if there's one place you can be sure of not finding his body, it's Summit Lake."

"It's frustrating, Jack. It makes me feel like a sap."

"Then think how you'll feel if you talk Plato Largis into dragging the lake and all he comes up with are old tires and tin cans." He gave me a poke on the arm, laughing at my long face. "Just forget about it, buddy. Going to the wedding?"

"What wedding?"

"Haven't you heard? Spangler and Beverly Keeler are getting hitched tomorrow. He asked me to be best man. Talk about guts. Wouldn't that look great on my agency record?"

45

Perhaps it shouldn't have, but the news left me stunned. The idea of a sweet girl like Beverly married to a thief didn't seem right. I convinced myself that my feelings had nothing to do with envy, and certainly not jealousy. For an instant the thought of trying to stop the wedding crossed my mind, then was quickly discarded. It was Sue Baney, not Beverly Keeler, who mattered in my life.

Rather than commenting on it, I went back to the original subject. "Jack, I still don't understand why you didn't let Plato Largis handle Reiner instead of tipping off Lynch."

"What could Largis have done? There wasn't any solid evidence to tie Reiner to either murder and never would be. Once the heat was off, Reiner would have started looking around for somebody else to help clean out Lynch's operation and no telling where that would have led."

For a while I sat quietly in a corner of Jack's office while he finished whatever he was doing. Of the two cases, the jewel robbery and Beverly Keeler's, Jack had zeroed in on the one of greater importance. Beverly, totally innocent of any wrongdoing, was no longer in danger of serving a prison sentence.

Victor Reiner had killed people in cold blood, but the law couldn't touch him. Perhaps Jack Eddy's way was best. Jerry Lynch took money from suckers, but if he were gone, someone else would move in and do the job.

Anderson Spangler was a different breed. He belonged in jail, but he didn't leave dead bodies behind. His real victims were insurance companies.

If Beverly Keeler's case hadn't come along, would Jack have done more on the jewel robbery? But what, for instance?

In the outer office a radio was softly playing Tommy Dorsey's "Once In a While," the top tune on that week's Hit Parade. I looked up suddenly and said, "Will you?"

"Huh?"

"Once in a while will you give one little thought to Anderson Spangler?"

"What brought that on?"

"Admit it, Jack, he outfoxed you again."

For a moment he scowled at me, then switched to a grin. "So maybe Spangler won another round. That doesn't mean the fight's over."

"If you nail him someday, it'll make his bride happy, won't it?"

"His problem, not mine."

"It really steams me, Jack. Either you or the cops should have done something about him before now."

He leaned back on his chair, hands locked behind his head, contemplating the ceiling. When he looked toward me again he said, "You're halfway intelligent, Bram, and thanks to your job you know your way around a police station. How many times would you say Plato Largis or any other cop in the country knows exactly how a job was pulled and could name every man involved, yet can't do a thing about it? We both know it happens all the time. When they say crime doesn't pay, they're talking about the dummies."

"That's not very satisfying." After a moment I grudgingly added, "Okay, I suppose you're right."

"You know I'm right. Even if we caught Spangler's boys in the act, they'd clam up tight. He wouldn't work with a squealer. Sure, we could put a man on him and know his every move, but so what? He might hit a place next week or maybe it'll be a year. So he goes into fifty jewelry stores, noses around, and maybe even buys something. What do we do, stake out every one of them indefinitely? Then when one gets hit he'll be a hundred miles away with an air-tight alibi."

"In other words he'll go on thumbing his nose at you and the agency until the day he dies."

"Maybe, maybe not. Remember that ball game we went to up in Cleveland when the Yankees were in town last summer? Lyn Lary was at shortstop for the Indians, a guy who handles ninety-six out of a hundred chances and makes it look easy. So DiMaggio tops the ball and hits an easy roller out to Lary, but at the last second it takes a funny little hop and bounces off his glove because he was nonchalanting it, just going through the same old motions. Sometimes you can be too good for your own good."

I thought about it, finally conceding that he was right. "You know," I said, "if Spangler hadn't come to Akron with larceny in mind, none of the rest of it would have happened. Does that make him the white knight?"

"It's okay by me if that'll help you wrap it up in a neat package. You know what your problem is, buddy? It's your job. You go out in the morning and dig up a few stories, go back and write them and that's it. The next day you start over with a clean slate. Everything nice and tidy. That's not the way it is in the real world, but you expect it to be."

"It's not that simple, Jack. A lot of stories carry over."

"No, they don't, they just give you a starting point for the next day. Then when all the empty space on those pages is filled up and the presses start to roll the editors and reporters sit back and say well, we did it again. Here it is, Akron, everything you need to know in forty-eight pages. Not an empty inch to leave you wondering what's missing."

Getting out a newspaper was more complex than that, yet there was a good deal of truth in what he said. Rather than arguing the point I said, "Can you give me a lift home?"

"Where's your car?"

"I had to drop it off at the shop. They say it needs a valve job, but since I just bought it, I'll get a twenty per cent discount."

When he wanted it that way, Jack Eddy's laugh could be downright nasty.

# DEATH ON THE DEVIL STRIP

When a burly stranger, a bear of a man, followed Jack Eddy into the parlor there was no reason to believe it was the opening scene of a drama in which I would play a starring role, one that would come close to killing me before the final curtain fell. I had been waiting expectantly to see who had rung the doorbell and asked for Jack. In the nine months he had lived at the boardinghouse on Dudley Street it was the first time such a thing had happened.

From the expression on Jack's face he would gladly have waited another nine. He looked toward me, rolling his eyes as if to say, "Why me?" After motioning the unkempt visitor to an empty chair he said, "Folks, meet Joe Kurtz."

I said, "Hi, Joe, I'm Bram Geary." Our landlord, Bus Bauer, hunched over with his ear close to the stately Grunow console radio that dominated the room, growled a warning that we were interrupting *Amos 'n' Andy*.

Mr. Reimer, the retired druggist, nodded tentatively while straight-laced Miss Ferrabee looked Kurtz up and down before grunting, "Humph!" From where he was lying on the floor with the latest issue of *Famous Funnies* 12-year-old Artie Bauer glanced up at the visitor, saw nothing of interest, and returned to his comic book.

Pudgy Mabel Klosterman giggled, then began a greeting that got as far as "Hell –" before her voice broke.

Miss Ferrabee swung around to face her. "Really, Mabel!"

Undeterred, Mabel wiped away the beads of perspiration that had formed on her upper lip and tried again. "Hello, Joe, I'm Miss Klosterman, but please call me Mabel."

For the life of me I couldn't think of a reason why he'd have need to call her anything. His meaty face looked as if it had spent forty years absorbing one discouraging blow after another, more than a few from the strong right fist of Joe Louis. His watery eyes spoke of past tragedies. Goodwill would have turned up its nose if offered his lint-speckled overcoat, and what I could see of his suit made my own look like something from Hart, Schaffner & Marx. Both of his socks were blue, but not mates, and the sole of his left shoe was coming apart from the scuffed upper.

After a silence that threatened to become embarrassing he said in a surprisingly gentle voice, "Uh, like I was starting to say, Mr. Eddy, I just wanted to stop by and thank you for steering that case my way. It's been, uh, kind of slow lately so I appreciate the recommendation."

Jack squirmed uncomfortably. "Think nothing of it, Joe. Anyhow, I wouldn't say I actually recommended you. After I told the lady that Wellington's National Detective Agency doesn't accept domestic cases, she asked if you were reliable and I said I never heard otherwise."

"Ooh," gushed Mabel, "you're a private detective like Jack!"

As unlikely as it seemed, Joe Kurtz blushed. "Well, uh, I wouldn't say I was in Mr. Eddy's class or anywhere close."

"Now, Joe, there's no need to be modest," said Mabel. "You're among friends, you know."

Miss Ferrabee arose abruptly and left the room.

Joe Kurtz stood up too. "Well, uh, I'd better be going. Like I said, Mr. Eddy, I just wanted to thank –"

"No need to, Joe," Jack interjected, "no need to."

Mabel followed Kurtz to the door saying, "It's too bad you have to rush off, Joe. Be sure to come back soon."

When she accompanied him out onto the porch, coatless despite the frigid January air, I glanced at Jack Eddy. It was the first time I could recall seeing him nonplussed.


I never learned how it came about, but after supper the next evening Mabel Klosterman went up to her room and a short time later came down again all dolled-up for a date with Joe Kurtz. I peered out the window and watched them drive off in Joe's battered old Durant coupe that was missing a rear fender and God only knows what else.

When she arrived home a few hours later Mabel's face was glowing, and not because of the bitterly cold weather that had settled on Akron in the early days of 1938. Joe had taken her to the Rialto, she said, but when Mrs. Bauer asked what picture had been playing, she couldn't remember.

On my way home the next afternoon I saw Mabel coming out of a beauty parlor on East Market Street, her reddish hair done up in curls that made her look like an aged, overfed Shirley Temple. That night when she was ready for another date with Kurtz she was wearing a new dress so tight that I feared something would give way at any second. Mabel Klosterman and tight dresses were never meant for each other, but she flushed with long-awaited delight when Jack Eddy gave a wolf whistle.

A few days later I had finished checking my stories in the first edition when Jack walked into the *Times-Press* city room. What I had written was error-free, but the rest of the world was in distress. The Samoan Clipper had exploded in the air near Pago Pago. A Northwest Airlines plane had crashed in the Bridger Mountains fourteen miles north of Bozeman, Montana, killing everyone aboard. In Toledo an oversize hole in the nipple of a baby bottle had caused a three-month-old girl to drown.

Unaware of all this, Jack smiled and waved to a few people, then gave city editor Ben Goldsmith a cheery greeting. Still it was apparent something was bothering him. He helped himself to a cigarette from the pack of Spuds on my desk, then as usual perched on a corner of it, one leg swinging back and forth. After flipping his match toward my ashtray and missing he said, "Remember Joe Kurtz?"

"Who could forget him?"

"He's got troubles, buddy. His client's husband was knocked off last night. While Joe was shagging him, or was trying to. The guy gave Joe the slip, then turned up dead an hour later. The big lug found him again about five minutes after the cops arrived at the scene. Now Joe thinks he's the number two suspect on their list."

"Who's number one?"

"His client."

"This happened last night? Then he was working for Milan Jelinek's wife? That was the only murder in town."

Jack nodded absently, taking off his hat and running long fingers through sandy brown hair that was growing thin on top although he was only in his mid twenties. His usual cockiness was missing.

I said, "Plato Largis is the detective handling the case. He didn't mention a shamus being involved."

Jack answered with a short, derisive laugh. "You're not green enough to believe he tells you everything."

"So where do you fit into the picture?"

"I don't. That is I don't except that Joe called me and he's all tied up in knots. I'm not responsible, buddy, you know that, and yet I can't help feeling that way."

"You're going soft, Jack. You didn't even recommend him to the woman, just said you hadn't heard he wasn't reliable."

"Hell, friend, I never heard of him at all until she mentioned his name. After she left I looked him up in the phone book. He doesn't even have a display ad."

"So what's your problem? Are you out of cases of your own to worry about?"

"Actually we're busier than usual." He stroked his jaw, then shrugged one shoulder. "It's just that the big lummox seems so helpless. You know what I mean, buddy."

I did indeed.

"Then on top of that there's Mabel. She's really gone for him in a big way."

Despite my best effort to bottle it up I burst out laughing. Tough, hard-bitten Jack Eddy, assistant manager of a large detective agency, a man driven by ambition to reach the top and determined to ride roughshod over anyone who got in his way, was all mixed up over a down-at-the-heels loner and a giddy, love-starved woman with romance on her mind. A less likely cupid couldn't be imagined.

"If you take him on as a client, who's going to foot the bill? Or is Wellington's taking charity cases these days?"

"He says he'll come up with the dough."

"What kind of retainer did he hand you?"

A scowl darkened Jack's angular features. "What's it to you, anyway? You auditing the agency books or what?"

"So you didn't get a cent in advance."

He straightened up and stalked off in a huff. "I haven't even decided if I'll take the case, fella."

"Yes you have, Jack. You have."


Milan Jelinek was – or had been – a production worker at the Miller Rubber Company. A daughter of the firm's founder had married Thomas Edison. The family, including Edison early in their marriage, lived in a big house on a hill overlooking downtown Akron.

Jelinek had married Sophie Kosla, a sales clerk at Akron Dry Goods. The childless couple lived in a small house on Lovers Lane, a street running east and west through a working-class neighborhood on the southeast side of town. Some time in the distant past the name must have been significant to Akronites. During the Great Depression the only lovers seen on Lovers Lane were waiting for a bus headed downtown.

Shots from a slow-moving car had killed Jelinek as he left a South Arlington Street tavern not far from where he lived. He had staggered a few steps toward home, then collapsed on the devil strip. That's how I had written it. Many years later I would learn that only in Akron is the grass between curb and sidewalk called the devil strip.

Arlington is the main north-south thoroughfare on Akron's east side, so there were witnesses. By a count of seven to one they favored a black sedan as the car carrying the shooter. Three said it was a 1937 Terraplane, the others a Buick, Dodge, DeSoto and Studebaker. One elderly gentleman insisted the shots had come from a crimson Ford convertible.

Plato Largis settled on the Terraplane. The witnesses who identified it as such said it had been parked just north of the tavern and began moving as Jelinek came out the door. They agreed there had been two men in the car, but none had gotten a look at their faces.

A distinctive teardrop grill made it difficult to mistake a 1937 Terraplane for any other make. The problem was there were dozens in the Akron area, the majority black sedans. On the positive side, the stories indicated Jelinek had been a specific target rather than one chosen at random.

When Jack Eddy left I returned to police headquarters in City Hall. After running down Plato Largis I said, "You didn't tell me a private eye had been shadowing Jelinek."

"You didn't ask."

"Come on, Plato, it's hardly a routine question. Did you mention it to Tom Kennedy?" My counterpart on the rival *Beacon Journal* would have gloated over a detail I'd missed.

"Up to now I haven't told anyone. How'd you find out?"

"From Jack Eddy."

Largis curled a lip in disgust. "I might have known. It wasn't a Wellington op, so how did he get in on the act?"

"Joe Kurtz called him. He thinks he's a suspect."

"Kurtz is something special. He came charging up about the time I got there. Know what he said? He looked down at the body and said, 'It's Jelinek. I thought I'd lost him.'"

"How'd Kurtz happen to go to that particular bar?"

"It was Jelinek's hangout. He wasn't much of a drinker, but he'd gotten in the habit of dropping in every day."

"Kurtz drives an old Durant, not a Terraplane."

"What's that prove? The fact is, though, Kurtz isn't on my list. I don't see him as a killer, and I doubt if he could hit the side of a barn with a .38."

"He could have been the driver."

"Whose side are you on, anyway? But I learned something new since I talked to you this morning. Jelinek was laid off at Miller Rubber Company three months ago."

"So? You can find ten laid-off rubberworkers on any street corner in town."

"Right," said Largis, a sly grin spreading over his broad jowly face, "but their wives know about it. Jelinek's didn't."

"How can you keep a thing like that secret? When the money stops coming in —"

"That's the point, kid, it didn't stop coming in. He went off to work every morning, at least his wife thought he did, and came home on payday with his pockets lined."

I had more questions, but a senior detective came up and led Largis away to a private office. When I tried to tag along, the door was slammed in my face.


After supper – Boston baked beans and knockwurst so tender it melted in your mouth – I followed Jack Eddy upstairs to his room. He was still a little sore, but he wasn't a door slammer. I said, "Largis doesn't consider Joe Kurtz a suspect."

"Try convincing Kurtz of that."

"So I was right, you're taking him on as a client."

"Not officially. I told him I'd check around a little. Want to run out to that bar where Jelinek copped it?"

"I was thinking about giving Sue Baney a ring."

"It'll keep, buddy. We'll take your car."

Curiosity won out over female companionship.

The tavern was no different than dozens of others in Akron, a dingy place where rubber workers drank in silence or argued loudly over union activities. The bartender was younger than most, surprisingly friendly and talkative. When Jack asked if anyone was around who had known Jelinek he said, "Everybody did by sight. The guy wasn't big on socializing." He looked up and down the bar, then nodded toward a man drinking alone near the rear of the long, narrow room. "Jelinek and Pete back there talked sometimes."

Pete looked us over suspiciously as we approached. "You guys cops? I already talked to one."

Jack signaled for another bottle of Erin Brew for the man. "Not cops, Pete, I'm private. A buddy of mine had been tailing Jelinek, so now he's a suspect."

"Tailing Milan? How come?"

"His wife thought he was running around."

Pete laughed scoffingly. "Broads, ain't they somethin'? Mine was always accusin' me of playin' the field, then one day she run off with the choir director at church."

I stifled a chuckle. Jack said, "Jelinek had been going out about every night lately. If he didn't have a tomato stashed away someplace, where was he?"

"Right here most of the time, workin' when he wasn't."

"Working? I heard he was laid off."

Pete nodded, finishing his fresh beer. After Jack called for another Pete said, "Sure, from Miller a few months back. But he picked up a part-time job right after that."

"Where?"

"At some garage, or maybe a car agency. I mean somebody tells you a thing like that, who remembers exactly? Anyway I'm not sure he ever mentioned the name of the place."

"Was Jelinek a mechanic?"

"Naw, he drove cars to Cleveland."

"Drove cars to Cleveland? What kind of a job's that?"

"One that pays the rent. That's all I know, chief."

Jack tugged on an ear, then gave a shrug of acceptance even though it was obvious he wasn't satisfied. He said, "Any of those witnesses to the shooting here tonight?"

"Ask Freddie."

"Who's Freddie?"

"You were talkin' to him a minute ago. The bartender."

We went to a pair of vacant stools up front. Jack sent still another beer back to Pete and ordered a couple for us. Freddie said, "Pete do you any good?"

"A little," Jack replied. "He said Jelinek found a part-time job after he was laid off."

"Right. They'd call him here when they had something for him to do."

"Know who did the calling?"

Freddie shook his head. "They'd just ask for Jelinek, and he never said. Sometimes I heard enough to know they were telling him when to come in to work."

"Did he leave right away?"

"Once or twice, maybe. Can't say for sure. I think they were telling him what time to come in the next day."

"Anybody around who witnessed the shooting?"

"None of them ever come in here, but I can tell you where to find one. Know that little grocery in the next block? See the guy who owns it. He lives up the street someplace and walks back and forth a lot. He's been telling everybody he'd just gone past when it happened."

The grocery was still open. The owner wasn't there, but he walked in while Jack was talking to the clerk. His name was Rushton, a mousy little man who turned garrulous when Jack mentioned murder. "It was a narrow escape," he said. "Thirty seconds sooner and they might have got me, too."

"Tell us about it," said Jack.

Rushton couldn't wait. "I had just closed up for the night and was walking home. I noticed the parked car, a Terraplane sedan, because the motor was running. There were two men in front, but away from the streetlight so I didn't get a real look at them. Anyway, the car started moving as I passed. Real slow, like they were lost or something. Then I heard the shots and swung around just as they took off fast and turned onto Lovers Lane. This Jelinek was staggering along the sidewalk, reaching out like he was trying to get to something, then fell face down on the devil strip."

"You're sure the car was a Terraplane?"

"Positive. A 1937 model, black. My brother-in-law has one just like it. Sounds like a truck and rides like one."

Jack was deep in thought while we walked back to my car. As I unlocked the door he said, "What I can't figure is this job of Jelinek's and why he was so close-mouthed about it. Not broadcasting the details around a bar is one thing, I can understand that, but why keep it a secret from his wife? Above all, why didn't he tell her he was laid off from the rubber company? It's nothing to be ashamed of."

"It shouldn't be, but some men see it as failure on their part. Or it might be he didn't want her worrying."

"Could be, friend. Maybe Jelinek hoped to come up with something to tide them over until he was recalled. In the meantime he didn't want to upset his wife so he kept quiet about the layoff, but then instead of telling her when he did find a part-time job he still kept mum. The only reason I can see for that is he was ashamed of what he was doing, knew she wouldn't approve."

"There's a hundred ways she might have found out he wasn't still at Miller. If she had, then explaining where his money was coming from would have been twice as hard. Oh what a tangled web we weave when ... ouch, that hurt."

Jack had punched my arm just below the shoulder. He said, "Can the recitation, buddy, but keep your ears open downtown tomorrow. This setup doesn't smell right."

It was still early when we got home so I called Sue Baney. After picking her up at her Massillon Road apartment, I drove back to Arlington for hamburgers and coffee at the Spotless Spot, telling her the story along the way.

"Poor Mabel," she said when I finished. "It doesn't sound like she's made much of a catch."

"What would you expect, one of Harvey Firestone's boys falling for somebody like her?"

"That's not nice, Bram. Mabel may not be a raving beauty, but she's a sweet person."

"She sweats a lot. And giggles."

"I didn't think you were so cold and unfeeling. Some people might not think you're another Fredric March. And what about me? I'm not exactly Claudette Colbert."

"You're better looking than Claudette Colbert. Anyway, comparing you with Mabel Klosterman is like comparing a Rembrandt to a Norman Rockwell magazine cover."

Sue wrinkled her nose. "Personally I prefer Rockwell. But why would the police suspect Mrs. Jelinek? What woman would hire a private detective to follow her husband and then get somebody else to kill him while he's under surveillance?"

"At the beginning a wife or husband is always under suspicion in a murder case. After doing some checking, Largis doesn't think she or Joe Kurtz had anything to do with it."

"Then why is Jack Eddy sticking his nose in?"

"Because Kurtz is worried."

Sue laughed contemptuously. "Who isn't these days? I'll admit one thing, it would be interesting to know why anybody would pay someone to drive cars to Cleveland."

"Car dealers do that. Say somebody wants a green Plymouth coupe and the dealer doesn't have one but another does. They work some kind of deal, or maybe swap cars."

"You can't tell me that happens often enough for a man to make as much money as he did at a rubber shop. For one thing, who's selling that many cars today?"

"Have you got a better answer?"

"I think Jelinek was involved in something crooked and that's what got him killed."

"Could be, I guess. Jack said about the same thing."

Knowing it annoyed me when she turned syrupy, Sue held her upraised arms close to her body and in a Betty Boop cutesy tone said, "Oh goody goody. If Jack Eddy says so, little me-ums must be right." Then sounding like a drill sergeant: "I wish you'd stay away from that man."

"You're forgetting one thing, Sue. If I hadn't been along on one of his jobs, I wouldn't have met you."

She wrinkled her nose again and gave me one of her pixieish smiles. "For that I'll give the devil his due."


To check the status of the big story in town, one that had been on page one for days, Ben Goldsmith had only to walk to the windows overlooking East Exchange and High streets. In a formidable old mansion on the northeast corner, Miss Augusta Kaiser, eighty-two, was holding out against all attempts to evict her from the home built in the 1870s by her father, a prominent manufacturer of stoves.

She claimed a fraudulent real estate deal had caused her to lose title to the property. A grand jury had indicted two men for embezzlement in the case, yet a judge ordered her out. The chief deputy sheriff and his men had knocked on Miss Kaiser's door but refused to break it down and put her out in the snow. Akronites cried, "Bravo!"

After reading the latest blow-by-blow account, I skimmed over the rest of the news. Another battle was being fought in Hollywood. Barbara Stanwyck's ex-husband had been granted visitation rights with their young son, but the actress demurred on grounds that she entertained Robert Taylor at the house and didn't want her former hubby around. His lawyers countered with a charge that Taylor had given the boy a fifty-dollar check for Christmas and it bounced.

I checked out our competition, the *Beacon Journal*. On page one was a photo of the German freighter S.S. *Crefeld* at a pier in Gibbstown, N.J. Bombs were being loaded for delivery to Japan for its war against China. The bombs had been made by Atlas Powder Works, a subsidiary of Du Pont.

That was enough for one day; I cast the papers aside and went home. What a wonderful world, and such beautiful people.

Mrs. Bauer's roast beef hash was delicious, but supper was a somber affair. I blamed it on romance. Kitty Bauer, vivacious daughter of the household, was in a snit because Jack Eddy had been too busy to take her out since New Year's Eve. Joe Kurtz hadn't been around for several days so Mabel Klosterman, usually a voracious eater, picked at her food without once raising her eyes from the table.

After dessert, having noted that Mrs. Bauer gave me the smallest piece of angel food cake, I retreated to my room. A moment later Jack Eddy knocked on the door and entered without waiting for an invitation. "I'm going to run out and talk to Milan Jelinek's wife," he said. "Want to go along?"

I had nothing better to do. And was nosey, of course.

When Sophie Jelinek opened the door at the house on Lovers Lane, I was a little taken aback. I had pictured her as a femme fatale; instead she was a plump but firm woman in a housedress with a faded floral pattern. Her eyes were bright and lively, her black hair shiny in the lamplight.

She said, "Yes?" without enthusiasm, then recognized Jack Eddy, perked up, and added, "Oh, it's you."

He removed his hat and said, "I'm sorry about your husband, Mrs. Jelinek. Joe Kurtz is all broken up so I'm lending him a hand. Can we talk a minute?"

"I suppose so. Come on in." She stepped aside so we could enter a narrow hallway with a staircase straight ahead. We followed her into a small living room furnished with inexpensive pieces. Everything was spotlessly clean. It wasn't much of a house, but it received loving care.

Studio portraits taken a decade earlier rested on each side of a mantel above a gas fireplace. Looking out from one was a younger Milan Jelinek, thin with slicked-back dark hair, the sheik look of the 'twenties.

When we were seated on opposite ends of an overstuffed couch, Jack said, "What gave you the idea your husband was running around?"

Sophie Jelinek hesitated, patting her dark curls and then straightening a doily on the arm of her chair. "I don't suppose talking about it can do any more harm. The past few months Milan had become withdrawn, very distant. He started going out nearly every night. Sometimes he was late getting home in the afternoon, and he never used to do that. When I'd ask him about it he was evasive. What else was I to think?"

"He didn't say anything about being laid off?"

"Not a word. It probably seems strange to you, but Milan was that way. Being out of work would have been very embarrassing for him, even with me. Especially with me."

"Why wouldn't he have told you about his part-time job?"

"I don't have an answer. It still would have been embarrassing, I suppose. I would have thought he'd tell me once there wasn't reason to worry about the house payment."

"Don't take this wrong, but had your husband ever been involved in anything illegal?"

"Milan?" She smiled, shaking her head. "For heaven's sake, no. To do that he'd have to have been desperate."

Jack asked a few more questions, none that led anywhere.

When we were out in the car again he said, "One thing doesn't add up, buddy. If Joe Kurtz was shagging him, how come he didn't tell her Jelinek wasn't going to work in the morning?"

The next afternoon I stopped by the Wellington office in the Metropolitan Building and found Kurtz on a chair in the reception area. He was staring at the floor, nervously twisting the brim of his battered gray fedora in his ham-like hands. Jack Eddy came out from his private office and said, "C'mon back, Joe." He beckoned to me. "You too, Bram."

Kurtz, still mangling the brim of his hat, eased down onto the chair beside Jack's desk. I went to another in a dark corner.

After lighting a cigarette Jack leaned back, folded his hands behind his head and said, "You don't need me, Joe. I've talked to Plato Largis and so has Bram. "You're at the bottom of the list of suspects, if you're on it at all. Put it out of your mind."

Joe Kurtz wasn't comforted. His face and eyes brought to mind a basset hound in one of its unhappier moments. "It's nice of you to say so, Mr. Eddy but, uh, I'd feel better if you stayed on the case."

"For crying out loud, Joe, there isn't a case." Jack's patience, which never amounted to much, was wearing thin. "I haven't done a thing, haven't even made out an assignment sheet. Let's just chalk it up as a favor and forget it."

"Well, uh, the thing is I feel kind of responsible. About Jelinek getting knocked off, I mean."

Jack's expression was turning ugly. "Now listen to me, Joe. You were hired to shag Jelinek and report to his wife. Nobody was paying you to be his bodyguard."

"Yeah, but –"

"There's no buts about it. I said to forget it."

"Okay, if you say so. But what about, uh, Mrs. Jelinek? I'd hate to see them pin it on a nice lady like her."

"Nobody's going to. She was on Largis' list at the beginning as any spouse would be. Now she's an also ran."

"Uh, Joe," I said. Now he had me uh-ing. "What exactly did Jelinek do while you were tailing him?"

"In the daytime he mostly just, uh, kind of hung around downtown. After supper he'd go to that bar on Arlington."

"That was all?" I said.

"Well, uh, this one day he took a ride out in the country but, uh..."

"But what, Joe?" Jack asked agitatedly.

"Well, uh, it's kind of embarrassing. That's why I didn't mention it to the police. You see my car, uh, it's not in such good shape, so I lost him. Couldn't keep up."

Jack turned away in disgust. Had poor Joe been one of his operatives he would have been out of a job at that point. Jack had lost interest, but I was still curious, so I said, "Which way was Jelinek headed when he took this ride?"

"Uh, north. I lost him on the Akron-Peninsula Road. After we got to that straight stretch out past the disposal plant, he put her to the floor. I, uh, well, I couldn't keep up with that Cord he was driving."

Jack looked at him again, frowning. "Cord? You mean that's what Jelinek drove?"

"Well, uh, it wasn't his car. He had a '34 Ford, but I figured he was having trouble with it."

"Why was that, Joe?" I asked. Pulling teeth would have been easier than prying around in his mind for information.

"Well, uh, he dropped the Ford off at a garage, and I figured they loaned him the Cord while they worked on it."

"Where is this place?" said Jack. "I'd like to patronize a shop that gives you a Cord for a loaner."

"Maybe he was, uh, thinking about buying it or something. I mean, I wasn't sure it was a loaner."

"Joe, I asked you where this shop is, remember?"

"Yeah, sure, it's on Front Street up in Cuyahoga Falls. A Hupmobile agency."

"And you thought this laid-off rubber worker might be buying a Cord? Was it one of the late coffin-nose models?"

"Yeah, a bright yellow job."

"Speaking of jobs, Joe," I said, "what did Sophie Jelinek say when you told her her husband wasn't working?"

"Well, uh, I never mentioned that. I mean he could of been on vacation or something." He paused to run fingers shaped like fat cigars through his tousled hair. "Besides, I wasn't, uh, going to report to her till the end of the week."

"Just out of curiosity," said Jack, "what did you do after you lost Jelinek?"

"Went on to Peninsula, but he wasn't anywhere around. I came back to town on Riverview Road but didn't see him."

"Ever think he might have taken Riverview north to Canal Road if he was going to Cleveland? So what did you do when you got back to town, wait for him at that Hupmobile agency?"

"Yeah, how'd you guess? I hung around till they closed up for the day, but he didn't come back."

"When did you pick him up again?"

"Not till the next morning. He didn't show up at the bar that night."

"What was he driving the next morning?"

"His Ford. I thought it was kind of funny at first, then I figured he, uh, beat me back to the garage and was gone by the time I got there."

Jack sighed a long-suffering sigh. "I don't suppose you checked to see if his Ford was still there or not? Well, I guess it doesn't matter. Look, Joe, it's been nice talking to you. I have to get busy now, but keep in mind what I said about being off the list of suspects."

Kurtz left reluctantly. I went out with him to make certain he didn't change his mind. On the sidewalk I turned south when Joe headed north, then when he was out of sight I returned to the Metropolitan Building. When I was seated in the chair formerly occupied by Kurtz, Jack said, "How do you suppose a guy can be that dumb and live as long as he has?"

"You can tell by looking that it hasn't been easy. He's a nice guy, though. I can't help feeling sorry for him. He tries, you have to admit that."

"Sure, and some guys try going over Niagara Falls in a barrel. It's his clients I feel sorry for." Jack laughed then. "He probably gets about three or four a year."

"We learned a few things, Jack. First, Kurtz hadn't reported to Sophie Jelinek, so she was telling the truth when she said the first she heard that her husband wasn't working was when Plato Largis told her. The big thing, though, is now we know who Jelinek was driving cars to Cleveland for. It's hard to believe Kurtz didn't tell Plato about that."

"No it isn't. Nothing's more humiliating than lousing up a tail. What's hard to believe is he told us."

"We'd better let Plato know."

"And get Kurtz in hot water? It's up to Largis to find out, buddy. That's his job, not ours."

"He'll be steamed if he finds out we knew and didn't tell him. If we don't, then the next thing we have to do is find out why Jelinek was driving those cars to Cleveland."

"Are you kidding, buddy? What difference does it make?"

"Like you said, something doesn't smell right about the setup. Learning the score will be interesting."

"Forget it, ace. I've already wasted enough time fooling around on this."

"Are you telling me you aren't curious about it?"

"Look, friend, if somebody walks in the door and explains it to me, I'll probably listen. If you're thinking I'm curious enough to go out on my own time to check it out, you're not a whole lot brighter than Joe Kurtz."

"Any particular reason we're going to Cuyahoga Falls?" Sue Baney asked as we dipped down the hill and crossed the narrow bridge over the river. She made it sound like a long trip when in reality the Falls was just an extension of Akron's north side. At that point the Cuyahoga River told you when you left one and entered the other; at some places a stranger would never have known the difference.

"The agency that Milan Jelinek drove cars to Cleveland for is up here. I want to see what it looks like."

"For yourself or Jack Eddy?"

"Jack's not interested, Sue. He's off the case, if he ever was on it. There's the place up ahead."

As I pulled to the curb on the opposite side of the street Sue said, "*That's* it?  Good grief, Bram, it's a dump. I'll bet they haven't sold a car since Christmas."

She was right, Harry Jett's dealership across from the abandoned Marathon Rubber Company factory on Front Street reeked of failure. That wasn't remarkable, conditions being what they were in 1938, but the dirty showroom windows showed a lack of trying on Jett's part. It appeared that he was one of many who had finally given up after eight years of battling insurmountable odds.

Three cars were in the showroom, new six- and eight-cylinder Hupmobile sedans and between them a used Dodge. Another dozen used cars were on the lot, most in need of washing.  An overhead door opened on a service garage at the rear of the brick building. Beside it were two walk-in grease

65

pits, both filthy. Even the Sinclair gas pump at the curb looked neglected.

Sue did her best to appear interested as I began reciting the history of the Hupp Motor Car Company. Rather than mentioning that I had done a little research at the library, I let her think I kept such information stored in my head.

Bobby Hupp was one of Ransom E. Olds's boy wonders who had overcome serious problems to put Oldsmobile across to the motoring public early in this century. Like many industrial pioneers, Hupp was eager to have a free hand in the pursuit of fame and fortune, so he borrowed twenty-five thousand dollars and started his own company. In choosing a name, he followed the example set by his former boss but dropped the final letter of his name in calling his car the Hupmobile.

During the teens and twenties Hupmobile became increasingly important in the automotive industry, one of many small and medium-sized manufacturers that didn't threaten Ford or General Motors but kept them on their toes.

That ended abruptly late in 1929 when Wall Street took its nosedive. That year Hupmobile sold more than fifty thousand cars, in 1930 fewer than eighteen thousand. The company struggled on, producing its most attractive models in the early years of the Depression. People weren't buying so dealers who until then had been making money found themselves in trouble. Many went under, as did numerous manufacturers in competition with Hupmobile.

In the mid-1930's Hupmobile went a year and a half without building a car. It was a devastating blow to those dealers, Harry Jett among them, who had managed to stay alive during the leanest years of the Depression. Shortly before the stock market crash, Hupmobile had taken over the Chandler car company in Cleveland and started building its lower priced cars in the Chandler factory. When I was through playing history professor Sue said, "Do you think Milan Jelinek could have been picking cars up at the factory and driving them to dealerships?"

"I doubt it. I imagine they use transporter trucks like everybody else. And even if he was, it wouldn't explain why he was driving cars from here to Cleveland unless Jett was wholesaling used cars up there. Obviously he doesn't sell many new Hupmobiles, so where would he be getting decent trade-ins for that? Joe Kurtz said Jelinek was driving a Cord the day he lost him, and Cords don't come cheap."

"You know what I'd do if I were you?"

"What?"

"Tomorrow I'd check the stolen car reports."

Not wanting to sound like a know-it-all, I didn't tell her that was something I had been planning to do.


Cars were being stolen in Akron, but not as many as I would have believed. The majority were cheapies taken by kids out for a joyride, and they turned up again in a hurry. It wasn't that way with the more expensive models. A few were recovered, most were gone for good.

That didn't tell me much more than I had known to begin with. I had hoped to find a yellow Cord on the list but drew a blank. The result was the same at the Summit County sheriff's office. I drove south to Barberton and checked with the police, then north again to Cuyahoga Falls and did the same. No Cords, yellow or otherwise.

All that driving was getting expensive so I turned to the telephone for the smaller communities making up Greater Akron. It seemed a waste of time until I talked to someone at the police station in Kent. After explaining what I was after, I said, "Any Cords? I'm looking for a yellow one."

"Alliance."

"Huh?"

"Try Alliance. I got a buddy on the department down there, and he was telling me about a professor at Mt. Union College raising hell because his Cord was stolen."

I thanked him and dialed Alliance. The tip was a good one. "Yeah," said the policeman on the desk, "a bright yellow that'd knock your eyes out. Everybody in town knew it by sight. That's what the guy wanted, he's a big showoff."

"When was it stolen?"

"A week or so ago. I'll check the date for you."

"Don't bother, that's close enough."

So I had something. It seemed likely that by now the yellow Cord was another color and had a new owner. I couldn't wait to get to Jack Eddy's office with the news. When I arrived, he was out, of course.

It was still early, four o'clock. Two hours until Mrs. Bauer would call, "Supper's on the table."

Under a threatening blanket of gray cloud I drove to Harry Jett's Hupmobile agency. A lone salesman was killing the hours staring out the showroom window. He fit the familiar caricature of a used car salesman: flashy sport coat, pasted-on smile, hint of a cheap cigar on his breath. I was greeted like a long-lost pal.

After we agreed that the weather was cold and commented on the snow earlier in the week, the heaviest in eleven years, he said, "Looking for something nice in a used car, are you?"

I nodded, a little annoyed that he had sized me up as a nonstarter in the new car market.

He slapped a front fender of the Dodge on display between the new Hupmobiles. "Here's a real cream puff. Isn't she a beaut?"

"Not bad. How much?"

"We can work a deal for you on this baby. What're you driving?"

"A '32 Chevy."

The salesman held out his hand. "Gimme the keys and I'll have one of the boys in back take her for a spin around the block, see what he says."

I pretended to look at my watch. "No time right now. Do you do your own servicing?"

He wasn't interested in that end of the business. "You bet. Now if you think this Dodge might be a little rich for your blood I've got some jewels out on the lot." His hand was out again. "It'll only take a minute for a test run. Let me have your keys, and we'll know where we stand."

If he got his hands on my keys, I knew I'd have to climb up on the roof to get them back. Customers were too scarce to let a live one drive away. "Like I told you, I don't have time right now. Let's take a look at your service area."

He grudgingly led me to a pair of swinging doors and on to the garage. A mechanic was working, under the hood of an ancient Hupmobile. That was the only activity. Old parts, mostly junk, were scattered around, and over in a corner a soft tarpaulin covered everything but the wheels of a long-hooded car. Before the salesman could stop me, I threw the tarp aside, revealing a striking convertible, a blue and gray job I didn't recognize. I gave a whistle of appreciation. "Now there's a real doozie. Is that what it is, a Duesenberg?"

In a disinterested monotone my escort replied, "Naw, it's a Reo Flying Cloud, '33 or '34."

"A Reo? I didn't know Reo ever made anything this snazzy. First one like it I've seen. What're you asking?"

"This one's not for sale. It's in for repair."

I could just picture the owner of a car like that bringing it to Harry Jett's dump for servicing, and the mechanics covering it with a tarp. But the Reo was exactly what I'd been hoping to see. I took another look at my watch and said, "Have to run, but I'll try to stop back tomorrow. Got a business card so I can be sure of talking to you?"

"Don't worry, I'll be here." The pasted-on smile had vanished along with the rest of his cordiality.


I was waiting at the front door when Jack Eddy parked his sleek Auburn in front of the boardinghouse. I hurried out to meet him. "Have I got news for you, Jack. Let's go down to the corner, there's time for a beer before supper."

At the Lenox Cafe the six o clock shift was stoking up for a night at Goodyear Plant One across the street. We had to take our bottles of Burkhardt's and stand beside a wall. Jack was only mildly interested when I told him about the stolen Cord and my visit to Harry Jett's.

"You could be on to something, buddy," he said, "but you're a little shy on proof."

"How many yellow Cords have you seen driving around town? And that Reo was as out of place in that crummy garage as you'd be at a garden club meeting."

"So you think somebody snatched cars off the street, took them there and Jelinek drove them to Cleveland. Why?"

"To sell, what else?"

"Isn't thirty-five miles a little close? People from here drive up to Cleveland all the time, and vice versa. If you were talking about Fords or Chevies it might make sense, but how long would it be before somebody spotted that yellow Cord and got curious, knowing one like it had been stolen?"

"Then what's your answer?"

"I'm not knocking your idea, buddy, but I'll bet they sell them somewhere else."

"Maybe, but if they sold the Cord in Cleveland, what are the odds against it being spotted? There's a certain amount of risk, sure, but if that was all it took to scare people away from crime we wouldn't need cops or people like you."

Jack laughed and gave me a punch just below the shoulder, a habit of his that kept my arms black and blue. "Okay," he said, "I concede the point. It never pays to transfer your own logic to the mind of a criminal."

The rubber workers were starting to drift out the door. Jack finished his beer and deposited the empty on the bar. "Let's go or we'll be late for supper and have Mrs. Bauer in a tizzy." As we headed home along Willard Street he said, "If you're right about this, friend, you're on thin ice. Lay it out to the police in Cuyahoga Falls, let them handle it."

"Without more to go on than I've got? If you were on a case, is that what you'd do at this point?"

I knew the answer even before he said, "That's different."


After stuffing myself on Mrs. Bauer's city chicken and mashed potatoes I called Sue Baney and told her I wouldn't be around that evening. She took the news with better grace than I would have preferred.

I parked down the street from the dimly-lit Hupmobile agency. There was no sign of life at the place. Nor was there much life left in me after a couple of hours of sitting in a cold car. I didn't want to burn gas by keeping the motor running, and even if I had, the heater wasn't much good. By nine-thirty I was ready to throw in the towel. By ten my fingers looked like cherry Popsicles, so I drove home, steering most of the way with the palms of my hands.

After standing as close to a radiator as possible for five minutes I climbed the stairs and knocked on Jack Eddy's door. He was stretched out on the bed reading the latest *Black Mask*, warm and comfortable in undershirt and shorts.

"Nothing going on up there tonight," I said.

Jack lowered his magazine. "You had Jett's place staked out? In your car?"

"I was half a block away."

"Any other cars parked along there?"

"No."

"If something had been in the works, you think you wouldn't have been spotted? You're an amateur at this game, friend. Drop it like I said, or you'll wind up a dead one."

"So how would you have handled it, smart guy?"

"I'd have found a place off the street. If there wasn't one, I'd have parked around the corner and done it on foot."

"It was cold out there, Jack. I'd have frozen on foot."

"That goes with the territory, buddy. Anyway, I think you were there at the wrong time and for too short a time. If you think they're going to move that Reo after dark, you should have spent the night there. But I think they'll do it during the day."

"Why?"

"Don't you remember the Dillinger gang's routine? People figure outlaws move at night in big powerful cars, but that's when the streets are empty and cops notice everything. Dillinger and his boys traveled in the daytime and used inconspicuous cars.

"At a busy time of day maybe a flashy Reo would be noticed in traffic, but that's all. At night on a deserted street you might as well be driving an army tank."

"That's swell. I have to work most of the day."

"I had the idea you were working out there tonight. Are you trying to come up with a story or just doing this out of idle curiosity?"

"You know I'm after a story."

"Then tell Ben Goldsmith about it and spend the next few days up there; let somebody else cover the police beat. Sell him on the idea that you're onto a big story and you won't have to ask permission to follow it up, he'll insist on it."

He was right, of course. In the morning I laid it out for Goldsmith. He felt as Jack did, it was something I should turn over to the police. It didn't impress him when I said there wasn't enough to go on for that. I played my ace, reminding him there would be no story at all if a visit by the cops didn't turn up evidence for an arrest but scared Jett into shutting down the operation.

"All right, I'll give you a day. Convince me it's worthwhile tomorrow morning, and maybe I'll give you more."


A few cars were parked on Front Street, so I pulled up close behind one on the opposite side of the street half a block from the dealership. It was seven-thirty, earlier than anyone was likely to have reported for work, so I walked to the garage at the rear of the building and peered in a window. Despite the grime on the pane of glass and the lack of light inside, I could make out the Reo in the far corner.

Funny it should be a Reo. Bobby Hupp's old boss, Ransom E. Olds, had been squeezed out of Oldsmobile, so he too started another company. In naming the car, he used his initials, REO.

I went back to my car and waited. It was still cold, but not as bad as the night before. I was better prepared too, having put on most of the clothes in my wardrobe.

As the work day began, there was more activity at Harry Jett's Hupmobile agency than at the abandoned rubber factory across the street, but not much more. Goodyear had bought Marathon Rubber Company in the mid 1920's, then shut it down early in the Great Depression. The only reminder of what it once had been was a green sign with yellow lettering along the top of the five-story building.

My friendly salesman reported for work, then a middle-aged woman who appeared to be an office worker. Two men dressed like mechanics went in a small door beside the

72

overhead one leading to the garage. Later a wiry man of about forty-five parked a new Hupmobile on the lot and hurried inside. He was wearing an expensive gray suit but no overcoat. I had never seen Harry Jett but was certain this was him.

In midmorning an elderly man arrived on foot and a few minutes later came out driving the old jalopy that was being serviced the previous afternoon. Shortly after that a well-dressed man drove a new Hupmobile up to the garage door and honked. When he came out again, he walked north on Front Street toward the small Cuyahoga Falls business district.

That was the extent of the morning's excitement. I wondered how the salesman survived the boredom of his days, but more than that I wondered what I was going to do about lunch. The answer was nothing. By two o'clock I had decided that even if someone offered me a hundred dollars a week I wouldn't trade my job for Jack Eddy's. Not if this was how a private eye spent a goodly share of his time.

I began debating the advisability of going a few blocks north and having a sandwich and cup of hot coffee at Isaly's. My stomach was scoring most of the points. As I reached to switch on the ignition, a stocky man wearing a flat cap and mackinaw turned the corner off Sackett Avenue and went into Jett's garage. That scotched my lunch plans.

Twenty minutes later the garage door rolled up and out came the Reo, the recent arrival behind the wheel. He was twenty-eight or thirty, a thin-lipped man with narrow eyes set too close together. A two-bit thug if I ever saw one. As he headed north on Front Street, I fell in behind.

At the business district the Reo turned left at Portage Trail. I barely had time to make the light. That scared me, so I hugged his rear bumper until we were past the remaining lights and the road narrowed to two lanes. After Fourteenth Street there was nothing but vacant land on both sides so I eased up, allowing a fair amount of space to open up between us.

When he reached State Road, Route 8, the driver of the Reo had two choices, continuing straight ahead and following the Cuyahoga Valley to Cleveland or turning right onto the state highway. He turned right. After going down a dip and passing

73

the Old Mill we were on a brick highway with room for three cars side by side.

The suicide lane in the middle always had an adverse effect on my nervous system. Not so with the man ahead. I didn't know what was under the long hood of the Reo, but it enabled the driver to make a mockery of any speed limit. He passed cars and trucks with little regard for his own safety and even less for mine. He always seemed to have a clear shot at the center lane, but when I'd try to pull out to keep pace, someone coming the other way would beat me to it.

Along with that my Chevy made frightening noises and developed a nasty shimmy when the speedometer climbed above sixty-five. The highway narrowed to two lanes of blacktop at Boston Heights, but by then the Reo was long out of sight.

On the way home I stopped at Harry Jett's agency, avoiding the salesman by going in the garage door. Both mechanics were busy, didn't even bother to look up as I entered. Someone else had been busy during my absence: a late model metallic green Packard sedan was in the space previously occupied by the Reo.


Explaining my day to Jack Eddy didn't prove as difficult as anticipated. The boardinghouse at 38 Dudley Street was quiet for a change, and we had the parlor to ourselves. The only activity was in the kitchen where Mrs. Bauer was busy preparing supper. The fragrance of pork and sauerkraut drifted our way. My stomach rumbled in anticipation.

"I'm to blame, buddy," said Jack. "I should have realized your bucket of bolts couldn't keep pace with a hot car like that and said something."

"It's a good car, Jack. At seventy-five it purred along like a kitten."

"I'll bet. Like a kitten with somebody standing on its tail. Tomorrow we'll swap cars, give you a fighting chance."

Sue Baney was less understanding. She sipped a chocolate soda at the big Isaly's on East Market Street while I told her the story between bites of a banana split.

She said, "And now you're going to use Jack Eddy's big car so you can be just as childish as that other driver? Honestly, Bram, you must be losing your mind. Does Ben Goldsmith know about this? I can't believe he'd allow it."

"I called him at home after supper. He thinks I'm onto something good. I'm free to work on it the rest of the week if I have to."

"All newspapermen are fools. Do you know Charlie Klein?"

"Chuck Klein, the Phillies outfielder?"

"Of course not. The man who works at my office."

"That mealy-mouthed guy you introduced me to a few months ago? What about him, what's he got to do with anything?"

"He asked me out to dinner Friday night, and I think I'll accept. It would be a nice change to spend time with someone who leads an ordinary life, a mature person who thinks there's excitement enough in pleasant companionship and everyday pastimes. There *are* men like that, you know."

"Now look, Sue, I'm just doing my job. If you'd rather spend your time with some timid little squirt, it's your funeral. But you'll be sorry."

"Is that a threat?"

"No. I meant it might spoil things for us."

"So would having you in traction at City Hospital. Or how would you like me to spend the rest of my life sitting home alone and taking flowers to a cemetery on Sunday? If you think that's my idea of living, you really are crazy."

"Okay, go out to dinner with your Mr. Milquetoast."

"All right, I will." She stood up and started toward the door. "And you don't have to drive me home, I'll walk."

I overtook her, convinced her that walking would be foolish. Or maybe it was the wind and flakes of snow swirling in the air. Whatever, she accepted a ride but pulled away when I tried to kiss her goodnight, slammed the door behind her, and went into her apartment building without a word.

I drove home wondering what life would be like in the French Foreign Legion.

75

The timetable was like the previous day's. When the same plug-ugly headed north in the green Packard, I had no trouble keeping up. I might have done the job on a bicycle because this time he drove as sedately as an elderly woman making her weekly run to the grocery in a Baker Electric. After a few miles I decided Milan Jelinek's replacement had been warned about his driving habits. Getting a speeding ticket wouldn't make his employer happy.

The Packard continued north through the eastern suburbs to Mayfield Road, then west toward downtown Cleveland. As we approached Murray Hill in the neighborhood known as Little Italy, it turned in at an auto agency that was a far cry from Harry Jett's. The immaculate showroom was large enough for six cars. Another twenty or so were displayed on the lot. All of them, both inside and out, were high-priced models from the previous few years and looked as though they had come straight from the factory.

I went on by, parked well down the street, and returned on foot. The area brought one thing to mind, the Murray Hill Mob, an important cog in the unsavory element of society that people were just beginning to call organized crime.

Average citizens thought the name referred to a nationwide network of criminals, for the most part Italian, Irish, and Jewish ex-bootleggers who had branched out into many fields. They were right, of course, but there was a second and equally important definition. The Murray Hill Mob and others like it were organizations that included specialists in every aspect of criminal activity. Aside from the hierarchy, the majority worked at everyday jobs until their skills were needed.

If plans called for holding up a jewelry store, it was cased in advance by an expert. A phone call alerted men ready to steal a car whenever one was needed. They didn't pick one at random but had selected cars in mind, ones parked in factory or office lots. Day or night they could on short notice deliver a cheap, mid-range or expensive model and know how many hours would elapse before it would be missed and reported stolen. Specialists in armed robbery would take over from there, then someone else would dispose of the loot. A paymaster distributed the proceeds, most of which remained with the men on top.

These were the men who controlled gambling, the numbers racket, prostitution, drugs, after-hours sale of liquor, any other illegal but lucrative activity. They also made money on legitimate businesses that served as fronts for their real interests. Once such an operation was in place, there could be power struggles within and territorial warfare with other gangs, but while law enforcement agencies might chip away at the edges or occasionally nail one of the big boys, bringing the organization down was all but impossible.

As I approached the car lot, I was thinking of the members of the gang whose specialty was killing on command. I wasn't in friendly territory.

By pure luck my timing was ideal. A transporter truck was being loaded, and among the three cars already aboard was the familiar Reo Flying Cloud. Failing to include their destination would leave a gaping hole in my story, but I wasn't keen on setting foot on the agency lot. For a few minutes I lingered indecisively on the sidewalk.

Someone was checking out the radio in a Lincoln Zephyr parked in the front row. The Larry Clinton band, a favorite of mine, was swinging one of the new hit tunes, "I Double Dare You." As Bea Wain warbled the lyrics, she seemed to be taunting me: I double dare you to step over here.

So I did. As far as I could tell, no one was paying the slightest attention to me. Even the inevitable salesman was nowhere to be seen. While the driver was securing a sporty Chrysler convertible on the transporter tracks I said, "Some real beauties on this load. Where're they headed?"

Without turning from his work he replied, "Baltimore."

There wasn't anything more I could hope to learn, so I went back to Jack Eddy's Auburn, as good looking a car as any on the dealer's lot. Rather than taking the same route home I followed Woodhill, East 93rd, and Warner Road to the Cuyahoga Valley, then Canal Road to Riverview. Once I had left the congested area behind, it was a relaxing ride through beautiful wooded countryside laced with rugged ravines, precipitous cliffs, and towering glacial rock formations. Only rarely did an approaching car disturb my thoughts.

I was going to have to talk to Harry Jett. Not alone if I could help it, so various ways of luring Jack Eddy into going along were flashing through my mind when a speeding car appeared in the rearview mirror. It swung out to pass me on a deserted section of road, then suddenly slowed to my speed and cut me off. Alarmed, I swung to the right and bumped along the berm until I was able to stop the big Auburn just short of the ditch.

The offending car screeched to a halt ahead of me. Two men got out and walked back. I was thinking they wanted to see if I was all right until I saw that one was the driver I had followed to Cleveland and the other had a gun in his hand. I knew I was in trouble but didn't realize how much until they ordered me out of the Auburn and I was frog-marched to their car, a black 1937 Terraplane sedan.

The man with the gun shared the back seat with me as we finished the drive to town. He was about six inches shorter than me, probably five-nine, and skinny as a hamburger at Ptomaine Tommie's. An unruly shock of black hair kept falling over one eye, and he'd toss his head to get it back in place. I asked a couple of questions but was given the silent treatment. As I anticipated, we followed the shortest route to Front Street and turned in at Harry Jett's Hupmobile agency. When the overhead door went up and we drove into the garage, my hope of leaving alive was dim indeed.

It was after five; the employees had gone home. Only the man I had earlier decided was Harry Jett remained to welcome us. I was pushed down onto a wooden chair, and he began firing questions at me, all relating to who else knew what I was doing and where I was at the moment.

Jett wasn't as well informed as I would have believed. He was surprised to hear I was with the *Times-Press* and wasn't aware that Joe Kurtz had been tailing Milan Jelinek. He wasn't happy to learn that Kurtz knew of Jelinek's connection to himself, and above all that Wellington's National Detective Agency was involved.

He was a novice at the game, a petty criminal who had gotten in over his head. Like an animal backed into a corner, he was confused and struck out wildly without regard to consequences. When he looked at the man with the gun and nodded toward the Terraplane, his message was obvious. There seemed little point in it, but I stalled for time by asking a question of my own: "Why did you have Milan Jelinek killed?"

He had every reason to believe his answer wouldn't be repeated, so after only a momentary pause he said, "Jelinek had a big nose, and he got greedy."

"I don't get you."

"Instead of being grateful for having a job, he started thinking too much. He wasn't as dumb as I thought and figured it all out, then wanted more money."

"Figuring it out would have been easy. There must have been more to it than that."

"He got on the wrong side of certain people. The last time he drove to Cleveland for me, he nosed around and found bullet holes in a car he had driven up earlier. The car wasn't anything special, a Cadillac sedan not worth shipping out, but it was stashed away where nobody should have seen it. Jelinek did, put two and two together, and decided it fit the description of one used in a bank job in Lakewood."

"The one a few weeks back when there was a shootout and a bank guard was killed?"

"Right. I had nothing to do with that, but the people up there were upset, told me to get rid of Jelinek. They meant permanently, and you don't argue with their kind."

He was enjoying the role of big shot, so I kept asking questions. "Why did you hire Jelinek in the first place?"

"We're a small operation, and the boys here are busy with other things. Having some down-and-outer do the driving made sense at the time. I had a cover story worked out in case he got picked up along the way."

"Why bring the cars here instead of taking them straight to Cleveland?"

"So we can clean them up, get more money that way."

"You mean you just sell them at Murray Hill? You're not part of the Cleveland set-up?"

"Me? I don't speak their language. I managed to struggle along until Hupmobile quit building cars for better than a year; then it was either branch out or go under. The boys here line up a car, then I call and see if they're interested in Cleveland. If they are, we pick up the car."

"So until you killed Jelinek, you hadn't done anything more than steal cars. Pretty stupid, wasn't it? One squeeze of your boy's trigger finger, and you jumped from petty criminal to capital offender. All that and it still leaves you a minor leaguer trying to play with the big boys."

The truth was upsetting. He looked to his hired gunman again and said, "Get him out of here."

"Kill me and it'll double your chances of getting strapped in the hot seat. If I don't make it home for supper, you'll be behind bars before midnight."

Jett was frightened, but he had his mind made up and there wasn't a thing I could do about it. I was hustled back into the Terraplane, the man with the gun at my side again.

Jett raised the overhead door and we started off to some lonely place free of prying eyes. But before we got to the street, the driver hit the brakes as a car off to the side suddenly shot forward and blocked the drive. I may have been more surprised than anyone because the car was my own.

I saw Jack Eddy leap out, and without looking knew the man beside me had jumped from the Terraplane. I turned to see him level his gun, but Jack had one, too, and he was first to fire. The thug spun halfway around and hit the ground hard. His own shot, wide of its target, made a pinging sound as it struck metal. I got out fast, jerked the gun from his hand, and looked up in time to see Harry Jett run back inside the garage.

I tossed the gun into the nearest grease pit and sprinted after Jett. He was twice my age and out of shape, so it was no contest. I brought him down with the best tackle I had made since nailing a Central High all-city halfback for a five-yard loss while playing end for East.

Now it was my turn to frog-march someone. When we got to the door, I pulled up short, mouth agape. The Chevy, mine for only a month, was in flames. Jack Eddy was dragging the downed man away from the fire with one hand, the other holding the gun on the Terraplane's driver.

"What happened, Jack?"

"This mug hit your gas tank, and I had just tossed my cigarette on the ground. I hope your insurance is paid up."

In the distance I could hear a siren, then another much closer. The Cuyahoga Falls fire station was only a couple of blocks north, but if it had been in the same building, the firemen couldn't have saved my car.

The police arrived close behind the fire engine; then came an ambulance from the Weller Funeral Home next door to the firehouse. The gunman, his shoulder ripped up by Jack's bullet, was quickly loaded onto a stretcher. Everything happened in such rapid succession that it was a little overwhelming.

Jack Eddy said something I didn't catch. I said, Huh?"

"My car, dammit. Where is it?"

"Out in the Valley. Riverview Road."

"Wrecked?"

"It's fine, Jack, just fine."

He exhaled audibly. "Lucky for you, sport."

Luckier, though, that he had shown up when he did. I said, "How'd you happen to be here, Jack?"

"I got curious and decided to come out and see how you were doing. You were nowhere in sight, but about ten minutes after I arrived you came riding up in that Terraplane."

"How'd you happen to have a gun? You hardly ever do."

"Just a hunch. It paid off."

"It sure did. I'm glad you got here when you did."

"That makes two of us. Otherwise, how would I have found my car? No telling what might have happened to it. It might even have ended up in Harry Jett's pipeline to Cleveland."

One thing about Jack Eddy, there were times when you couldn't tell if he was serious or just kidding around.


We were late for supper. Missed it, in fact. After hearing about the shootout and all that went with it, Mrs. Bauer said, "Well, you could at least have taken time to call and let me know you wouldn't be here."

On the way into the house we had barely escaped being trampled by Mabel Klosterman as she rushed out to meet Joe Kurtz at the Rialto. After our session with Mrs. Bauer, Jack went into the parlor and pulled Kitty up from her chair. "Powder your nose, kiddo," he said. "I'll grab a sandwich somewhere, and then we're going out on the town." Romance had returned to the boardinghouse.

I changed out of my dirty clothes and started the lonely walk to the Coney Island Lunch, then turned and went back and dialed Sue Baney's number. When she answered, I said, "I missed supper, so I'm going out to get a bite. I was wondering if you might want to go along? The thing is, I don't have a car, so we'd have to meet somewhere on the bus line."

"What's wrong with your car, Bram?"

"It's out of commission."

"You mean it's in the shop again? You bought a lemon."

"It's not in the shop. It burned up."

"*What*? What have you been up to now, Bram? Don't tell me over the phone, I want to hear this in person. I'll meet you down by the corner at the New Era Cafe."

She listened to the story, but instead of delivering the expected tirade didn't say a word, just kept shaking her head. Her only comment, when it finally came, was, "So Milan Jelinek's wife was wrong. He was a crook like the others."

"I don't think so. Not like the others anyway. His problem, what got him in trouble, was he loved his wife. That witness to the shooting said it looked like he was reaching out for something as he fell on the devil strip. I'll bet he was reaching out for Sophie."

"That's sad, but I'm not sure I understand."

"Jelinek was scared. Not for himself, for Sophie. He couldn't bear the thought of losing the house, knowing how much it meant to her. A lot of men are in the same fix today, but no matter how hard they try, the opportunity to do something about it never comes along. For Jelinek it did."

My mind was busy as I ate the last bite of waxy cherry pie. "When you think about it, Harry Jett wasn't much different. He has a big house in Silver Lake and probably was afraid of losing it along with everything else."

82

"A lot of people with big houses in Silver Lake can't afford to pay the paper boy. I don't sympathize with them, it's those like Jelinek and his wife I feel sorry for."

"All kinds of people have been hit by this Depression, Sue. Conditions are a lot better since Roosevelt was elected, but I wonder what it's going to take to end it for once and for all?" I didn't add a conviction that had been building in my mind: a big war would end it.

For a while we sipped coffee in silence. Eventually I said, "Are you still going out to dinner with that creep?"

"He isn't a creep, he's a nice person."

"Okay, so are you going out with that nice person?"

"No. I told him maybe some other time. But that doesn't mean I've forgiven you for the things you said or that I've changed my mind." Without the least warning she started crying. It was a first, and I didn't know what to do. After a minute or so she said, "Oh, Bram, you really are a silly fool. I wish I didn't care about you, but I do."

That was all that mattered. I felt much better.


Ben Goldsmith wasn't overly pleased. He lectured me on the role of a reporter, telling me to keep myself out of the story. He said a reporter observes and reports, he doesn't participate. One more thing Harry Jett hadn't been aware of.

Jett and his pair of thugs faced murder charges. The triggerman hadn't even had the sense to get rid of the gun he used to kill Milan Jelinek. All of them were afraid to talk, however, knowing the result if they did. My testimony would be hearsay, and what I had seen in Cleveland was meaningless. The Murray Hill people were in the clear.

Miss Augusta Kaiser, though, had been granted a reprieve from eviction until the weather warmed up in April. She would lose in the end, of course, but nearly everyone does.

For the second time in little more than a month I started making the rounds of the used car lots. At the last of them I recalled how Sue Baney often said I was too easily influenced by my surroundings and experiences. Perhaps she was right. Listening to polkas on the radio – they filled the airwaves in

Northeast Ohio – made me gay and lively, but five minutes of wailing violins on *The Hungarian Hour* and I was ready to end it all. I'd pick out something on a menu; then, when Sue ordered something that sounded better than my selection I'd switch. And one afternoon I drove home in a four-year-old Hupmobile sedan with a sloping grille and oval headlights. The body was an eye-catching olive green, the fenders black. I hadn't bought it at Harry Jett's place, of course.

# NIGHTMARE ON NORTH HILL

We were discussing spring training, wondering if Lou Gehrig was beginning to slow down and if Bob Feller, the rifle-armed high school kid from Iowa, might lead the Indians to a pennant, when Jack Eddy casually mentioned that he had taken on the case of Pop Bannister.

I was shocked. Bannister was on death row at the Ohio State Penitentiary in Columbus, his date with Old Sparky only two weeks away. Further proof, I thought, that Jack Eddy was the sort of man who would do anything for money or publicity that might further his career. Preferably publicity. In the eleven months since he had taken a room at Mrs. Bauer's boardinghouse on Dudley Street I had found Jack Eddy totally ruthless in going after the thing that mattered most to him, moving up the ladder at Wellington's National Detective Agency. During that time he had risen from operative to assistant manager at the Akron office, which didn't begin to satisfy him. He wanted to be top dog at one of the thirty-three branches, then have a private office on mahogany row at the agency's New York headquarters.

As police reporter for the Akron *Times-Press* I had enjoyed a close-up view of his methods. He had used me in every possible way, taken advantage of my connections, pumped me for inside information. At times I resented this, but always went along with it. For selfish reasons, so I suppose we had more in common than I liked to believe. Whatever, acting as his stooge had led me to some great stories, enabled me to scoop the competition on numerous occasions.

My first words once the shock had worn off were, "You can't be serious, Jack. It was an open-and-shut case. The jury came back with a verdict in twenty minutes. Besides, it happened in the summer of 1936, nearly two years ago, so what can you hope to find out now? Another thing, who's footing the bill? As I remember it, the old guy didn't even have money to pay his attorney."

"That's what convinced me to take it on."

"What, that he was broke? Look, Jack, this wasn't your run-of-the-mill murder. Bannister killed an innocent young woman in cold blood, then stuffed her body in a furnace to cover his tracks. My God, the man's a monster."

"Are you finished, friend? Is the sermon over, has the collection plate been passed? Is it okay now for me to tell you what I meant?"

When I nodded, he said, " I was talking about another matter with his lawyer, Amos Dooby, when Dooby told me he's been working on the case free gratis all this time but is running out of hope. Then just jokingly he said he was a topnotch lawyer but right now would trade all his skills for my know-how as an investigator."

"And after that lathering on of compliments I suppose you told him you'd be glad to lend a hand, also free gratis. For crying out loud, Jack, you were conned by an expert."

"Look, smart guy, would you care to hear why a lawyer would donate his services the way Dooby has? Think of it a minute, a lawyer working for nothing. That's more astonishing than having Eleanor Roosevelt come out in favor of free love or repealing the child labor laws."

I was curious, but used a shrug to feign disinterest. "Okay, I haven't heard a good fairy tale for a long time."

"It's like this, Dooby and Bannister have been friends since they were kids. Grew up next door to each other right here in East Akron back when it was still called Middlebury. They had dinner together at *La Paix* a couple of hours after the murder took place. Do you think Dooby wouldn't have recognized the signs if his old friend had just killed somebody?"

"That's it? A couple of old geezers get together for a meal, and because one doesn't break down and confess to murder, it proves he's innocent? I can see Dooby convincing himself of that, but you, Jack, I thought you'd been around too much to fall for something so ridiculous."

"Look, sport, no one can top me when it comes to judging character. Dooby may be getting up there, but he's nobody's fool. In the morning he's going to show me everything he's got on Bannister, but what I want to do right now is run down to the *Times-Press* so you can dig out the file on the case."

"Sorry, Jack. I'm picking up Sue Baney in twenty minutes. We're going to that show at the Colonial."

"It can wait. Tell her you'll take her tomorrow."

"You don't just break a date that way at the last minute. Anyway, I'm taking Artie Bauer to an East High basketball game tomorrow night."

"You know, buddy, you must have the busiest social calendar in Akron. Okay, I'll tell you what. I'll follow you and Sue downtown, then we'll run into the paper and you can pull the file for me. You go on to the movie and when I'm finished I'll leave the folder on your desk."

I should have known it would end that way. Once Jack Eddy's mind was set on something, you might just as well have tried reasoning with a bulldog that had sunk his teeth into the seat of your pants. If tenacity was an investigator's strong suit, Jack would soon be running the entire agency.

Sue Baney wasn't pleased when I pulled to the curb in front of the *Times-Press* building at Exchange and High streets. "You didn't tell me we had to stop here first," she said. "I don't want to arrive after the main feature starts."

"I won't be a minute, Sue. I just have to pull a file." I didn't mention that it was for Jack Eddy, knowing how Sue disapproved of him, believed he was a bad influence on me. My attempt at playing coy fell flat; as I was walking around the car, Jack swung his big Auburn into the space ahead, honking his horn and waving as if we somehow might fail to notice him.

Sue opened her door and started to get out, in her haste causing my heart to skip a beat by showing more leg than usual. "Bram Geary, if you think I'm going to sit here waiting while you and that Jack Eddy –"

She was cut off by Jack's friendly, "Hi, kid." He thrust a paper bag toward her. "Here's something to enjoy during the show."

Two packages of Necco wafers and a Clark bar, her favorites. How had he known that? Sue murmured a weak thank you and drew her legs back inside the car.

The file was on my desk in the morning reminding me again of the day I had performed the most onerous task facing a reporter: knocking on a door and asking the bereaved for a photo of an accident or crime victim. Staring up from page one of the old newspaper was the picture I had obtained, one of a dark-haired young woman. A plain-Jane at first glance, but on closer examination a little pretty. Shy, introverted, yet still attractive. The kind of girl brought up to believe that satisfaction should be found in church, not a theater or a dance hall. Instead it was death that Sarah Kleiner had found in church.

It was a pleasantly warm June afternoon when at three o'clock she had gone to a large church on Akron's North Hill to practice the organ music she would play during Sunday service. When she failed to return to her York Street home for supper, a search was launched by her family. The following day the Akron police joined in and quickly solved the mystery. Starting about four o'clock neighbors had noticed smoke pouring from the church's high chimney. Despite the temperature outside they had paid it little heed until detectives began asking questions. Dental records confirmed that the remains of a body found in the furnace were those of Sarah Kleiner. The coroner had little else to work with, so the autopsy, such as it was, proved nothing.

Pop Bannister was arrested and charged the following day. The janitor, a widower, said he had left the church shortly after noon the day of the murder, walked to his modest home on Carpenter Street, and remained there until it was time to catch a six o'clock bus headed downtown. Two people recalled seeing him walking home; no one had seen him the rest of the day.

The Reverend Thomas Yarger said only four keys existed to the church's side door. He had one, Bannister another, and the two remaining were in the possession of Sarah Kleiner and the choir director, a man with the unlikely name of Simon Pourficte. The first time I heard it I vowed that never again would I complain because my parents, long dead now in an auto accident, had given me a name impossible to live up to,

Abraham Lincoln Geary. Even Lincoln's staunchest admirers never claimed he was perfect.

Neither Yarger nor Pourficte could produce anyone able to verify his whereabouts from three to five on the afternoon of the murder. It wasn't important; in those days who would have suspected a minister or a choir director? Yarger claimed to have taken the afternoon off to go fishing on the banks of the Cuyahoga River near an area known as the Chuckery. A century earlier someone had been touting a new community on the site, a town to be called Summit City. A potential investor asked a nearby resident what the population of Summit City happened to be, and the man replied, "Ten thousand. One human being and nine thousand nine hundred and ninety-nine woodchucks." While the proposed Summit City died aborning and was quickly forgotten, most Akronites could tell you where to find the Chuckery.

Despite the fact that carp were about the only thing swimming in the Cuyahoga in 1936 and few people were enthusiastic about eating them, Yarger's alibi was accepted. As for Pourficte, he said he was in Cleveland browsing through used bookstores in search of old hymnals and religious sheet music. For all the people who remembered him he might as well have been on the moon. Pourficte was the sort of person who could have walked past a thousand people and thirty seconds later, if asked about him, they would all have replied, "Man? What man?" He was that forgettable.

Not that it mattered; the police had already zeroed in on Pop Bannister. One reason was that no one else was familiar with the furnace and its operation. Dooby, Pop's lawyer, had rightfully argued that aside from being larger the coal-fired furnace was little different from those found in nearly every house in Akron and the rest of the country. No one paid attention, minds were already made up.

At that time it wasn't considered proper to discuss such things, at least not in mixed company, so motive was seldom talked about. Everyone knew, of course, and the fact that it was an elderly man and a young woman made it all the more revolting. Guilty or innocent, Pop Bannister was convicted from the first day onward. People who had always liked him began remembering his strange and sinister actions, such as chasing away the kids who had broken a stained-glass window and from then on refusing to allow them to play ball in the small lot beside the church. Or paying little attention to people but feeding every stray dog and cat on North Hill.

Doubters, and there were only a few, were always answered with one question: if not Bannister, then who? Surely not a man of the cloth. Surely not a choir director. And the premise that only four keys existed was taken as gospel, so to speak. The idea that Sarah Kleiner might have opened the door to someone was broached by Bannister's lawyer, but ignored. Nor at the time was any consideration given to the first point raised by Jack Eddy when I stopped by his office in the Metropolitan Building after he had gone over Amos Dooby's material: "It's a big church, buddy. Anyone could have been hiding inside for hours, even days."

Jack was on the verge of driving out to talk to the Reverend Yarger at the rectory next door to the church, so I rode along. The man was still as I remembered him, large, awkward, and untidy, a boisterous back-slapper, the kind with a certain appeal to those less forward and outgoing. He told us nothing new, but reluctantly admitted that someone could have been hiding in the church with little fear of discovery.

"Did anyone ever come with her when she practiced?" asked Jack.

"No, of course not. Sarah wasn't that sort of girl."

"What sort's that?"

One who would bring a man along."

"Who said anything about a man?"

"Surely you're not implying a woman was responsible?"

"I'm not implying anything, chief. Look, you all used the side door to come and go, but what about the front door? I thought churches were always open so people could pray and light candles, stuff like that."

"I believe you're thinking of Roman Catholics," replied Yarger in the tone he might have used in speaking of Attila the Hun and his hordes. Or of Jack Eddy, because Yarger had obviously taken an instant dislike to him. "We might have done the same at one time as well, but in this day and age we keep the doors locked and barred."

"Suppose someone knocked on the back door, could Sarah have heard the knocking from the bench at the organ?"

Rather than answering, Yarger took us across the yard to the church so we could see, or hear, for ourselves. They left me standing outside to pound on the door, which I did repeatedly until they came back and said it was no use, they hadn't heard a thing.

"You were up by the organ, right? How do you know she might not have been here just inside the door?"

"For what possible purpose?" Yarger answered condescendingly.

"To let her boyfriend in," said Jack. "Or because she had just come in herself."

Jack hadn't mentioned his next step, but I felt sure it was paying a visit to Simon Pourficte. He was saved the trouble by the man's arrival. If there are such things as generic faces and personalities, Simon Pourficte possessed both. Even his own dog probably didn't remember him when he arrived home at night.

Jack asked the expected questions. As I listened to the answers, the title for a book about Pourficte leaped to mind: *The Man Who Knew Nothing.*

Jack's final question was put to both Yarger and Pourficte: "Do you think Pop Bannister should get the chair?"

Their answers, if either included one somewhere among the verbiage, made me wonder why both weren't in politics.

We had wasted the better part of an hour, at least in my opinion, but as we drove back downtown Jack Eddy was exuberant. "I told you, buddy," he said. "I told you there was more to this business than meets the eye."

"Like what, for Pete's sake?"

He laughed and gave me a one-knuckle punch on the arm that brought tears to my eyes. "You're a card, friend. You can be kidding around and sound so serious you almost have me fooled."

Kidding around? If someone had been, it wasn't me.

"Look, Artie, just take my word for it." As I spoke, a March wind from hell was propelling us eastward along Market Street, enough of an irritant in itself without lip from a kid. "It doesn't matter how they pronounce it in Kentucky, in Ohio there's no Louie in Louisville."

Like most kids of twelve, Artie Bauer resisted any onslaught against his ignorance. We were bound for Goodyear Gym and the second night of the 1938 sectional basketball tournament. Starting at six o'clock, five games were scheduled fifty minutes apart, and in one of them our team, the East High Orientals, would play Louisville, a small town east of Canton.

Mrs. Bauer, being the good mother and landlady that she was, had packed sandwiches and a Thermos of hot chocolate for us. Grumbling all the while, however. She couldn't understand why we had to leave an hour before suppertime when East didn't play until eight thirty.

"There'll be a big crowd," I told her. "We want to be sure of getting good seats."

"Won't some of those whose teams lose in the first three games leave early?"

She had a point, of course. Explaining that we wanted to see *all* the games would have been fruitless. Mrs. Bauer understood Artie's interest but felt there was something strange about a man of twenty-four who enjoyed watching a bunch of high school boys run around in short pants and undershirts.

It was a ten-minute walk past lunchrooms, beer joints, pool halls, a theater, the East Akron Cemetery, and across the street, Goodyear Plant One. To the west was a cheap hotel and vibrant business district. A man could enjoy a full life without ever leaving the neighborhood, even when he died.

Artie and I joined an impatient crowd waiting on the sidewalk until the doors opened. They opened outward, of course, and the crowd was packed tightly against them. There was an interesting moment or two when those inside began pushing while the people outside couldn't give ground because others behind them were pressing forward. I knew from experience that small people were at a disadvantage, so I kept Artie in front of me and maintained a firm grip on his shoulders. A nearby woman about his size was less fortunate, being gradually squeezed upward until she towered above the mob, all the time beating at heads with her purse and shouting, "Let me down!"

East easily defeated a Louisville team long on spirit, short on talent. We stayed for most of the Ravenna-Stow game, so it was past ten when we arrived home. After a lecture from Mrs. Bauer on the evils of keeping a young boy out so late I climbed that stairs and knocked on the door of Jack Eddy's room. He was stretched out in his street clothes but swung his legs off the bed as I entered.

"Keep your hat on, buddy," he said. "We're going out to see the Kleiners."

"At *this* hour?"

"They're expecting us."

My protests of being tired and having to get up early went unheeded. We took my new four-year-old olive green Hupmobile, allowing Jack to sit back, hands locked behind his head, mouth going a mile a minute. We followed the short route through the mist-shrouded valley at Old Forge, up the steep Dan Street hill and east on Tallmadge Avenue past North High, arriving at the Kleiner residence in fifteen minutes. The porch light was on, and as we climbed the steps, the pebbled-glass front door was opened by Matthew Kleiner, the victim's father. He was a big man, close to my own six-three, but bent and haggard from thirty years of leaning over machinery at Star Drill.

The same years that had given Matthew Kleiner his stoop had added too many pounds to his wife Edina. The woman sat rigidly in a chair beside a gas fireplace with a large crucifix mounted above it. A younger man with the same tightlipped, unforgiving expression as his parents arose from a couch as we entered. Even at that late hour Peter Kleiner wore the cheap suit and conservative necktie that stamped him as a clerk at a rubber shop or downtown office.

The sparsely furnished room was warm, the atmosphere chilly, Decent and God fearing is how its occupants would have described themselves, but they were not the kind you would reach out to when in need. Upstanding citizens, the kind who took "God helps those who help themselves" as their motto. Despite their Bible's admonition, they would be the first to cast stones. Their eyes held the same glint of self-righteousness found in portraits of a former Akronite, abolitionist John Brown.

The Kleiners answered Jack Eddy's questions without any display of emotion. I had to remind myself that it was the murder of their daughter, not some stranger, that was being discussed. Jack had introduced me by name, not occupation. Mrs Kleiner showed no sign of remembering me as the man who had come for Sarah's photograph. For that I was grateful.

"We eat at six," Mr Kleiner was saying when I put my thoughts aside and began listening. "Peter was off work with a summer head cold, and Sarah said she'd be home by suppertime. When she wasn't, we went ahead without her, but when she hadn't arrived at quarter to seven, we decided something might be wrong. Mrs Kleiner called Sarah's friend Maxine Cahill, but she hadn't seen her. Then I rang the preacher. He went over to the church, then called back to say she wasn't there." He paused before adding resentfully, "The man didn't seem concerned about Sarah but was upset because the janitor had started the furnace but had forgotten to turn the damper down, so it was going full blast."

"He didn't open the furnace door?"

"He didn't mention it at the time, but later he said he hadn't. Might have saved us a lot of time and trouble if he had."

Not to mention giving the police a jump on finding out what had happened. But saving time and trouble, was that the important thing to Kleiner?

Jack also had picked up on it. His voice was sharp-edged as he asked, "So what did you do next?"

"Walked over to the church myself. Couldn't get in, but thought maybe I'd see some sign of Sarah along the way. About the time I started out, Peter phoned his friend Bob Quill, thinking he might help look for her. He was out, but he got the message and came to the house soon after I got back. First thing he thought of was that fellow who'd been bothering Sarah, that Mike Savage."

"Bothering her? How?"

"Calling up here all the time. Going to places where he thought she might be, always pestering her to go out with him. Picture shows, dancing, roller skating that sort of thing. Frivolities we don't hold with in this household."

I could tell Jack was itching to challenge him on that statement but managed to contain himself. It wasn't often that he allowed good sense to stand in the way of a barbed comment, so I was impressed by his restraint.

He turned to Peter. "Bob Quill, he's an old friend, is he?"

"We've known each other since grade school."

"What did you do after he mentioned this Savage?"

It took me a second or two to remember it was a name, not a description. It always had that effect on me.

Peter, whose round face, pug nose, and thick lips put me in mind of a frog, blinked his eyes rapidly. "We went looking for him."

"And?"

"We stopped by the place where he worked, but he wasn't there."

"And then?"

"He had a room up on Dayton Street near Jennings School. His landlady said she'd been out all day and hadn't seen him."

"So you didn't find him?"

"No."

"What next, then?" Jack's impatience with short answers was starting to show.

"Drove around looking in places where she might have been. Isaly's, places like that."

"What made you think she might be at Isaly's?"

"Maybe stopped for a Coke or ice cream, something like that."

"And stayed there for what…two hours or more?"

"We didn't know what else to do." Peter was starting to get his back up. "What would you have done? Where would you have looked?"

Jack gave him a placating smile. "Probably the same spots you did. Did you go in your car?"

95

"In Bob's. I don't have one."

Jack looked back to Mr. Kleiner. "This Savage, where did it turn out he was that night?"

"Summit Beach Park. With a girl, naturally."

"And during the afternoon?"

"Working, he said. Pumps gas at a station on Tallmadge Avenue, or did at the time."

"That's only a few blocks from the church, isn't it?"

"It is, but the boss claimed Savage was there all afternoon. Well, except for a short time when he ran a customer's car back to him after a brake job."

Jack turned to Edina Kleiner. "Your husband mentioned Sarah's friend. Maxine Cahill, was it? She had other friends, didn't she?"

The woman's lips barely moved. "I'm sure you wouldn't know young women of Sarah's kind. She was very discriminating when it came to who she associated with."

With Herculean effort I suppressed the laughter fighting to burst forth. A beautiful putdown, one that wasn't lost on Jack Eddy. But what had we learned? Little if anything we hadn't known from reading the *Times-Press* file. Jack wound it up with a final pair of questions addressed to Kleiner.

"Do you think Pop Bannister is guilty?"

"'Judge not, that ye be not judged.'"

"Do you think he should get the chair?"

"'An eye for an eye, says the Lord.'"

On that happy note we took our leave. As we crossed the long North Hill Viaduct that took us downtown I said, "Admit it, Jack, that was a complete waste of time."

"Not at all, buddy. Now we know the kind of people we're dealing with first-hand."

"I'd hate to have to throw myself on the mercy of that bunch. Why are some religious people so self-righteous?"

"You don't have to be religious to be that way, friend. Granted, when people who believe their way is the way for everybody go overboard on religion, or anything else for that matter, the result isn't pretty. Just be thankful they're a minority. If the time ever comes when they aren't, I don't want to be around."

After talking to Plato Largis on another matter at the police station the next morning, I mentioned Pop Bannister's upcoming date with the chair. "You're convinced he's guilty, Plato? Beyond a shadow of a doubt?"

The portly detective fixed his penetrating dark eyes on me a moment, then gave a slight shrug. "I don't have to be. It wasn't my case, remember?"

"I know, but you must have an opinion."

He grinned and gave me a friendly poke in the stomach. "What're you trying to do, boy, get me to second-guess a colleague? I can see the banner headline now: DETECTIVE SAYS BANNISTER NOT GUILTY."

"Too many words, Plato. Wouldn't fit on one line."

"Get me to say I have doubts and that hard-nosed city editor of yours would turn the whole front page into a headline. But seriously, Bram, I wasn't close enough to the case to form an opinion. I mean one based on something more than what little talk I heard. I'll tell you one thing, but it's strictly off the record, Okay?"

After a nod from me he said, "Nobody's said anything, understand, but there're a couple of boys around here would feel a whole lot better if they hadn't come down with the death penalty. From what I make of it, everything pointed to the janitor. But concrete evidence - I mean if you had said reasonable  doubt, then maybe, but when you start talking about not a shadow of a doubt, well…"

After deadline I gave Sue Baney a ring at her office and asked if she could meet me for lunch at Ptomaine Tommie's. She said she was busy and didn't know when she could get away. A little later as I walked north on Main Street I bumped into Helen Suder as she dashed out of Polsky's department store. Helen who worked in the *Times-Press* society department, asked if I was on my way to lunch, which she called dinner, then fell into step beside me. I'm sure Tommie's wasn't on her list of select dining establishments, but she didn't complain when we went inside, just sniffed and murmured something about proper ventilation.

We finished our burgers and lingered a few minutes over coffee, Helen rattling on the entire time about some high society event she had attended the previous night. She was the kind who would be speechless if she couldn't use her hands. She also used them for touching to emphasize a point, laying them on your arm or hand or whatever part of your body was most convenient. She was leaning close, her hand on mine as she related some juicy tidbit about society people I'd never heard of, when Sue Baney walked in, did a double-take, then turned and stalked out again.

Wherever she went, we met her coming the other way as we walked back to the paper. She gave me an overly sweet smile, the kind dripping venom. "I saw you at the lunch counter and was going to come over but was afraid I might be interrupting something."

Before I could think of a reply, she was gone, lost in the noontime crowd. Helen looked over her shoulder and said, "Who was *that*?"

"Oh, just a girl I know."

Helen's laugh was more of a shrick, the piercing kind of sound that can break crystal at twenty yards. "Just a girl you know? A girl you've been quite intimate with, I'm sure."

In the 1930's saying someone had been intimate with a girl had an entirely different connotation than it did in later years. Not only was I being wrongly charged, I knew the story would be embellished and related to everyone at the *Times-Press.*

My day, a washout so far, didn't grow brighter when I slumped down at my desk to look over the first edition. A flood in California dominated page one. They had recovered a hundred and four bodies, ten of them sightseers who had drowned when a pedestrian bridge collapsed at Long Beach. The governor had issued orders to shoot looters on sight. Cheery stuff, the kind that made me wonder why anyone chose to live in a state where earthquakes, floods, mudslides, and forest fires took turns in wreaking havoc.

The only good news was on the sports page. The Goodyear Wingfoots had won the National Basketball League championship for the second year in a row. Even that was tempered by my being reminded that East High's next

98

tournament foe would be the tough Massillon Tigers. I sighed, pushed the paper aside, and turned to the window, wondering what else might happen to make my day a bit more sour. It began raining.

It was late evening before I saw Jack Eddy. He had called Mrs. Bauer to say he wouldn't make it for supper, remembering for once that failing to do so was at the top of her sin list. Busy on the Pop Bannister case, I had assumed, but when I asked about developments, he said, "Didn't have time for it today, buddy. Been in Kenmore since early morning helping Cal Andres finish up a different job."

Before I could say something I might have wished I hadn't, Kitty Bauer came flouncing down the stairs. The voluptuous daughter of the household stopped in front of us, hands on hips, glaring at Jack. She held the pose a moment before saying, "I really appreciate being stood up, Mr. Eddy. You forgot we were going dancing, didn't you?"

Jack held out his hands, palms upward, the picture of innocence unless you knew this master of the con job. "Hey, kiddo, I called and told your mother I wouldn't be here for supper."

That made Kitty angrier yet. "You talked to my mother and that was good enough, was it?" After this you can take *her* dancing."

She turned and went back up the stairs, pausing at the landing. "I guess I know where I stand with you, Jack Eddy."

"Look, doll, I'm sorry. I'll make it up to –"

"Don't bother on my account!"

Jack turned to me with a bewildered look that quickly gave way to a grin. "Women! Who can understand 'em?"

"It's your own fault, Jack." I was thinking, though of how I had dialed Sue Baney's number four times and heard four busy signals. She wan't that much of a talker, the receiver was off the hook. I went to the phone and tried again. Busy signal.

The next afternoon Jack Eddy called to ask if I wanted to go along when he talked to Mike Savage, Sarah Kleiner's unwelcome suitor. As soon as I was off the phone, Ben Goldsmith said, "That was Jack Eddy, wasn't it? What's he working on that involves you?"

How did the testy old city editor always know who I had on the line? With him hovering around, a man had no privacy at all. Ben's nose was even better than his ears: he could smell a story at five hundred yards. Reluctantly I said, "The Pop Bannister case"

It tool a moment for the name to register; then the light dawned. "That janitor who killed the girl? Isn't his date with the chair coming up?"

"A week from Tuesday."

"What's new on it, Geary? How come you haven't kept me informed?"

"There's nothing new, Ben. Jack's just going over it again to satisfy Amos Dooby, Bannister's lawyer."

"Don't try to snow me, fella. Jack Eddy wouldn't put his pants on in the morning if there wasn't something in it for him. I want to be kept on top of this, understand? When can I expect something from you?"

For once I blew up under his relentless pressure. I slammed the dictionary I had been using down on the desk and headed for the door. "A week from Tuesday," I called over my shoulder. "You'll get the story that Bannister was strapped in the chair and fried that morning."

Sitting back in Jack Eddy's stately Auburn sedan helped ease the tension, lowered my blood pressure. It took only a few minutes to reach North Hill, a predominantly Italian area severed from the rest of Akron by the wide valley of the Little Cuyahoga River. Odd, it seemed to me, that with so many first- and second-generation Italians living on the Hill not a single one was involved in the case. It didn't matter, of course, so I put the thought aside as Jack pulled into the filling station that was our destination.

"So I called her a few times, so what?" said Mike Savage. A smear of grease on one cheek of his narrow face highlighted his unclean appearance, went well with the dirt under his fingernails. Such things were part of his job, but Savage was the kind who could step out of a shower looking like he needed another. He wasn't happy about being questioned and kept glancing out at the pumps, hoping someone would pull in for gas.

Jack Eddy pressed on. "Why her? Sarah Kleiner wasn't exactly the belle of the Hill, was she?"

It wasn't a fair question. Popular girls wouldn't waste two seconds on the likes of Savage. Beneath the grime his face flushed as he tried to express the plight faced by all the Mike Savages of the world when they yearned for female companionship. "She wasn't too bad. I seen her when we was at North High, and, well, nobody ever asked her out. I thought maybe, well, you know…"

"You didn't get to first base, right?"

"Uh, no. She was always busy."

"But you took a chick to Summit Beach the night Sarah was killed, didn't you?"

The questions kept getting more embarrassing for the poor guy. "Well, I didn't exactly take her. She was there alone, and well, you know, we got to talking. I mean we went on a couple of rides together, but then she said she had to go home." The story of his life in three sentences.

"That afternoon you delivered a car to a customer's house. Where exactly?"

"Up on Wall Street."

"Did the owner give you a lift back?"

Savage hesitated, more distressed by each succeeding question. I understood why the latest bothered him when he said, "Not that guy. It steams me the way he wants special treatment but never hands out a tip and always expects you to walk back."

So there went his alibi. Depending upon the route taken, it meant he would have passed within a block or two of the church. Might even have walked past the front door.

When we left the thoroughly miserable Savage, Jack wanted to see for himself. We drove to Wall Street, a workingman's residential street bearing no resemblance to the one of the same name several hundred miles to the east, then back past the church. Poor Mike, no alibi but an obvious motive. I didn't see him as a killer, though, at least not the cool variety who wouldn't have cracked during the first five minutes of interrogation by detectives. Those who had done the interrogating apparently felt the same way.

"Now what?" I said when we were back on Main Street.

"That's it for today, buddy. I've got another matter to attend to right now, so I'll drop you at the office."

He wasn't really trying, at least not that I could see. I kept my thoughts to myself, even when he pulled into an empty space across from the Metropolitan Building. Jack was dropping me off at *his* office, not mine.

I tagged along again the next afternoon when he returned to North Hill to talk to Bob Quill, Peter Kleiner's old friend. Along the way I decided it was time to express my feelings. "You're damned casual about this case, Jack. Here it is Saturday, just a little more than a week left, and you aren't exactly knocking yourself out, are you?"

He laughed, aware that it would irritate me. "You don't know the half of it, buddy. I'll be out of town next week."

"Out of town? Where?"

"New York. The agency has a special training session for some of the top men around the country."

"And you're one of them, huh? I just hope Amos Dooby didn't tell Bannister you're supposed to be digging up new stuff. No matter what the man's done, it would be cruel to raise his hopes, then toy around with the case this way."

"I'm not toying around with it, friend. Cal Andres has a few days off, but starting Monday he'll be working on it."

"That's swell, isn't it? Another one starting from scratch and without a prayer. I told you the first day you should keep your nose out of it. What have you accomplished, Jack? Nothing, not a solitary thing."

He laughed again but didn't comment.

Bob Quill was a far cry from what I expected. A real dude dressed to the nines in the middle of a Saturday afternoon. And he smelled of brilliantine or a potent shaving lotion, something dangerously close to perfume. In a hardworking town like Akron a man might smell of honest sweat, nothing more. What could Quill have in common with a stick-in-the-mud like Peter Kleiner? It was surprising that the elder Kleiner even allowed him in the house.

Our visit seemed almost a joke to him. He sat smiling, legs crossed, stroking his Gable-style mustache in the only comfortable chair in his Schiller Avenue apartment. A stone's throw away was the church where Sarah Kleiner had died. He laughed when Jack asked, "Did you ever date Sarah?"

"Me date Sarah? You must be kidding, fella. Obviously you didn't know her."

"That bad, huh?"

"Now, don't get me wrong. She wasn't a dog, nothing like that, but if you were looking for a girl to take out for a good time, her name wouldn't have leaped to mind."

Jack gave him a wicked grin. "Some men might see that as a challenge. Someone who thinks every woman should go into a swoon at the sight of him."

Someone like Bob Quill, that was Jack's message.

Quill didn't get it. Or maybe he did but didn't think it applied to him. His type wouldn't care for similar men, those who thought all females went weak in the knees in their presence. Anyone believing that of himself would look with scorn upon mere pretenders.

"Sarah didn't know anybody like that." He said. "Her old man would have chased them off with a club."

"But he thinks you're a swell guy, does he?"

"Why not?" said Quill, running a finger along the thin line of hair above his self-satisfied smirk. He was the sort of man you wanted to slug for no reason other than that he was there. "Me and Pete have been pals since grade school," he continued. "I'm like one of the family."

The weird thing was that it seemed to be true. Oil and water, who said they don't mix? Oily Bob Quill, the colorless Kleiners. Even Jack Eddy was thrown for a loss by that unlikely combination. He had only one more question: "So where were you the afternoon Sarah died?"

"Me?" That anyone should ask seemed to surprise Quill. I had read the answer on police reports long before he said, "Hoisting a few with the boys in a bar at Temple Square."

Jack had read the same reports. Still, he didn't press the issue even though none of "the boys" could say for sure that Quill was there after three o'clock.

We made one more stop, this one at the home of Maxine Cahill, Sarah Kleiner's lone friend. She was expecting us, had gotten all dolled up for the occasion. The effect wasn't what she had hoped for. She brought Mabel Klosterman at the boardinghouse to mind. A little too plump, a little too fleshy abut the face, a little too much makeup ineptly applied, a dress that might have been worn successfully by some young women but was grotesque on her. Features and taste little different from those of attractive girls, yet that difference was monumental.

She had made coffee and brought each of us a cup after we were seated in the oversized living room of the house on Vesper Street. Aware of her uneasiness, Jack Eddy made an effort to be gentle in drawing her out on a subject that was obviously painful. In the first few minutes we learned that she was an only child and had a part-time job in a nearby grocery store. Throughout the Depression her mother had had steady work in an office at the courthouse. Her father, in common with so many Akronites, had recently found a job in a print shop after being out of work for several years.

Jack carefully led her to speak of Sarah Kleiner, avoiding the unpleasant topic that eventually would have to be raised. "So you and Sarah were friends from way back?"

Since first grade at Findley School."

"Visited back and forth a lot, did you?"

Maxine shook her head. "Sarah always came over here. Her parents…" There was no need to finish the thought. We understood.

"Go out to places together?"

"Sometimes. We'd walk up to the Dayton Theater once in a while, but without her parents' knowing about it. They were funny about things like that. Sometimes we'd go somewhere for a Coke or to look at clothes, things like that."

"Either of you go out much with boys?"

The question made her blush. "No. Sarah never did and I, well not too often."

She meant never. If offered the chance she would have jumped at it. Why couldn't the Maxine Cahills and the Mike Savages cross paths? They might have made each other happy.

"Mightn't Sarah have had a boyfriend without your knowing about it?"

"No, she would have told me." Tears suddenly welled up in Maxine's eyes. "I wish you'd stop asking me questions about Sarah. Can't you just let her rest in peace?"

"Tell me something, kid, would she rest easy if the wrong man gets the chair and her killer walks around free?"

Maxine dabbed at her cheeks with a frilly handkerchief. "Okay, you've made your point. But why did any of it have to happen? Why did she ever let a man…"

Only the ticking of a clock on the fireplace mantel disturbed the hush that had fallen over the room. Even Jack Eddy needed time to absorb Maxine's last statement. When he had he quietly said, "Let a man do what?"

"You know. Get her that way."

After another moment of shocked silence Jack said, "Are you saying Sarash was pregnant?"

You had to be watching closely to see the unhappy girl's brief nod. "Nobody else knew, I was the only one she told. Well, the only one except the man responsible. He wanted her to, uh, to get rid of it, even arranged with somebody to have it done, but Sarah refused."

"This man, who was he?"

"Sarah wouldn't tell me. Whenever I asked, she'd shake her head and change the subject."

"Didn't she drop a hint? Come on, sweetie, think. It's important."

"I'm telling you she didn't. She wouldn't say a thing about that part of it."

The distraught girl seemed on the verge of hysteria. Jack went over and sat on the arm of her chair, patting her shoulder.

"Okay, don't get yourself all worked up. Look, you knew her better than anyone else. Don't you have some idea of your own? Sarah wasn't the kind of girl always out running around, so how many men could there have been in her life?"

"There weren't any that I knew about."

"Tell me this, then, was there someone else she might have confided in?"

"No. No one at all, I was her only close friend, the only one she would have talked to about a thing like that."

"How about her mother?"

"Never! She's the last person in the world Sarah would have told."

"And after what happened, you didn't tell anyone abut it? Not her parents, or yours? Not the police?"

The idea horrified her. "No, and now I wish I hadn't told you. Why did you have to pressure me like this? Even the police didn't do that.'

"Maybe they should have. Look, kiddo, I hate having to upset you like this, but a man's life is at sake. You wouldn't want it on your conscience that you might have done something to save him, but didn't. And think about this, if someone else killed her, he just might kill again. Then how would you feel? You did the right thing, so quit feeling guilty."

There was nothing more to be gained, so we left a few minutes later. Jack had managed to soothe the unfortunate girl, make her feel better about what she saw as the betrayal of a confidence. Now I was the one who felt low.

Nice girls like Maxine Cahill, why were they so often dealt a bum hand? And her friend Sarah, what kind of a hand had she been given to play? A normal girl raised to believe that anything enjoyable had to be evil, how could that idea make sense to anyone?

Jack drummed his fingers against the steering wheel, lost in thought as we descended the steep incline on Howard Street. The downtown buildings towered over us in thw distance. Just before bottoming out at the bridge over the Little Cuyahoga he glanced at me and said. "Tell me something, buddy. Why would Sarah confide in the only real friend she had, the one person she was able to talk to about it, but hold back on naming the man involved?"

"Too embarrassing, I guess."

"Come on, ace, use your head for a change. For a shy, introverted girl like Sarah wouldn't the most embarrassing thing be confessing she was pregnant? Wouldn't naming the man be the easiest part?"

"Look, Jack, how would I know how a girl would feel about something like that?"

"You've got an imagination, don't you? The way I see it, it has to be someone we know. If it was Bob Quill or Mike Savage, I don't think Sarah would have had any problem telling Maxine. The same applies to the minister or the choir director. I don't think she'd have hesitated a minute."

"So who does that leave? You're not suggesting—"

"Damn right I'm suggesting it wasn't the usual case of a boy and girl going too far, then having to face the consequences. It was something worse than that for Sarah."

"How about this, Jack. Savage, or someone like him, is the kind a lot of girls find repugnant. Admitting to a friend that you'd let someone like that . . . well, you know what I mean."

"It's a legitimate point. But there's no reason to believe Sarah Kleiner had anything more to do with Savage than turn him down on the telephone or at some soda fountain. Even then I think she would have come out with it, making it sound like she was unwilling but he managed to have his way. No, this was something far more embarrassing."

"Do you realize what you're saying, Jack? By eliminating everyone else you've narrowed the possibilities down to her own brother or father. Surely you can't—"

He cut me off with a loud snap of his fingers. "No, you're wrong. Damn, the answer's so obvious, why didn't I tumble to it right off the bat?"

"Tumble to what?"

"Give me time, friend. I just thought of an angle I want to check out, that's all."

"Yeah, sure. Quit playing cute and tell me what it is."

"I told you to hold your horses."

"Come off it, Jack. You won't tell me about this brainstorm because you're afraid of being wrong. Admit it, you're afraid of being embarrassed."

He laughed and gave me another of his one-knuckle punches on the arm. "When in hell did you get your degree in psychiatry? Me embarrassed, that's a good one."

But it was the truth. He knew it and he knew that I knew it. Jack Eddy could handle just about anything that came his way, but he couldn't handle being wrong, not if someone else knew about it.

We finished the ride in silence. This time he dropped me off at the lot where I had parked my car rather than making me walk the better part of a mile. I had one foot on the running board when he said, "By the way, buddy, I want you to drive me to Cleveland tomorrow. I'm catching the Twentieth Century Limited."

Leave it to Jack Eddy to pass up all the trains heading east from Akron and pick one that went through Cleveland. And to take it for granted that I had nothing better to do than act as his chauffeur.

Artie Bauer and I were back at Goodyear Gym that evening cheering wildly as the East Orientals battled Massillon for a berth in the following week's district tournament. East jumped out to a lead, and I watched fascinated as Paul Brown, the Massillon coach, appeared to be ignoring the action on the floor. At heart Brown was a football coach, of course. In those Depression years, few schools could afford more than one coach, so for Brown and others it was an all-sport job.

Brown was rewriting the book on coaching football. The things he originated would in later years be routine practice at ever level of the game. In the 1930's his Massillon Tigers were playing the best teams from as far away as Nebraska and Massachusetts, whipping them all by astronomical scores. Even so, no one dreamed that someday he would be the founder of two professional teams, dress them both in Massillon orange, and lend his name to the one representing Cleveland.

Now with Massillon trailing, the slim man dressed in brown ran a hand over his thinning hair, leaned back, and casually began filing his fingernails. The message of his discontent came across to his players more forcibly than any amount of shouting or wild antics. The Tigers fought desperately, but to no avail. East won 38-32; Artie and I headed home hoarse but happy.

I dialed Sue Baney's number to tell her the news and see if she wanted to go somewhere for a soda or sandwich. Her line was busy.

The following days passed in dreary fashion. Not just because Jack Eddy was off living it up in New York, or because Sue Baney was in a snit over a perfectly innocent occurrence. It just seemed that the whole world had turned sour. But damn Jack Eddy for making me believe Pop Bannister might be innocent, then going merrily on his way while I was left to stew over the rapidly approaching date of execution.

After supper I took long, lonely walks past rubber factories – Goodyear, Mohawk, General – all sharing the same air of desolation in the chill March darkness. I'd stop occasionally in some dim bar where rubber-workers drank beside those without jobs, men sitting quietly nursing their cheap beers to make them last as long as possible. Better that than go home and face the reproachful looks of wives who couldn't conceal their despair.

The men knew they were blameless, yet they felt the burden of responsibility. For some that burden induced guilt, and the guilt led to anger. The anger spread to those still working when Goodrich threatened to take five thousand jobs out of Akron unless the employees agreed to a substantial cut in wages already too low for anything more than survival. If that wasn't enough to have Akronites seething, Goodyear was ignoring seniority in announcing new layoffs.

So I was far from being alone in finding little joy. The Industrial Valley wasn't the place to look for it as winter grudgingly gave way to spring in 1938.

I spent part of one evening at home but couldn't get interested in the radio show the others were enjoying. Bus Bauer had his ear glued to the big Grunow console, afraid of missing a single word as The Shadow solved the case of the White Legion. Even straitlaced Miss Ferrabee had dropped her knitting, totally absorbed by the story. Old Mr. Reimer, the retired druggist, wasn't concentrating on the book in his hands while Mabel Klosterman was wide-eyed and beginning to perspire.

So why wasn't I caught up in the emoting of Orson Welles and Agnes Moorehead? My thoughts kept wandering without going anywhere in particular. The show was nearly over and all I could really recall were the commercials for Blue Coal. Did Pennsylvania anthracite really burn with a blue flame? No one I knew could afford to use it. And why didn't The Shadow pay a visit to Akron? He knew the evil that lurks in the hearts of men, but in whose heart would he find it?

Orson Welles was thanking the audience for tuning in for the final show of the season when I walked out of the room, picked up the phone in the hallway, and once again dialed Sue Baney's number. I felt like a fool persisting that that way, consoled only by the fact that no one else, Sue included, knew I was doing so.

Not getting a busy signal was so surprising that I was momentarily at a loss for words when Sue answered on the second ring. "Uh, Sue" I finally stammered, "it's Bram Geary."

"You needn't elaborate, you're the only Bram I'm acquainted with. Anyway, I recognized your voice. What do you want?"

"Uh, nothing in particular. Just wondered how you were. Want to go out for a soda or something"

"I have company, Bram. What's the problem, is your girlfriend busy this evening?" Or is there more than one, do I need to be more specific?"

"Now look, Sue, that wasn't my girlfriend. You know that as well as I do. And who's there with you, a man or woman?"

"I hardly think that's any of your concern. I have to go now."

"Well then, how about –" I was talking to myself, she had hung up, I looked around to see if anyone was within hearing distance. No one was, but even so I said goodbye before replacing the receiver. Having a conversation end so abruptly was embarrassing even when no one but yourself was there to know about it.

Jack Eddy arrived home on Friday evening while Artie and I were out watching East beat Scienceville. I had never heard of the place, and from what little I could discover, Scienceville was just a neighborhood on the north side of Youngstown. Now the Orientals were just a game away from a trip to the sixteen-team state finals.

Jack had dropped off his suitcase, then left again for his office. I was fast asleep before he returned, so I never did hear

110

how he got back from Cleveland, or if he had come home on one of the trains passing through Akron..

It was the Depression, I believe, that kept most of us from paying real attention to what was happening in the rest of the world. When the wolf is at your door, or skulking somewhere just down the street, you don't worry about the tiger on the prowl far beyond an ocean.

There was one time-honored exception. The starving children of India had a way of turning up in conversation whenever Artie Bauer or some other mother's child complained about having to eat succotash or dandelion greens for supper.

All that changed on Saturday morning. The first stories were coming over the wire when I walked into the newsroom a few minutes before seven. The German army had marched into Austria, Hitler was on the move. Only the most naïve could believe this wasn't just the first step, that more wouldn't quickly follow. The Beast of Berlin had started down the road to war, a war that eventually would involve us all.

A vision of myself in uniform exchanging fire with goose-stepping stormtroopers hit me. I shook it off, only to have it return periodically throughout the day. The resulting glumness persisted, even when Artie and I went back to Goodyear Gym that evening to see East beat Euclid Shore. The Orientals had won a district championship and a trip to the state finals in Columbus. I should have been celebrating, not shuffling around in a blue funk.

I spent Sunday morning poring over the newspapers, looking up now and then as Mr. Reimer clucked his tongue while reading of Hitler's easy conquest of his native land. Shortly before noon I dialed Sue Baney's number. There was no answer. After going upstairs and making my bed I prowled around the boardinghouse, restless and undecided about going out somewhere for a sandwich. I hated quiet Sundays.

It was a phone call from Jack Eddy that settled my plans for the afternoon. "Better get off your duff, buddy, and come down to the agency." He said. I asked why. "Caleb Cahill, Maxine's old man, is coming in at one o'clock."

"What for?"

"Look, friend, leave the questions to me. Just be here."

A direct order no less, and the prospect of obeying it was underwhelming. Nothing better came to mind, though, so I drove downtown, stopping along the way for a quick sandwich at a little joint where Buchtel Avenue crossed Market Street at an angle. The counterman was frying a hamburger for the lone customer, so I ordered the same. While sipping coffee I watched a roach crawl out from a crack near the grill, then up onto the cook's hot spatula. At that moment the man picked it up without looking, slipped it under the hamburger and flipped the meat onto a waiting bun, then slid the plate down the counter to the unsuspecting customer.

I opened my mouth to say something, but what? Pardon me, sir, there's a roach in your sandwich. The man took a bite. Now it was too late. I leaned back and watched him eat with gusto but kept one eye on that spatula.

Aside from a few early arrivals for the movie at the Keith-Albee Palace, Main Street was deserted as usual on a Sunday afternoon. I parked in front of the Metropolitan Building, rode the elevator to the fifth floor, walked into the Wellington Agency a few minutes before one. Cliff Austin was the operative pulling floor duty. I was passing the time of day with him when a man hesitantly opened the door, a cadaverous looking fellow of about forty-five with smudged wire-rimmed glasses and thinning red hair that stood out in little tufts when he took off his sweat-stained fedora.

Jack Eddy must have been listening. Before anyone could say a work, he came down the hall from his private office and greeted the man with an outstretched hand. "Mr. Cahill?" Come on back." Taking Cahill's arm, he guided him along the hallway. Over his shoulder he called, "You too, Bram."

Jack helped Cahill out of his overcoat, hung it on a peg, seated the man in a chair near his cluttered desk. I went to another beside a low table in a dark corner. I knew Jack Eddy, knew such exaggerated politeness wasn't like him. Was the man being softened up for the kill?"

A few boring moments passed with Jack telling about our talk with Maxine, her surprising revelation concerning Sarah Kleiner. I perked up a little when he finally got to the point.

"The thing is, Mr. Cahill, Sarah wouldn't name the man responsible, I thought maybe you could help us with that."

"I don't see how." They were the first words spoken by Cahill since he'd arrived. He had been tense up to then; Jack's friendly approach was helping him relax.

"The problem, as I'm sure you know, is that Sarah had limited contact with men. We've eliminated most of them: Reverend Yarger, the choir director, Bob Quill, a would be suitor named Mike Savage."

"What's the point in this? That janitor, Bannister, killed Sarah. Why are you dragging it up again?"

"We don't think Pop Bannister is guilty, Mr. Cahill. In fact we're sure of it. So who does that leave? Sarah's father and her brother." Jack leaned far back in his chair, locking his hands behind his head and smiling like that wolf lurking down the street. "And you, of course."

"Me?" Cahill stiffened, taken aback.

Jack went on being uncharacteristically polite. "You would have had the opportunity wouldn't you?" Maxine said Sarah often came over while she was out and waited for her. Maxine was never comfortable at the Kleiners', which is under-standable, so they always got together at your place."

"Yes, she told me about the atmosphere at Sarah's home." He gave a quick, high-pitched laugh, trying to appear at ease, not quite succeeding. "But to even think that I ... well, the idea's preposterous."

"Is it really, Mr. Cahill? Sarah was an attractive girl. A little repressed and shy but still appealing. Men noticed her, which was natural. With you being out of a job and Mrs. Cahill working all day at the courthouse, it must have been a temptation being alone with Sarah that way."

"It didn't happen often. I wasn't always home, you know. For you to think that I would have made advances –"

Jack suddenly leaned forward, his cordiality vanishing in a flash. "We don't *think* it, Cahill, we *know*. It wasn't difficult, was it? A girl like Sarah, not knowing much about men yet having normal curiosity and desires. An easy mark, wasn't she?"

"I don't –"

"Just be quiet and listen. We know exactly what happened. It started tentatively, a little seemingly harmless banter that soon led to bigger things. Sarah began coming over when she knew Maxine wouldn't be there and the two of you had all the time in the world. But you were stupid about it, didn't take the precautions you should have. You were frantic when you learned she was pregnant. So was Sarah. She had to confide in someone, so she told her only real friend, Maxine, but she couldn't bring herself to tell her it was her own father who was responsible.

"So you lined up some quack to perform a back alley abortion, but Sarah either was afraid or wouldn't go along with the idea because of her religious beliefs. Time was running out, and you became more and more desperate. She wouldn't come to the house any more unless she was certain Maxine was home. You wouldn't have dared go to her house, so you went to the church when you knew she'd be there. You were lucky, or maybe unlucky, because no one else was around. Sarah wouldn't listen, though, still refused to go along with your plans. You got more and more worked up, and suddenly things got out of control. You didn't plan to kill her, it just happened. Then you thought you could cover it up, figured you had a way to keep anyone from knowing what became of her. In you state of mind you forgot one thing, you forgot that no one fires up a furnace in late June."

Cahill was on his feet, pale and shaky but trying to bluff his way through. "This is unbelievable. I don't have to stay here and listen to this nonsense."

"That's right, you don't." Jack reached for the telephone, resting his hand on the receiver without picking it up. "But maybe you should sit down and listen a minute before I turn it over to the cops."

Cahill slumped down on the chair, frightened by the thought of facing the police. Jack let him stew a moment before saying, "Have you ever been in the back room at a police station, Cahill? And do you know what it means to go around the horn?"

"Sailing around the tip of South America. Or maybe it's Africa, I can't remember."

"To some people, yes. In this part of the country it means taking a trip to Cleveland. Do you know how many precinct houses they have up there? You start at the station downtown. They blindfold you and take you to one of the precincts by car. The boys there work you over, work you over good. Then they take you to another precinct and the same thing happens. On and on that way, that's how it goes. When you get back downtown, you don't know where you've been and you didn't see a single face. In other words, it never happened, so there's no use complaining to anyone."

Cahill was badly shaken. Beads of sweat that earlier had formed on his forehead were now streaming down his face.

Jack lit a cigarette, exhaled a cloud of smoke, then handed the pack of Camels to Cahill. "One other thing. That's the way it works with thieves and robbers, those who won't talk. What do you think they'd do with somebody who murdered a young girl and stuffed her body in a furnace and then was going to let an innocent man fry?"

The prospect was too much for Cahill. In a shaky voice he said, "My God, it was an accident. It was the last thing in the world... And don't you think it's been driving me crazy about Bannister, but what could I do? It's bee a nightmare for me, cant's you see that?"

Jack eyed him with contempt. "Sure, I see. I'm not so sure you do, though. You say it's been a nightmare for you, but what about the Kleiners, what abut Pop Bannister?" Jack picked up the phone. "And how about Maxine and your wife? Do you think that from now on it's going to be happy dreams for them?"

In retrospect I decided Jack had been right. It should have become obvious while we were talking to Maxine. He woke up to it quickly, and that, I suppose, is why he was a detective and I just stood back and observed. It occurred to me, too, that he had deliberately waited until the last minute in order to achieve the maximum dramatic effect.

The official word reached Columbus Monday morning, twenty-one hours before Pop Bannister was slated to take his last short walk. Akronites heard the news Sunday night, at least those who bought the Extra published by the *Times-Press.*

It was big news, but I hadn't expected an extra. Perhaps I should have; it was the only way to beat the Monday editions of the *Beacon Journal* and *Plain Dealer*.

I doubt if anyone else even noticed the point that gave me the most satisfaction. My story had pushed Hitler out of the headlines and down below the fold on page one. His first setback, even if he didn't know about it.

For a few hours the excitement banished the blues that had been nagging me, then they came creeping back. Was it the fault of the man in Berlin, the apprehension over what lay ahead, or was it the unavailability of Sue Baney? I wasn't certain, but I knew that life had lost its zest.

Even going to Columbus to see East play Hamilton in the state finals wasn't the fun it should have been. Sunday was to have been my day off, so Ben Goldsmith agreed to give me Thursday as compensatory time. Artie Bauer wasn't as fortunate. All his begging and pleading didn't convince Mrs. Bauer that he should be allowed to skip school and go with me. He didn't miss much; in a mid-afternoon game the Hamilton Big Blue eliminated the Orientals, 17-12.

I arrived back home just too late for supper. Before going out somewhere for a bite I dialed Sue Baney's number on impulse, and this time she answered. She had already eaten but agreed somewhat reluctantly to have a cup of coffee at the New Era Café just down the street from her apartment. It didn't go well, was about as enjoyable as watching East get sidelined in the tournament.

A few months later Caleb Cahill was found guilty. He was handed a life sentence rather than given the chair. The narrow escape of Pop Bannister seemed to scare Akron judges and juries off death sentences for a while. Soon after the trial Maxine and her mother left town.

Pop Bannister never returned to Akron. His friend Amos Dooby sold the house on Carpenter Street for him, then shipped his possessions to an address in Piqua, where for reasons unknown Pop had decided to settle. All I knew about Piqua was that it was in the western part of the state and was the hometown of the Mills Brothers, the popular signing group. I wasn't even sure how to pronounce its name.

Bannister was the big winner in it all, of course. Jack Eddy fared well, too, the nationwide publicity enabling him to take a giant step on his climb toward the top. Now that things had quieted down, he and Kitty had made up and were out dancing their shoes off several nights a week.

Scoring a big scoop over the competition meant I was another in the winner's circle. So why wasn't I happy?

Ben Goldsmith may have provided the answer when he joined me one afternoon while I was sitting alone at the bar in Stone's Grill on Main Street. "Been down in the dumps lately, haven't you Geary?" he said.

"I guess."

"Guess, my foot. You know what your trouble is, don't you?"

When I shook my head, he said, "You've grown up, kid. You've been in this game long enough to come down with the old newspaperman's affliction. You've learned about people."

JACK EDDY'S 1932 AUBURN SEDAN

# THE PHANTOM OF JOHNNYCAKE LOCK

*I*t was a bittersweet melody, haunting in its simplicity. A song of the times, melancholy, reflective, introspective. A hush fell when it began playing. Conversations trailed off, memories of old loves blurred by the passing years grew sharp and clear again.

When Jimmy Medlin heard it for the first time it was fresh and new, a popular hit of the day. Even young listeners who preferred the upbeat bands, scorned the mushy offerings of Lombardo and Jan Garber, fell under the spell of the latest release by Wayne King and His Orchestra. At the ballrooms and pavilions dancers clung tightly to their partners, lost for a while in a tranquil, secure world quite unlike the one awaiting them outside. And Jimmy Medlin would never forget that "The Waltz You Saved for Me" was playing the night he finally worked up the courage to pop the big question and Audrey Blaine said yes.

There was no other girl quite like her, Jimmy was certain of that. None quite so pretty, so pleasant, so much fun in a loving, subdued way. He couldn't think of a single thing about her that he would change, and now that he had found her he couldn't imagine life without Audrey Blaine.

What a difference six months had made. He had been jobless, without prospects, alone and frightened. In common with so many young people in that grim, hopeless year of 1931, Jimmy Medlin was embroiled in a daily struggle just to survive, a battle that pushed all thoughts of the future aside. But now he had accomplished the next to impossible, found a decent job, and found the one girl meant for him. Another popular song of the time seemed to play continually in his mind: "It's the Girl." Yes, that was what made his life worthwhile, The Girl.

I couldn't recall the names of those involved, but for nearly seven years the incident remained tucked away in some remote corner of my mind. A freak accident they called it at the time. The deer had leaped aside a split second before the hunter fired; the bullet somehow passed unhindered through several hundred yards of trees before striking the driver of a car on Riverview Road. A one-in-a-million happenstance, the sort of thing the best marksman in the world couldn't have accomplished deliberately had he fired a thousand rounds in the attempt.

The hunter hadn't come forward, later claiming he hadn't been aware of the deadly result of his shot. A persistent sheriff's deputy familiar with the area and its people eventually tracked him down. No charges were filed – what would have been the use? – but knowing the man's identity marked the case closed and put minds at rest.

All but one mind. The day the hunter's name appeared in the newspapers he had been viciously assaulted by the victim's fiancé. Had others present not restrained him it would have been murder. The assailant was arrested but never went to trial. Instead he was shipped off to Lima, committed to the state hospital for the criminally insane.

The events of seven years earlier came back to me only because the shooting had taken place not far from the spot where the dismembered body of a young man had been found. After pulling the old file from the *Times-Press* morgue and refreshing my memory, I did a sidebar on the all-but-forgotten case. It added spice, a touch of color, to my story of the mystery surrounding the body at Lock 27 on the long-abandoned Ohio and Erie Canal.

The gruesome killing resulted in some wild speculation in the Akron area. Many felt Cleveland's serial killer, the Mad Butcher of Kingsbury Run, had shifted his sphere of operation twenty miles south to the remote Cuyahoga Valley. The police and medics knew better. The murders in Cleveland were the work of skilled hands. The copycat was a rank amateur with a hacksaw, not a doctor, veterinarian, or butcher. Reporters covering the police beat, and I was one of them, could write that particular truth until doomsday, but a large segment of the population would remain unconvinced.

Only those who lived in northeast Ohio during the late years of the Great Depression could ever appreciate the fear inspired by the Mad Butcher. It was irrational, as most of us were well aware. The killer who periodically deposited bodies along the railroad tracks running through a desolate industrial area near downtown Cleveland picked his victims with great care. Most were derelicts or transients who frequented the rough, often dangerous saloons in the Third Police Precinct, the "Roaring Third." When they vanished, no one missed them, no one cared. With one or two exceptions they would remain forever unidentified.

Yes, we all knew that. Still the sound of footsteps in the dark of night banished reason from even the most pragmatic mind. And imaginative kids – all it took to send them flying for home was a glimpse of a stranger dressed in black and carrying a satchel that might contain a large knife.


I returned to the boardinghouse on Dudley Street after a late evening walk, shook the March drizzle from my coat and climbed the stairs to the second floor, ready to hop into bed. Then on impulse I knocked on the door across from mine, the door of Jack Eddy's room. He snarled something that I took for an invitation. The assistant manager of the Akron branch of Wellington's National Detective Agency was stretched out on his bed but still dressed for the street.

I said, "How about a quick beer down at the Lenox?"

For a moment he lay scowling at me, then swung his legs to the floor. "Okay, why not?"

Those were the last words he uttered until we had spent five minutes on stools at the East Market Street bar a block from home. He wouldn't have spoken then if I hadn't said, "What's eating you, anyway?"

"What're you talking about?"

"You've been out of sorts for three days, that's what."

"Keeping count, are you?"

"How could I avoid it? So what's up?"

He polished off a half-full bottle of Burkhardt beer at a single gulp, signaled for another, and then gave a shrug of resignation. "If it'll get you off my back, I can't locate a guy named Garland Skeen who came to town six weeks ago from Sandusky, then dropped out of sight. His mother's in a real tizzy, calls the agency every few hours. A thirty-one year-old man and she acts like he's a baby. Anyway, Cal Andres spent three days trying to run him down, then I took over myself."

"And struck out, right? Even knowing it was a mistake, I couldn't keep a smirk off my face. "Mighty Casey advances to the bat and goes down swinging on three pitches. Cal Andres must be laughing up his sleeve."

He turned on my. "Think it's funny, do you? For two cents I'd –" He cut it off short and stalked out the door, leaving me to wonder just what it was he'd do for two cents. I had a pretty good idea, of course, so I lingered at the Lenox until he had time to get home and into bed. Needling a man like Jack Eddy was foolhardy even when he was in a good mood. When he wasn't, baiting a coiled rattlesnake would have been less risky.

The second body was discovered early the next morning at the village of Everett close by the crumbling lock on the old canal. The first had been found just to the south at a place where the canal had once crossed Furnace Run on an aqueduct.

As was true of many of the forty-two locks that lowered the canal about four hundred feet between Akron and Cleveland, Lock 27 was better known by its nickname, Johnnycake Lock. Some of the names merely pinpointed a location; others told, or hinted at, a story. When a washout stranded a boat at Lock 27 for several days, the passengers had nothing to eat but the form of cornbread known as johnnycake. For the same reason the next one south was Pancake Lock, and a little beyond it was the Mudcatcher. Lonesome Lock nestled beside a desolate swamp, while a nearby distillery made Whiskey Lock a popular layover point.

Brawls over right of way were commonplace at the locks, so when a young muleskinner named Jim Garfield was on the losing side in one and ended up in the murky water, they didn't name the lock for him. They might have, had anyone realized he would go on to be president of the United States.

Why the killer picked Johnnycake Lock as a dumping ground was a mystery. It was visible from several houses in the quiet village of Everett. The aqueduct that had carried the canal over Furnace Run had long since disappeared, so approaching from the south on what remained of the towpath was next to impossible. At certain other locks the killer's gruesome work might have gone undiscovered for quite some time, but perhaps he didn't want it that way.

Finding the bodies hardly inspired an appetite for johnnycake or anything else. There is no point in going into detail, but in each case they found a little bit here, a little bit there. The latest – the one Jack Eddy and many others assumed was his quarry – was missing a vital clue to his identity, a head. Garland Skeen had never been fingerprinted and had no distinguishing marks or scars, but the reassembled body was about the right age and size. It seemed reasonable to believe that Jack could close his file.

It was the loose, uninformed talk about the Mad Butcher of Kingsbury Run that led me into trouble. At twenty-four I was young enough and naïve enough to believe the copycat killer deserved a name of his own. A police reporter with competition from two other newspapers needs to be creative now and then, but life would have been simpler had I just written a routine story. Instead, my lead read, "The Phantom of Johnnycake Lock struck again Tuesday night. An Everett man walking his dog Wednesday morning discovered the dismembered body of a white male at Lock 27 on the old Ohio and Erie Canal. In February the body of Pat Monahan, an itinerant recently arrived in the Akron area, was found in similar condition a short distance south of the lock."

Actually it was the dog that made the discovery. When I first wrote it that way, *Times-Press* city editor Ben Goldsmith bellowed, "Come on, Geary, try using your head for something besides a hat rack. Let's keep good taste in mind." His unfortunate choice of words set up a howl in the newsroom.

But Goldsmith loved the "Phantom" touch. It gave us an edge, he believed, over the Cleveland *Plain Dealer* and the Akron *Beacon Journal*, our rivals in the circulation wars.

It certainly attracted attention. More than that, it aroused the ire of the entire community. I was castigated for being a scaremonger by three mayors, two chiefs of police, the sheriff, and more preachers than Summit County had churches. In the days that followed, the man who handled the letters to the editor threatened to quit if he wasn't given either a helper or a fat raise. Goldsmith ran a full page of them one day, all hostile. I never really understood what all the fuss was about.

Even Sue Baney looked at me askance when I picked her up the evening the story appeared. It was our first date in several weeks and I was hoping to work my way back into her good graces. She had grown angry over a perfectly innocent occurrence, but had reluctantly agreed to dinner and a movie.

Before settling on the seat of my recently purchased Hupmobile sedan she said, "Was it Goldsmith who coined that disgusting name? I'm sure it couldn't have been you, Bram. Now everyone's using it, even the radio announcers, without thinking of the frightening effect it will have on children. It was Goldsmith, wasn't it? He's such a crude person."

"Well, uh … he thought it was a great idea."

"What's that supposed to mean? "

"Uh, to tell the truth, Sue, I thought we needed to distinguish him from the Mad Butcher of Kingsbury Run so –"

"My God, Bram, you mean you *are* responsible? I never would have believed it. What were you thinking of?"

"Selling newspapers, I guess. I mean that's my job, isn't it?"

"So selling your product justifies having the moral standards of an ape? You know what they call a woman like that, don't you?"

"Now look, Sue –"

"Oh, just shut up, Bram!" She opened the door again, slammed it behind her, and went marching back into her Massillon Road apartment.

I waited a few minutes to see if she'd come out again, then drove off in a huff. So much for a reconciliation. And where was the justice in life? It was me, not the killer, who was seen as the villain.


After the first edition was on the street and things had quieted down the next day, I asked Goldsmith to give me first crack at any other beat that opened up in the future. He laughed.

"What's the matter, Geary, no guts? Rather join the tea drinkers covering the county commissioners or school board meetings?"

"Look, Ben, I'm sick of the police beat. Sick of murders and getting phone calls in the middle of the night to go out to the scene of a plane crash or a fatal accident. It gets to you after a while."

He turned sympathetic. "Look, kid, I understand. I put in my time on the police beat in Chicago back during Prohibition when the gangs used each other for target practice. And anybody else who happened to get in the way. A hot meal and a good night's sleep and you'll be ready to tackle anything that comes your way."

Somehow I preferred him when he was his usual nasty self. Besides, I knew that his reporting days had been spent in Pittsburgh, not with some paper in Chicago.

He was right, though, as usual. A heaping platterful of Mrs. Bauer's corned beef hash did wonders for my morale. After supper I took a long walk through the East Akron business district, then past the Children's Home where I had grown up. I thought about dull evenings at school board meetings and decided I wasn't so bad off after all. As for women, from now on they'd just have to do without my company.


Soon after the first edition deadline Jack Eddy, his usual cocky self again, came striding into the newsroom and clapped me on the back. Harder than necessary, I thought. "Get off your duff, buddy," he said. "Let's grab some chow."

He had forgotten he was mad at me. I followed him out, thinking we were headed for Ptomaine Tommie's as usual. At six-feet-three I stood four inches taller than Jack Eddy, yet always had to walk faster than usual to keep pace with him. Rather than turning north toward Tommie's at Main Street, he pulled a surprise by heading south. Across the street the red brick buildings of the Goodrich plant sprawled over several city blocks. On our side was a motley array of saloons, uninviting lunchrooms, and second-floor hotels that sent shivers along the spines of fastidious passersby, business places catering to people down on their luck.

It was half an hour after the factory's noon shift change, but groups of men, those who began and ended work with a shot and a beer at one of the nearby saloons, still crowded the sidewalks at the bus stops. I was about to raise a protest over the route we were taking when Jack turned in at a place with an "EATS" sign hanging at a precarious angle over the sidewalk, an Armenian joint I had noticed in passing but always avoided for the sake of my digestive system. It was typical of industrial area lunchstands, a narrow boxcar-like room with fifteen or twenty stools at a counter facing the grill and a few wooden booths along the opposite wall. Grease had turned the walls yellow; Goodrich grit crunched underfoot and streaked the once-blue linoleum on the floor. The décor of flyspecked girlie calendars was highlighted by a "No Spitting" sign.

The burly, hook-nosed owner sat at the register in front lovingly toting up the day's take to that point. A scarecrow-thin man with a face the color of old cement and droopy bags under his eyes was doing double duty as counterman and short order cook. He came over to where we had settled on stools and took a pencil from behind one ear and a pad of green checks from the pocket of an apron long overdue for a washing. After coughing, then clearing his throat, he said, "What'll it be, gents?"

"A burger with everything," said Jack, "but start us off with a couple of cups of java, Jimmy."

The man stared at Jack, blinking a few times while he tried to place him. I couldn't believe that Jack knew this human flotsam, had been there before and now returned for a second

126

shot at food poisoning. Figuring a hamburger was as safe a bet as anything on the menu board I said, "Make mine the same."

The man started toward the grill, but Jack stopped him by saying, "Hold on a sec, I want you to meet a friend of mine. Bram Geary, shake hands with Jimmy Medlin."

It took a minute for the name to register. After a limp and greasy handshake, I waited until the man had gone back to his grill before turning to Jack and whispering, "You mean he's *the* Jimmy Medlin? My God, Jack, he looks fifty."

"What do you expect after seven years at Lima? It's not the beach at Atlantic City, you know."

"How'd you learn he was out and working here?"

"A couple of phone calls, friend. The ones you should have made before you wrote that sidebar. Think you'll ever learn to tie up the loose ends of a story?"

"I was on deadline, Jack. There wasn't time. But why did *you* check him out? What's your interest?"

"Your memory must be going, too, buddy. I'm looking for a man who's dropped out of sight. Remember now, do you?"

"Didn't finding the second body satisfy your client? Anyway, you don't seriously think that pathetic wreck is the Phantom, do you?"

"At this point I don't think anything. Give me a day or two and maybe I'll let you know."

I took another long look at Jimmy Medlin, then said, "Poor guy, he lost the one thing that meant something in his life. I wonder how he got a job in a dump like this?"

"That's what he did at Lima, cooked for the other inmates. He didn't belong there, you know. He went off the deep end when his girl was killed, but he wasn't crazy. At least that's what they told me at the state hospital. Anyway, his sponsor or whatever they call it had a room on Yale Street and this job lined up for him before they turned him loose."

Sponsor? Who is he, an old friend or what?"

"A local businessman. Claims he thought Medlin got a raw deal. The authorities felt the same, I guess, so they jumped at the chance to put him back in circulation."

"Why didn't this businessman give him a job?"

"Nothing open, I suppose. Not in Medlin's line, at least. This Peter Hobensack runs a beauty supply operation. Medlin's hardly the type to make a hit in beauty shops."

"Sad, isn't it? I mean think what he must have been, then look at him now. Life handed him a raw deal, Jack."

"Right, friend. Him and a helluva lot of other people."

The big news hit Central Police Station while I was making my final rounds of the afternoon. The second body had been identified, and it wasn't Garland Skeen, the son of Jack Eddy's client in Sandusky. I hurried to the nearest phone booth and called Jack.

After being told he could resume his search for Skeen, Jack said, "Great, just what I wanted. Well, at least the guy's mother will be happy. So who was the victim, friend?"

"Hold onto your seat, Jack. It was Herb List, the man who accidentally killed Jimmy Medlin's girl."

After a low whistle from Jack there was a lengthy silence. I was about to ask if he was still on the line when he said, "I don't get it, buddy. Something doesn't smell right. You saw Medlin, saw what he's like. Can you picture him as your phantom?"

"Not really, but hatred can do strange things to a man."

"So tell me, buddy, what did Medlin have against the other victim? What was his name, Monahan?"

"Maybe he killed him as a cover-up. You know, throw the cops off the scent when he got the man he was really after."

After saying, "You don't have to tell me what a cover-up is," Jack laughed scornfully. "Better give that theory a little more thought, ace. Medlin could kill a dozen men, but if one of them *was* List, everything would still point to him. That damn story of yours may hang him."

"They don't hang people in Ohio. But come on, Jack, the police would have picked up on it anyway as soon as they checked out List's background."

"Correct, buddy. You just gave them a head start."

True. It wasn't my fault, yet I still felt uncomfortable. I checked my watch, saw it was about the time Jimmy Medlin

128

should be going off duty, and hurried off toward the lunchroom across from Goodrich. I wanted to see him again, see if I might have been mistaken and Medlin did fit the image of a killer. Whether he did or not, I knew my next day's story would have to mention his connection with the Phantom's second victim and this time say he was back in Akron. The odds were against either the *Beacon Journal* or *Plain Dealer* finding out he was in town by then, so it would mean another scoop for me. That should have pleased me, but it didn't.

He was seated at the far end of the counter, a mug of coffee in front of him, a cigarette in his left hand. The filthy apron was gone, replaced by a khaki windbreaker.

I stopped by the twin metal coffee vats. After Medlin's replacement had drawn a mug and handed it to me in exchange for a nickel, I went back and sat down beside him. He gave me a quick glance and a short nod, the kind a person gives someone they have seen before but can't quite place.

Before there was time for his thoughts to drift away again, I said, "Jimmy, I did a story on you in the *Times-Press* a while back. Did you see it?"

He took a long drag on his Lucky Strike, drawing the smoke deep into his lungs, then shook his head. "Don't look at the paper much." He wasn't interested, didn't care, not even if he was the subject of a story. He had withdrawn behind an invisible wall, safely hidden in a world he had built for himself, one far removed from that in which the rest of us traveled. Our world had hurt him, wounded him mortally. Now, even though his body moved among us, his mind didn't. We could see him, but he couldn't see us, not really.

He shifted a little so he was facing me, and I was surprised to see the start of a smile on his lips and a faint glow in his eyes. "I read books. Wodehouse, writers like that. That Jeeves is really something, isn't he? Has an answer for everything."

More of his make-believe world. A pair of humorous characters, situations grotesquely funny, a world that could amuse Akronites but was as alien to them as life on Mars. Reality was missing, and that made the stories amusing, even to a lost soul like Jimmy Medlin.

"Go to the movies?" I said.

"Sometimes."   Again the hint of a smile appeared. "William Powell and Myrna Loy, they're my favorites."

Another surprise.  Powell traveled on dark streets, and Loy was kept busy dragging him back into the light again.  As I thought about it, though, it was the same thing, more make-believe.  Come what may, Powell never lost his aplomb, Loy never gave in to despair, the happy ending was never in doubt. Perfect entertainment for Depression-weary audiences.  Or for a man who didn't savor unpleasant surprises.  Cagney, Bogart, Edward G. Robinson, their pictures were not for Jimmy Medlin.

His rejection of the world, the walls he had built, had restored a childlike innocence in Jimmy Medlin.  Could a man like this kill?   Of course, given the right circumstances. Anyone can.  But could he kill as the Phantom of Johnnycake Lock killed?  I had no training in psychology, yet knew beyond a shadow of a doubt that such acts were beyond the capability of the man beside me.

He had been set up, was being used for a patsy.  Bodies found only a few hundred yards from the spot where the girl he loved had been killed, one of them that of the man who had killed her, all within months of his release.  What could a lawyer say in his defense?  Who would believe it was mere coincidence, or that Jimmy Medlin had been framed to take the fall for someone else?

This Peter Hobensack, the man Jack Eddy called Medlin's sponsor, was he a good Samaritan – or a Judas?

Jack Eddy slammed the door behind him as he entered the boardinghouse the next evening.  From the arched entrance to the parlor he motioned with his head, a curt gesture telling me to follow him out to the hallway.

"The damn fools did it, buddy," he said.  "They picked up Jimmy Medlin an hour ago."

"You mean they're charging him with the murders?"

He cast a scornful glance my way.  "No, they invited him down for tea and crumpets."

"The sheriff's been under a lot of pressure, Jack. Guess he had little choice."

"Medlin needs a lawyer, and fast."

"The court will appoint someone to defend him."

"Yeah, some hack without clients of his own and all the free time in the world. I mean a good lawyer, the best."

"Who'll foot the bill?"

"Pick up your hat, buddy, and we'll pay a call on that sponsor of his. Maybe he'll be good for it."

We went in Jack's big Auburn sedan, a 1932 model that would have held its own in a collision with an army tank. Peter Hobensack lived in a century-old house on a hill in Tallmadge not far from the traffic circle, a roundabout that left those trying to enter it with the feeling of pulling out of the pits at Indianapolis with the full field bearing down on them.

We made the trip in silence, giving me time to wonder about Jack Eddy's role in the case. It no longer concerned the missing man from Sandusky. Why would someone driven by ambition care about a down-and-outer like Medlin? The answer, I decided, was that he didn't. He saw the case as another opportunity to show up the police, to grab a few headlines for Wellington's National Detective Agency. And himself, of course. Favorable material for his file at agency headquarters in New York. There was a chance that I was wrong, but it seemed a slim one.

Hobensack answered the ringing of the doorbell himself, a newspaper trailing from his left hand. A frail man pushing sixty, an unlikely Phantom. The paper had informed him of the second victim's identity, but he was shocked to hear of Medlin's arrest.

He led us to a living room with high ceilings and a wood fire burning. His wife brought coffee. Without being asked he explained how an acquaintance had told him the story of Jimmy Medlin, how it had aroused his interest so he had asked a doctor friend to make inquiries at the state hospital. That led Hobensack to make the three-hour drive to Lima, where he talked with Medlin and several hospital officials. The upshot of it was Medlin's release after Hobensack had found him a job and a place to live.

131

His voice began to waver. "It looks like I made a horrible mistake. I never dreamed he would do something like this."

"He didn't," said Jack. He set his cup aside and leaned forward. "You can bank on that, Mr. Hobensack. There was a time when he might have killed, but it would have been in the heat of passion. Medlin isn't a cold-blooded butcher. Trust me, he's been set up."

"Who would do such a thing? How many people would even have known he was a free man and back in Akron?"

"That I don't know. Not yet, but I intend to find out. In the meantime, Medlin needs a lawyer. Can you help there?"

Hobensack removed his rimless spectacles, which were spotless, and began polishing them with a handkerchief. "On the assumption you're right, I'll take care of it in the morning. After all, if it weren't for me he'd still be safely in Lima."

On the way home I said, "What do you think, Jack? Is Hobensack the upstanding citizen he appears to be, or is he a good actor with a big knife tucked away somewhere?"

"He's on the level, buddy. Cross him off your list."

"What list? I'm like you and everybody else, I haven't got a clue. From day one the county detectives haven't said boo, but the Akron police have been monitoring it in case it spills over into their territory. On the q.t., Plato Largis told me the county boys have two prime suspects, or did have."

"Who are they?"

"Plato didn't say. Maybe he didn't know."

"Then we'll have to find out for ourselves, buddy."

"What's your angle in this, Jack?"

He was a long time in answering. Finally after a curt laugh he said, "Maybe I'm going soft. That sidebar of yours on Medlin, it got me curious. I did some checking, and then when I took a look at the guy I couldn't help feeling sorry for him. He got one bad rap, friend, and now he's about to get another. It's got me steamed."

"I figured you for a tough guy, Jack. Now you want me to believe you're just another sentimental slob?"

He laughed and gave me a friendly punch on the arm. "Think whatever you like, friend."

Fine, except that I didn't know what to think. Any psychiatrist or psychologist trying to fit Jack Eddy into a preconceived niche would have gone off the deep end himself.

We had spent the afternoon wandering from place to place in the village of Peninsula. Now I was weary. Not Jack Eddy. He was as tireless as a bloodhound on the scent. It wouldn't have surprised me if he'd thrown his head back and bayed. It was that way every time I tagged along when he was working on a case. I'd be worn out and want to give up, he'd keep pressing ahead, and more often than not it turned out he was right and I was wrong. Sometimes I wondered if I was a natural born quitter.

It started as it usually did with Jack striding into the newsroom at lunchtime and telling me how I was going to spend my afternoon. This frequently led to a good story, so if I had dug my heels in and refused to go along, Ben Goldsmith would have been all over me. I had been skimming the first edition, taking time, though, to read the daily story on Hitler carefully. Now he was talking about a predominantly German section of Czechoslovakia, an area most people had never heard of, called the Sudetenland. Didn't the man ever take a day off from his ranting and threatening? Couldn't he sit back just for once and enjoy his unbroken string of successes and conquests?

"Why Peninsula?" I asked as we drove north in Jack's Auburn. "Nothing's happened in Peninsula since the last canal boat passed through. It's a good three miles from Johnnycake Lock, Jack."

"I want to find out more about this Pat Monahan. That was the genuine murder, buddy. The second was merely to cast suspicion on Medlin for both."

"Who says so?"

"I say so."

"The infallible Jack Eddy."

"Just for once try thinking a situation all the way through, sport. Everybody believes Jimmy Medlin killed this guy Herb List. If it had been a lone murder for revenge, that might make sense, but it would have been out of character for him to have killed a stranger first. Medlin isn't crafty; he's not a schemer who would have dreamed up a plan like that."

I agreed, but didn't say so. We made the rest of the ride along Akron-Peninsula Road in silence.

Our first stop was a saloon on the only highway passing through the picturesque little town. People tend to clam up if they know they're talking to a private eye, so Jack was an insurance man looking for a few answers before his company paid off a policy on Pat Monahan's life. It didn't seem like much of a pretext to me, but it worked. If anyone had asked, he would have said I was a new man learning the ropes. As usual, though, I could have been the Invisible Man for all the attention people paid to me when Jack Eddy was present.

I never understood why it was that an unfamiliar bartender would grow suspicious if I asked him the time of day but to Jack Eddy he eagerly poured out every bit of information in his head. The guy behind the bar in Peninsula was an interrogator's dream come true. A person couldn't drop into the local lunchstand for a cup of coffee without him knowing about it and looking for an ulterior motive.

Pat Monahan had been a regular at the tavern. From the sound of it he spent more time there than at the store up the street where he worked.

"He was a real mover, know what I mean?" said the bartender with a wink and the kind of leer that always made me glad I wasn't a female. With men like him on the prowl it was a wonder any woman made it to twenty-five.

"Chalked up the scores, did he?" said Jack.

The bartender laughed. "With Pat around, a man didn't dare let his wife or girlfriend outta sight, know what I mean? The couple that run the store where he got a job – the broad's not a bad looker for being on the wrong side of forty, and old Pat had her in a swoon before he'd been there an hour. Take it from me, she didn't have a secret left from any man in town after Pat spread the word."

"So he was a talker?"

"Was he ever. Then there was the rich old widow at that big farm east of town. Fifty if she's a day but what the old girls would call remarkably well preserved, know what I mean? Everybody figured Twombly Dietrich was about to walk her down the aisle and latch onto all that dough; then Monahan comes along and she's head over heels."

"Twombly? Helluva name for a man. What's he do, set hair for the ladies?"

They both laughed and cracked wise. It was the kind of talk that under normal circumstances made me get up and go elsewhere.

"Nah, he's not that kind," said the bartender. "Rick, that's what everybody calls him, has that lumberyard over Richfield way. Off the job he's a loner. Okay, I guess, but not my cup of tea. I'll say this for him, though, he looks after his kid brother."

"So who doesn't? That's not saying much for him."

"Yeah, but you don't know Tibbals. A real piece of work, he is. Nothing upstairs, know what I mean?"

"Tibbals? Their parents must have had weird senses of humor. Meet my sons, Twombly and Tibbals."

They laughed again, and even I had to smile over that. After they talked a little more, Jack said, "Guess it's not too surprising somebody took a knife to Monahan."

"Yeah, a guy like that makes a lot of enemies."

"How about the other one? Victim, I mean."

"Herb List? He was the last guy in the world you'd expect to end up that way. In here every night lapping 'em up by himself, then at closing time he'd barely be able to walk outta the place. Always sat down there at the end stool. You know what happened to him a few years back, don't you?"

Jack feigned ignorance, so we heard an embellished version of the shooting of Audrey Blaine.

As we walked toward a lunchstand down the street, Jack said, "Great guy, isn't he? The kind that makes you wonder if this Hitler bird isn't right and maybe we should exterminate mankind."

"You didn't come across much better."

Jack laughed and gave me a friendly poke in the midsection. "Just doing my job, buddy. Wouldn't get far playing the role of bluenose, would I?"

"You've got a lousy job, Jack. Whenever I get to feeling my line of work turns a man into a rat, I think about you and feel better."

Jack laughed. "You know something, ace, that's the first compliment you've ever paid me."

That was too ridiculous to warrant a response, so I said, "If nothing else, we know that bar was the hangout for both victims. So do the cops, though, so it's nothing new."

It never ceased to amaze me the way Jack Eddy would have women falling all over themselves to please him as soon as he walked through a doorway. His eyes were narrow, his lips thin, his brown hair growing sparse, so where was the appeal? I was taller, had a full thatch of hair, and was better looking all around, but after a quick glance they'd turn away. The young waitress at the otherwise empty lunchstand was typical, acted like she believed Jack was Prince Charming come to carry her off on his white charger.

One thing about Jack Eddy, he certainly could steer a conversation onto the right course. Before I was a third of the way through my cup of coffee, we had heard the full story of how furious Tom Kellums, the owner of the store where Monahan worked, had been over his wife's behavior with the hired help.

"Poor Mr. Kellums. It was scandalous," said the waitress, all wide-eyed and innocent. You didn't have to be an Einstein to tell it would have taken more than a noontime orgy on the street out front to scandalize her.

Somehow Jack turned the talk to Twombly Dietrich. He was right, it was a helluva name for a man.

The girl sniffed at the mention of it. "Mr. Dietrich is a cheapskate. No matter how much he eats, he never leaves more than a dime under his plate. Sometimes a nickel. I feel like tossing it back at him and saying, 'Keep it, you need it more than I do.'"

I was sure she always managed to overcome the urge.

Jack said, "Maybe he's one of those guys who banks too close."

The girl shrieked with laughter. "Banks too close? The only time Mr. Dietrich goes to the bank is to try to worm more money out of them."

"Down on his luck, is he?"

"Flat broke's more like it. That's why he was cosying up to that rich, nose-in-the-air widow woman. Everybody in town was laughing like crazy when she gave him the gate."

"I hear Pat Monahan cut him off at the final turn."

"You can say that again. Now there was a real gentleman. Well, maybe not a gentleman exactly, but a swell guy, a real sport. You didn't catch him leaving nickels and dimes. He knew how to treat people."

Right, provided the people were wearing skirts.

Jack was all business when we entered the store where Pat Monahan had worked. The owner, Tom Kellums, set his jaw at mention of Monahan. "Hard to believe someone like that would have an insurance policy."

"I understand he wasn't … well, a man of good character."

"He was scum."

"Some people figure he got what he deserved."

"Not really. Being chopped up in little pieces was too good for him."

"Hear he made a few enemies around here."

"Look, mister, if you've heard anything at all, you can quit beating around the bush and come right out with what you're thinking. You're no insurance man, you're another detective trying to play it cute. Sure, I had good reason to kill the bum, but I didn't. Didn't have the guts for it, I guess."

We hit a few more places, heard pretty much the same gossip. When we finally returned to Jack's Auburn and headed back to town, I said, "It's always this way, Jack. We spend hours hearing the same thing every cop within a hundred miles heard before us, then you take a wild guess and sometimes are lucky enough to come up with the right answer. So what is it this time?"

"Come on, buddy, you know it as well as I do. We need one more thing to nail Twombly Dietrich to the wall."

"And what exactly is that?"

"Proof that he heard Jimmy Medlin was back in town sometime between the two murders."

"And the police weren't clever enough to suspect Dietrich? Kellums, too, for that matter."

"Of course they were. Remember Plato Largis said they had two suspects? You can bet Kellums was one and Dietrich was at the top of the list, maybe on the verge of being pulled in. Why else would he have committed the second murder? And it's worked out just the way he figured, buddy. They forgot him and went after Medlin."

"Pure guesswork. As usual, you're jumping to conclusions, and this time it's based on nothing but idle gossip. Trouble with you, Jack, you think you know it all."

He laughed and gave me a one-knuckle punch on the arm, the kind that hurts. He had taken it as a compliment again.


We arrived home at the boardinghouse on Dudley Street an hour before suppertime. Artie Bauer, the youngest of the landlord's clan, was lying on the parlor floor in front of the big Grunow console radio listening to Jack Armstrong. The All-American Boy's theme song was playing, and "Wave the flag for Hudson High ..." filled the room at ear-shattering level. "Hey, Bram," Artie called as I passed in the hallway, "let's go up to Hudson sometime and talk to Jack Armstrong."

I paused in the doorway. "Artie, that's make-believe. They aren't singing about the school in that jerkwater town up north of Mid-City Airport."

"How do you know?"

"Because it's a song about Hudson anyplace, not Ohio."

"If it could be anyplace, how do you know it's not Ohio?"

"I just do, that's all."

He waved me on with a scornful, "Aw, you think you know it all." Familiar words. Had I been around Jack Eddy so long that I was beginning to act like him? It was a frightening thought.

After a dinner of beef and noodles with brown gravy over white bread on the side and lemon pie for dessert, I dialed Sue Baney's number and asked for a date. She turned me down flat. I went back to the parlor half angry, half sad and found Mr. Reimer, the retired druggist, discussing the fast approaching start of the 1938 baseball season with Jack Eddy. The elderly gentleman, who was never seen without a suit and tie, was an expert on the game except for one small detail: before the opening of every season he believed the Cleveland Indians were going to win the pennant. He might have been right, too, had the Yankees dropped out of the league.

Mabel Klosterman was all dolled up for a date with her sometimes boyfriend, the bumbling Joe Kurtz. The vivacious Kitty Bauer came downstairs and told Jack Eddy she was ready to head out for a night of dancing. Her brother Paul, a senior at East High, waved goodbye on his way to a date with a girl from Goodyear Heights. That left Artie, Mr. Reimer, and me dateless. Or so I thought until Mr. Reimer got up saying it was time to fetch the elderly neighbor lady for their weekly trip to dish night at the Norka Theater.

"Okay, Artie," I said, "tell your mother we're driving up to Hudson to look around for Jack Armstrong."


For lack of anything better to do, particularly anything involving female companionship, I stopped by Jack Eddy's office in the Metropolitan Building after completing my rounds the next afternoon. He was in his private office gleefully exchanging boisterous remarks with Cliff Austin. "I was about to call you, buddy," he said. "I found what I needed, somebody who can verify that Twombly Dietrich knew a week before the second murder that Jimmy Medlin was back in Akron."

"How'd you find this person?"

"I'll tell you later, but right now we've got to head out to Johnnycake Lock. You haven't heard the best part; Cliff just roped Dietrich into meeting him there. Told him he'd found something interesting at the lock and would turn it over to the cops unless Dietrich met him there at four o'clock with big bucks in hand."

"Where's Dietrich going to come up with big bucks?"

Jack threw his head back, laughing. "Don't you ever get the point, friend? It doesn't matter if he does or doesn't, all we wanted was for him to take the bait and meet Cliff there. If he shows up with a big knife in hand, so much the better."

"Maybe not for Cliff."

"Come off it, sport. Cliff could take him with one arm in a sling."

"How do you know? You've never seen Dietrich, have you?"

"Don't have to, I've seen Cliff. Now come on, we've got to be in position well before Dietrich arrives."

"Position for what, Jack? If you think I'm going to take part in some harebrained scheme, you've got another ..." He was pushing me out the door, not hearing a word I said.


From the big bend at Akron, the Cuyahoga River meanders leisurely northward through a wide valley bordered by wooded hills that from a distance appear gentle and friendly. In reality they are laced with deep ravines and glacial rock formations that can prove deadly to the unwary.

Seldom does the river follow a straight line for more than a short distance before eventually emptying into Lake Erie at Cleveland. The Indians called it the Crooked River. The Cuyahoga was part of their waterway connecting the lake with the Ohio River and points south. From the big bend they would portage their canoes to the Tuscarawas River, which would carry them to the Muskingum and then the Ohio, the Mississippi, and the Gulf of Mexico.

For a time the Cuyahoga was the western boundary of the United States. Later the Ohio and Erie Canal used its valley as a route between Akron and Cleveland and depended on it as a source of water. Factory and mill owners overlooked its beauty, seeing it merely as a cheap and convenient place to dump their poisonous waste. At its mouth great ships and ore boats used it as a loading and unloading point and a haven from Erie's deadly storms.

The building of the canal brought prosperity to Ohio farmers, who until then lacked a feasible way of marketing

140

their products in the East. When its route was announced, a new town sprang up at the highest point. Until then the site of the town they decided to call Akron was considered worthless, its hills, deep gorges, and shallow bedrock making farming impractical. Early settlers went elsewhere, leaving it to the wolves, panthers, bears, and rattlesnakes.

Following the old towpath wasn't very difficult in March. In summer the foliage would change that. The canal itself, devastated by the flood of 1913 and abandoned as too expensive to repair, might never have existed for all that could be seen of it in places. At others it was clearly defined, and here and there water stood in stagnant ponds or ran lazily toward Lake Erie. In Cleveland it was still used by the steel mills as a source of water.

With the aqueduct over Furnace Run long gone, Johnnycake Lock wasn't the easiest place to get to. A large field, cultivated during warm weather, lay to the east. Houses stood near the old west bank, private property whose owners didn't encourage sightseers, let alone murderers, parading through their yards. From the north, the lock could be approached by getting on the towpath where it ran near the Valley Line Railroad. That's the route we took, and it might have been the one used by the Phantom.

Despite the years of neglect the lock wasn't in very bad shape. Some were in better condition, others far worse. All things considered, it seemed an unlikely place for anyone to use as a dumping ground for bodies or anything else. While a few of the old locks were all but inaccessible, many were far easier to reach and not within sight of houses.

Just south of Johnnycake Lock were the remains of a stone edifice I couldn't identify, although the pile of rocks must have had something to do with the canal. A quarry was not too far away, but how had they managed to transport such huge stones before the days of modern equipment? I didn't have much time to ponder the question before Jack decided it would serve as our hiding place while Cliff Austin waited beside the lock. As a place of concealment it didn't impress me, but Jack didn't even deign to reply to my protest.

When I first heard the name Twombly Dietrich I had visualized the man as a skinny runt wearing wire-rimmed glasses, a real Mr. Milquetoast. I soon decided that couldn't be true. In order to reach manhood a kid called Twombly would have to be handy with his dukes. The picture in my mind changed to one of a man built along the lines of heavyweight champion Joe Louis, or the fighter from whom he had wrested the title a year earlier, Jim Braddock.

I was wrong on both counts. When Dietrich approached from the north, he turned out to be an average looking businessman in a blue suit and cheap overcoat, something I wished I was wearing that cool March afternoon. Hands in pockets, eyes on the ground, he ambled along like a man carrying the world's troubles on his shoulders.

When he reached the place where Cliff Austin waited, he said, "Look, it's going to take me a little while to come up with any money. What have you got? What did the boy leave behind?"

I turned to where Jack crouched, a puzzled look on his face. He stood up suddenly and went over to the others. "What're you talking about, Dietrich? What boy?"

Having us appear out of the blue caught Dietrich off guard. "My brother. Isn't that what this is about?" Then he realized something was wrong, that he'd been tricked. "Wait a minute, who are you guys?"

It wasn't funny, but I couldn't help myself. Jack turned on me, furious as I let out a roar of laughter. I stopped, though, when it dawned on me that the man's uncanny luck had come through for him again. His deduction had been dead wrong, yet Jack's ploy had paid off with an inadvertent admission of the Phantom's identity. Dietrich had been aware of it all along, but had been looking out for his kid brother, covering up for him.


At noon the next day I braved a biting March wind and walked alone to Ptomaine Tommie's. I was halfway through the usual burger with everything and crisp hash browns when Sue Baney came in and took the stool next to mine. After

142

gulping the food in my mouth I turned and said, "Hi, Sue. How've you been?"

"Fine," she said, then studied a menu she had to have known by heart. She suddenly tossed it down on the counter and said, "No, I haven't, Bram. I've been acting like a fool and I'm sorry. Will you forgive me?"

I suppose I should have played the tough guy and kept her guessing for a while. Bogart, maybe, lisping, "Look, kid, it's all over." Instead I was like a dog that's been kicked, then at the first kind word goes rushing back to the kicker with tail wagging.

A little later I walked up the street to the Wellington Detective Agency wanting to tell someone that Sue and I had made up and had a date that evening. When I tapped lightly on the open door of Jack Eddy's private office, he looked up, scowling. Report forms and assignment sheets were scattered haphazardly on his desk. A cigarette burned in the ashtray, another dangled from one corner of his mouth. He didn't bother to say hello, just, "whadda *you* want? I'm snowed, no time for idle chitchat."

Before I could tell him to go to hell, he leaned back in his chair, lacing his fingers behind his head, and said, "We found that bum Garland Skeen this morning, or rather Cal Andres did. Living off a woman, holed up at her house in Kenmore while she went out and earned the money to support him. Wasn't a bit guilty about not letting his mother know where he was."

"Nice guy."

"About what you'd expect, buddy. She's been doting on him all his life, making him think he's something special. Whenever he got in trouble, and it happened a lot, he'd go running to mommy, and she'd put things right instead of teaching him he was responsible for his own actions. I'll tell you one thing, friend, a professional criminal, a Dillinger or a Pretty Boy Floyd, is made of better stuff than these selfish, look-out-for-number-one boys."

Jack wasn't too thrilled that Sue and I were back together. "Lucky for you the next stool was empty," he said. "If she'd had to sit at the other end of the counter, it might have been beside her ideal man, which you're not. Like the guy who

143

ducks into a store for a pack of gum, then goes back outside and gets hit by a bus. Forget the gum and the bus is half a mile away when he crosses the street."

"You make it sound like a person isn't in charge of his own destiny."

Jack laughed at that. "Wise up, buddy. What control do you really have? Do all the right things, follow all the right rules, and you've got the world by the tail. Then you go into a store for a pack of gum."


The Phantom of Johnnycake Lock spent the rest of his life behind bars. Not in the state penitentiary but at the hospital for the criminally insane in Lima. Swapped places with Jimmy Medlin, more or less. Some Phantom he turned out to be. Too stupid to make it through high school, not crazy enough to lock up somewhere before it was too late.

They didn't charge his brother for covering up the truth. It had bothered him from the start, of course, but he felt a little responsible because he had complained at home about Pat Monahan.. Tibbals Dietrich, who had been fascinated by the Mad Butcher of Kingsbury Run, had decided to help his brother's love life by imitating the Clevelander with the sharp knife, then discovered he enjoyed it. List had merely been a convenient second victim when he wandered out of a bar one night in a drunken stupor. After Medlin's arrest, Twombly was guilt-stricken, yet had still been reluctant to hand over his not-too-bright brother.

Jack Eddy admitted one day that he hadn't found someone who knew Dietrich was aware that Jimmy Medlin was back in town. He had just taken a flyer and had Cliff Austin call with the cock and bull story that Dietrich had swallowed. In that sort of thing a private operative had the advantage over the police. He didn't have to worry about building a case to take to court, just used any means available to get where he wanted to go.

It was frightening, though, to think what might have happened had it not been for Jack Eddy's less-than-scrupulous action. Everyone had been looking for a logical solution, including Jack, and there had been none. That a warped mind was responsible came as no surprise, but still we had believed that logic came into play and it hadn't.

They never caught up with the Mad Butcher of Kingsbury Run. Eliot Ness, the Cleveland Safety Director who earlier had played a key role in sending Al Capone to prison, escaped the Butcher's knife but even so was one of his victims. Ness couldn't overcome the bitterness Clevelanders felt about his failure to capture the killer. He had come to town with a big reputation and big ideas. He worked wonders in cleaning up one of the country's most corrupt police departments. He inherited streets that were so deadly that even crossing one was an adventure, and quickly cut the death toll in half. But he couldn't catch the Mad Butcher. His attempts to do so were sometimes brutal, so his shiny reputation grew tarnished and eventually was destroyed. He later claimed he knew the Butcher's identity, but a publicity hound like Ness wouldn't have kept it a secret if that had been true.

The tangled wilderness around Johnnycake Lock and the other locks between Akron and Cleveland would one day become part of the National Parks system. Thousands of people would walk the restored towpath and more challenging trails wandering among the hills and glacial rock formations.

People would go on killing each other for little or no reason, of course, escalating the pace with each passing year. As they gained more possessions, they lost the compassion, the help-thy-neighbor outlook of the Great Depression. A tradeoff, I guess. One that made us richer, left us poorer.


After his release Jimmy Medlin went back to work at the lunchstand, then removed his apron one day in the middle of a shift, walked out the door, and dropped off the face of the earth. I'd gotten in the habit of stopping by once in a while just to talk with him a little and was there when it happened. Nothing unusual had occurred, so I've never understood why he suddenly left the way he did.

After hearing his story, Sue Baney wanted to meet him. With reservations about doing so, I took her there that day for

145

lunch. They didn't normally attract customers like Sue, so Jimmy took an immediate liking to her, came out of his shell a little. For some reason he even seemed to see me in a new and more favorable light.

We had finished our sandwiches and were drinking coffee, in no big hurry to leave. While Jimmy was serving someone down the counter, Sue said, "I like him, Bram. With a friend or two, I bet he'd soon forget all about the past."

I didn't agree, but kept my thoughts to myself. Sue seemed to have decided to make Jimmy's return to normality her private project, so I wasn't surprised when she said, "This place needs cheering up. It's so dreary and lifeless, Bram, and that awful sign about spitting. Play something on the jukebox."

I walked to the big machine at the rear of the room. Six plays for a quarter, so I dropped one in the slot and punched half a dozen buttons. Mostly current hits you'd hear all the time on the radio: "Once in a While," "Bei Mir Bist du Schoen," "The Dipsy Doodle," "Love Walked In," "Thanks for the Memory," and one oldie, "The Waltz You Saved for Me."

# MAYHEM ON MARKET STREET

The pathetic whining of the old dog Casey jarred me from a dreamless sleep. I had not closed my bedroom door tightly so the Bauer family's shaggy, streetwise mutt had nosed it open and now rested his chin on the edge of my bed. Tears streamed from his eyes – and from mine. Had it not been for the bewildered, unhappy dog I might have believed I had been struck down in my prime by some mysterious affliction that had set my eyes afire and had me crying like a baby.

Then I became aware of the noise outside: men shouting, guns firing. Tear gas, that was the cause of my crying. And Casey's too, of course. What was happening? This was friendly, familiar East Akron in the spring of 1938, not the Somme in 1916.

My reporter's instincts clicked into gear and I hurried into yesterday's clothes, descended the stairs two at a time, ran down the hallway and out onto Dudley Street. Not the most prudent move, all things considered, but one that would have met the approval of my boss, *Times-Press* city editor Ben Goldsmith.

A few men went running past, but beyond the chain-link fence where Dudley ended thirty yards away at Willard Street a real mob was on the loose in East Akron Cemetery. Several tombstones toppled in the time it took me to run to the corner, where a fresh wave of gas assaulted my eyes and nostrils.

I yelled, "What's happening?" at a man who came over the fence, ripping his pants and gashing his arm in the process.

He ran on, looking back over his shoulder to call: "The coppers come out of the plant and went for us. Better run for it!"

I did, but down Willard toward East Market Street a block away. It was a reporter's job to head for the action, not away from it. That's what I was paid to do.

When I stopped at the intersection across from Goodyear's Willard Street Gatehouse it was like nothing I had seen before.

The plate-glass window of the Lenox Café on the corner was shattered, blood ran in the gutters, company guards and city policemen wearing gas masks wielded their billy clubs and more than a few had guns in hand. Some of the civilians, Goodyear men, fought back with ball bats and tire chains.

We should have seen it coming. Goodrich had just signed an agreement with the union, leaving Goodyear as the lone holdout among the Big Three rubber companies in refusing to recognize or deal with the United Rubber Workers. Along with that, employees were disgruntled because the firm was laying off workers without regard to seniority. The previous day an unexpected sit-down strike had begun across the street at Plant One.

Now a full-blown riot was raging on the streets and among the graves in the cemetery. I watched open-mouthed, but not for long. From the corner of my eye I saw an Akron policeman sprinting toward me, nightstick swinging above his head. I started to raise my hand and call out that I was an observer, a newspaperman, but my protest was cut short by an explosion inside my head.

I was dimly aware of lying on the sidewalk, of hearing gunshots and cries of anger and fear. I heard the sound of feet pounding past me and I heard the twang of a bullet ricocheting off metal. I mustered what little strength was left to me and crawled back along Willard Street to a small lot behind the Lenox. Then the lights went out.

Dawn was breaking as I slowly came awake. Jack Eddy was kneeling beside me, cursing under his breath as he examined the wound on my head. In a semicircle behind him stood the resident's of Bauer's boardinghouse, including all of the Bauer family except Bus, the head of the household and an ardent union man at Goodyear.

"We can't find Daddy," said the vivacious Kitty, eldest of the family's three children. "Have you seen him?"

The question was absurd. Couldn't the empty-headed girl see the condition I was in? I lifted my head from the ground, seeing blood still collected in the gutter and more of it close by that was my own. "I haven't seen anybody. Not since that cop crowned me for no reason at all."

"Think you can walk, buddy?" asked Jack. He was hoisting me to my feet without waiting for an answer. My knees buckled after a couple of tentative steps, but he held on tight to keep me from falling.

He said, "Bram Geary, ace reporter, felled in the line of duty." Then he laughed.

If only a photographer had been there to capture the expressions on the faces around me. Sweat was rolling down pudgy Mabel Klosterman's ghastly pale cheeks, prim and proper Nora Ferrabee was as outraged as if some ragamuffin had lifted her skirt, old Mr. Reimer had the gray look of someone more dead than alive. Kitty was totally bewildered, but Mrs. Bauer and her oldest son, Paul, appeared ready to take on an army, preferably an army of Akron policemen. Twelve-year-old Artie Bauer, however, was having the time of his young life. And old Casey was back to normal, his tail wagging a little as he tried to understand why all the people in his usually tranquil world were behaving so strangely.

It wasn't far to the boardinghouse, not much more than a hundred yards, but it seemed like miles. Climbing the porch steps was like scaling Everest, but once inside I insisted on calling Ben Goldsmith before receiving any treatment.

He was less than sympathetic. "Get down here, Geary," he said. "We had three men and a photographer out there so you can work with them on adding a personal touch. First, though, drive around the area and see how things stand now."

That's what I did after Jack and Mabel had cleansed my wound and poured on something that burned like the fires of hell. "He should be in the hospital," said Mabel.

"What, for a little tap on the noggin?" replied Jack. "Forget it, he's okay." I guess that lack of concern was all that could be expected from a hard-bitten private eye.

As I started out I saw two round black marks on the side of the house where tear gas shells had hit. I checked my olive green Hupmobile sedan for damage. It had emerged unscathed.

East Market Street, usually alive with people, was deserted. A machine gun pointed downward from the Goodyear clock tower, another was mounted on the steps of the Goodyear State

Bank. Beneath the small bridge on Case Avenue a policeman's motorcycle lay on its side in the shallow water of the Little Cuyahoga River. Men who replaced window glass were going to have a field day.

As the day wore on, more of the story would come out. Housewives leaving the Rialto Theater after Bank Night found themselves in the middle of the melee and some were chased and beaten by policemen. More than a hundred people went to hospitals. Mayor Lee D. Schroy had sent his boys in blue to join company guards in staging the attack, thereby ingratiating himself with the city's industrialists and ensuring his defeat at the next election. Like residents of any blue-collar town, Akronites didn't look kindly on cops assaulting workers, let alone women coming out of a theater. Newspaper reporters ... well, maybe.

Jack Eddy had found Bus Bauer at a temporary union headquarters on Case Avenue. It had been hastily set up after the police had burned their headquarters across from Plant One. I drove east again on Market Street until I saw the rest of the Bauer clan and told them to go home, Bus was okay and would be there.

When I arrived at the *Times-Press* building downtown, Ben Goldsmith was trying to hide his disgust as he explained to the newsroom staff the manner in which the top brass had decided to play the story: the workers were to blame and the police were just doing their job of maintaining law and order.

That was a charade in which I refused to take part. Life on the police beat bore no resemblance to an afternoon tea at the Womens' Club, but I loved my job. Even so I was ready to hand Goldsmith my resignation when he looked up from where he was talking on the phone and said, "Drop that, Geary, let the others handle it. There's been a murder and I want you out there."

"Where?"

"Around the corner from that dump where you live. Willard Street."

Had all of East Akron gone suddenly mad? Riots, murders, what next?

"Was this connected with the riot?" I said.

"How the hell would I know? That's what I'm sending you to find out. Get moving."

Artie Bauer, on his way to Kent School, was bent over picking something up, then placing it in a cigar box as I turned off East Market onto Willard. I stopped to ask what he was doing.

"Pickin' up empty tear gas shells to take and show the girls. The ones that live over by Arlington Street and missed the fun." He showed me the box half filled with red cardboard casings.

"You'd better be careful, Artie. If you let kids smell those things and they get sick you could be in big trouble."

He laughed scornfully. "Just the girls. The pretty ones, I mean. They won't snitch on me."

Artie Bauer, Big Man for a day. Well, maybe I'd have done the same thing when I was his age and headed for another boring day in sixth grade at the decrepit old building on South Arlington.

Me and Hawkeye seen 'em before it started," he said.

"Saw what?"

"The guys on strike. We was comin' back from the Troop 45 scout meetin' up in Goodyear Heights and they had Market Street practically blocked off. Guys with clubs and tire chains, stuff like that."

"And you didn't tell me?" I was hot under the collar. "I could have been there right at the beginning. Thanks a lot, Artie."

He hung his head for a few seconds, then lifted it again and stared at me defiantly. "You was up in your room already when I got home. Besides, what'd you ever do for me?"

I could think of a hundred things, but when I opened the car door to start after him he took off on the dead run, stopping at the corner just long enough to raise one finger in the air and give me the raspberry.

The scene of the murder was near the far end of the street. I was hoping to find Plato Largis in charge of the investigation. Instead it was a young detective named Ed Mayhew. From the time of our first meeting we had taken a dislike to each other. He had no use for reporters and I didn't think much of his slipshod methods, his desire for a quick and easy solution to any assignment.

This case was right up his alley. Another sordid ending of a life when words failed and a gun was handy. In this instance the victim's own gun. He was a man of about fifty who lived with a grown daughter since divorcing his wife a year earlier. He had been shot twice from behind in the kitchen of the two-story house. I recognized Red Spivey as a man I had seen discussing union business with Bus Bauer at the boardinghouse. The daughter, Esther, was nowhere to be seen.

A gabby neighbor was giving Mayhew his view of what had happened even though he hadn't been there when the shots were fired. When Mayhew had heard enough, he sent the man on his way and headed for me, a supercilious grin on his face.

"Open and shut from the look of it," he said. "Spivey stomped the daylights out of the daughter's boyfriend and sent him packing yesterday evening. The girl took off in hysterics. Pretty obvious that the boyfriend, a kid named Andy Butler, came back and took care of the old man. He and the daughter have probably headed for the hills."

I bit my tongue to keep from saying, "Obvious to whom?" Mayhew had settled on the Butler youth as the killer without bothering to consider the daughter, the ex-wife, or that it might have had something to do with union business, the riot, or a hundred other possibilities. Unless the kid had an airtight alibi he was in for it when Mayhew tracked him down.

I went back to the newsroom and wrote the story, such as it was, without mentioning Mayhew's easy solution. It didn't matter, it would get short shrift on a day when the riot would dominate the pages of the *Times-Press* and the rival *Beacon Journal*. The latter's police reporter, Tom Kennedy, had been at the house while I was there and had shown the same enthusiasm for the story that I had. And like me he felt that sans-alibi, Andy Butler was a dead duck.

By the time I headed home late in the afternoon, Butler had been in custody for several hours. He had been picked up at the house on Talbot Street where he lived with his parents and two sisters. His face was a mess from the beating and he was covered with bruises. He said he had been despondent over being embarrassed in front of his girl and being ordered to never darken her door again. He had walked the streets for most of the night without seeing anyone he knew or stopping someplace where people might remember seeing him. As he told me this, Mayhew wore a self-satisfied smirk.

Esther Spivey went home after hearing about the murder while listening to the radio at a friend's house. She said she had fled after watching her boyfriend take a beating and, like Butler, had wanted to be alone so she had spent hours at a downtown theater. Again like Butler, she had seen no one she knew and lacked an alibi for the time of the killing. She told Mayhew that her father had kept his gun, a small-caliber pistol, in a kitchen table drawer. He had made a habit of showing it to nearly everyone who visited the house so its location was far from being a secret.

I went straight to bed after telling Mrs. Bauer not to call me for supper. Nothing could have convinced her that I was in bad shape as effectively as that. My last thought before my head hit the pillow was that a person needed to be very careful about spending time alone and unaccounted for just in case someone he knew happened to be murdered.

Luckily I had the next day off work so it was mid-morning before I showed my face downstairs. After giving me a critical looking over, Mrs. Bauer rushed to the kitchen and prepared a heaping breakfast of bacon and eggs, hash browns, sausage, orange juice and coffee for me. This was unheard of for boarders on any day other than Sunday. I still had little appetite, but my brain was functioning enough to keep that fact hidden from Ivy Bauer. Had I not eaten, or even just picked at my food, I'm sure an ambulance would have pulled up at the front door.

Sue Baney arrived shortly after I forced down the last of the food on my plate. Mabel Klosterman had phoned her to say that her sometimes-boyfriend was at death's door, or words to that effect. Apparently everyone had the day off work because what was left of the morning passed with Sue, Mabel, Kitty, Nora Ferrabee and Mrs. Bauer taking turns looking at me, clucking their tongues and shaking their heads. It would have been more relaxing for me if it had been a workday. I really wanted to go upstairs and lie down, but doing so would only have convinced them that I was a goner.

The riot had shaken both the union and company leaders. They reached an agreement on Sunday and everyone was back at work on Tuesday. After supper that evening Jack Eddy cornered me on the front porch and began pumping me for information on the Spivey murder.

Andy Butler's family, correctly believing that the police investigation was over, had hired Wellington's National Detective Agency to dig beyond the surface. As an assistant manager of the agency's Akron branch, Jack Eddy had assigned the case to Cliff Austin. An hour later Austin twisted his ankle while stepping off a curb, putting himself out of action for a week or more. The rest of the agency's operatives were either busy on other cases or lacked sufficient experience for a major assignment so Jack took over himself. Now he wanted to know what I could tell him that hadn't appeared in the newspaper.

"There's nothing to tell, Jack," I said. "How come you always manage to get your nose into these things?"

"Because we deliver the goods, buddy. We have a reputation. The public knows how we operate."

He was half right. Wellington's delivered, that was true, but the public had no idea of the way the agency operated. The police had rules and regulations to follow, Jack Eddy and his breed paid little more heed to the law than did the crooks and killers.

"Tell me something, Jack, have you ever had a client who was guilty?"

"Never," he said in that supremely confident, overbearing way of his that could be so annoying. "If we find one who is, we drop him like a hot potato."

That was another of his irritating habits, always working a cliché into everything he said. Whenever his name was mentioned the same picture leaped to mind: a cocksure expression on his square, thin-lipped face, a cigarette dangling from one corner of his mouth, his collar unbuttoned and necktie loosened, his fingers running through thinning sandy hair, statements pouring from his mouth with the staccato beat of a machine gun and often followed by a humorless laugh.

He was a hard and overly ambitious man, Jack Eddy. A reliable friend, though, and a fine detective, as well as a lucky one who always seemed to catch the breaks. He had put me on the trail of numerous big stories so I told him what I knew of the case that had gone unwritten. It wasn't enough to make a decent-size paragraph.

Jack left in pursuit of something or someone, so after listening to Kenny Baker sing *Love Walked In* on Bus Bauer's big Grunow radio I called Sue Baney, then picked her up at her apartment on Massillon Road. It wasn't much of a date, a movie at Loew's, a hamburger at a drive-in called *The Pilot* across from the airport, a goodnight kiss that ended with her slapping my hand and rushing inside without issuing an invitation for me to tag along.


I won a wager with myself the next day when Jack Eddy strolled into the newsroom just after deadline. His method of operating had become quite predictable to me after being around him for more than a year. He had other matters than just lunch in mind, of course, but we walked north on Main Street to my usual lunchroom, *Ptomaine Tommie's,* but it had changed hands and now was called *Kippy's*. Jack felt the new name was an improvement. I liked the old one better. It was unique, had distinction and character.

Jack allowed me to talk baseball for a minute or two, then broke into the middle of a sentence with: "The Spivey broad was no angel, you know."

"I didn't know, and I don't really care. No one in Akron cares."

"She and her old man fought like cats and dogs. He fixed her up with an out-of town union organizer and she wanted no part of the guy."

"And that makes her no angel? Come off it, Jack."

"Finish that 'burger, will you. We're going out to union headquarters, buddy."

155

"I have a job, Jack. It's time for my afternoon rounds and after that —"

"Later, friend, later. My car's parked just around the corner."

So we drove out to Case Avenue in his 1932 Auburn sedan, a car I secretly coveted. I liked my Hupmobile, a fine car and a beauty, but Jack's brown Auburn was a classic. To Jack Eddy it was just a means of getting from one place to another.

"What's this lover boy's name? I asked.

"Guido Minardi." He pronounced it *Gee-dough*.

"It's *Gwee*, not *Gee*. *Gwee-dough*."

"Well pardon me for living, pal. Just think, without you I might have committed a real *faux pas*." He pronounced it *fox paw*, but I kept my mouth shut. I had learned that when Jack Eddy called you buddy or friend, he meant it. When it was pal, sport, chief or Mac you knew you were not among his favorite people. It didn't matter; an hour later he would have forgotten about being mad. Or, as Jack would have put it in cliché-fashion, when it came to relationships he blew hot and cold.

Minardi was not there when we arrived. We were greeted by one of the local union officers, a big, strapping man named Nick Bicanic. "Red Spivey was a good union man," he said, "but a hothead. Beating up that kid was just like him. Hard to blame the kid for going back and getting even."

Jack let the inference pass. He said, "So Spivey must have made a lot of enemies, right?"

Bicanic smiled. He had a good smile, one that came across as sincere and friendly, but he was the hail-fellow-well-met type who talked loudly and emphatically so that whenever he spoke you could almost see the exclamation marks floating in the air. He was not the type of man I cared to be around. He said, "Red did his share of fighting, but the guys understood it was just his nature. Enemies? Naw, I can't think of a one."

"Well somebody sure didn't think he was a real prince," said Jack, " and it wasn't the Butler kid. Everybody who knows him says he was gentle as a lamb."

Bicanic gave us another smile. "Those quiet ones can fool you. Boy, can they ever."

Jack looked ready for an argument, but at that moment Guido Minardi walked in. Along with his other habits that didn't appeal to me, Bicanic was a back-slapper. He gave Jack a hard one, then said, "Here's the guy you're looking for," and made the introductions. Then he left for a late lunch so we were alone with Minardi, who it turned out had come over from Pittsburgh to help the local union boys get started.

He was a good-looking man in a slick, oily way. A salesman type, outgoing and probably persuasive with a lot of people. I wasn't any more fond of his kind than I was of Bicanic's, and I could see that Jack wasn't at all taken with him. He didn't even try to be polite or hide his antagonism. Doing so would not have been Jack Eddy's way.

"I hear you tried to make it with Esther Spivey," he said, "but she gave you the cold shoulder. Or did her old man change his mind about you and put the kibosh on it?"

Minardi's smile wasn't as pleasant as Bicanic's. "You couldn't be more wrong, fella. Esther and I didn't hit it off, sure, and Red was steamed about it, but he put the blame on her, not me. Gave her a bad time, but Red had the wrong idea. It was just a case where neither one of us went for the other. Know what I mean?"

Despite not caring for the man, I believed him. So did Jack, apparently, because we left soon after that and he was in a foul mood on the way back downtown.

Artie Bauer was bouncing a tennis ball off the side of the house and then catching it in his fielder's glove when I arrived home in late afternoon. He had been avoiding me since the tear gas episode but was all smiles when I said, "How about a game of catch?"

He ran to get a beat up old baseball covered with black friction tape while I went up to my room and rummaged around in the closet until I found my glove. We tossed the ball back and forth for half an hour, then I said it was time to take a break. We sat on the front steps, neither of us saying anything, until I felt the time was ripe and asked, "How's school going these days?"

"Same old boring stuff," he said, a look of disgust on his face. That changed to a grin as he added, "Only two more weeks 'til summer vacation."

"Ever think about what you want to do when you grow up?"

"Nope."

"You'll have to one of these days. What kind of a job would you like to have?"

He thought it over, then said, "An easy one . . . like yours."

I swallowed a retort that leaped to mind and instead said, "You'd like that, Artie. Lots of excitement, something different every day. You'd never get bored, that's for sure."

"Yeah, that's the kind of job I want."

"You could handle it, but there's something you have to do before they'd hire you. You have to learn to talk right, speak proper English. All those things they try to teach you in school are important so you'll have to work a lot harder in seventh grade."

"Sure, and have all the guys make fun of me."

"I studied hard when I went to Kent School and nobody made fun of me."

"Yeah, back in the Dark Ages." He started laughing. "How'd you get there, in a horse and buggy?"

That was enough for me. I gave up and went inside to get ready for supper. Jack Eddy was a real bear at the table, sullen and surly whenever anyone spoke to him. It was apparent he wasn't getting anywhere on the Spivey case. I couldn't help but feel a little satisfaction at seeing the mighty Jack Eddy traveling a hard road like the rest of us.

After enjoying a second helping of Ivy Bauer's incomparable beef stew topped off with lemon pie I joined most of the others in the living room. Kitty had beaten her father to the radio and was listening to music. The Ozzie Nelson band was backing up Harriet Hilliard on one of the hits of the day, *Says My Heart*. Harriet was bemoaning the fact that whenever romance was about to enter her life she ran for cover because her old school-teacher's heart kept ringing in false alarms. Like they said, things were tough all over.

I got up to leave when Rudy Vallee came on singing the off-beat *Vieni Vieni*, a song I could tolerate the first ten thousand times I heard it, but no longer. A good book, Christie's *Murder in Mesopotamia,* was waiting in my room, but I was only halfway up the stairs when Jack Eddy came charging out of his room, grabbed my arm and swung me around while saying, "Let's go, buddy. Beer time."

What he failed to say was that before heading for the Lenox Café by turning right on Willard Street, we were going to turn left and pay Esther Spivey a visit.

When I realized what he had in mind I said, "Why, Jack? I don't want to."

"Save it for another time, friend. Business before pleasure."

"It's not my business, Jack. That doesn't mean anything to you, does it?"

He didn't bother to answer, which wasn't a surprise. I was hoping she wouldn't be home. A vain hope, as it turned out, because I should have known Jack would have phoned her before starting out.

It was the first time I saw Esther Spivey. She wasn't an attractive girl, at least in my opinion. Her features were good, her figure too, but she was a little hard-bitten for my taste. That wasn't uncommon among East Akron girls, but unlike many of them she hadn't retained her femininity through rough times. To be charitable about it, I conceded that her recent times had been rougher than most.

Jack had talked to her on several earlier occasions without learning much of importance even though she wanted to help him get her boyfriend out of jail. All he could do was go over the same ground, hoping that some new angle might develop. I couldn't help wonder if she might want things to remain just as they were because it had been her finger on the trigger. Cynicism was an unpleasant trait developed by most reporters after they had been on the job for a while.

Jack led her through a minute-by-minute account of the day her father died. It was boring, hearing what she ate for breakfast, why she had the day off from her job as sales clerk at Akron Dry Goods, and on and on and on. But I decided to butt in with a question when she said Red Spivey had been in a particularly unpleasant mood that day. "Why?" I asked. "Being a big union man, I should think he would have been excited about the strike that had just started."

She hesitated a moment before saying, "Well, now that I think about it he had been that way all week. Mean and nasty, I mean. He didn't go into work until six in the evening – well, with the strike he didn't go in at all that day – but for days all he did was sit at the kitchen table going over union papers again and again. I asked what he was doing one day and he bit my head off."

"What kind of union papers?" asked Jack.

"How should I know? Just a big stack of papers. All columns of numbers, stuff like that. Before he'd leave for work he'd lock them up in a tin box, then first thing in the morning he'd get them out again."

"How about taking a look at what's in that box?"

Esther got up and walked to a large cabinet in the dining room, the kind some people called a breakfront. The room opened on the one we were in so she was visible to us. After opening a drawer, she turned to us and said, "It isn't here. This is where he always kept it." She rummaged through the rest of the cabinet, then shrugged and returned empty handed.

Jack Eddy had her go on reciting the rest of the day's events, and I was wondering if the telling wasn't going to take longer than the living had when he decided to knock off for the night. By then it was so late we passed up the beer at the Lenox.

Jack hadn't said anything on the walk home, but after we climbed the stairs to our rooms he gave me a painful one-knuckle punch on the arm and said, "That was a good question you asked, buddy. Should have thought of it myself."

"A better one is what happened to that tin box."

"Right. So the next question is how do we find out?"

The following morning I buttonholed Ed Mayhew while making my rounds at Central Police Station. He laughed when I told him he should check out what it was about the union that was bothering Red Spivey. "Because some shamus is nosing around? You're even dumber than I thought. That case is wrapped up and forgotten, fella."

True enough as far as he was concerned. Later on I took Plato Largis aside and asked if there wasn't a way to work around Mayhew's stonewalling. "Sure there is, go over his head to the top brass. But if you do, there isn't a cop in Akron who'll ever give you the time of day again. A man may be the most inept guy on the force, but if he catches heat from up above because of an outsider they'll close ranks behind him."

He was right, of course. The only way to open up Mayhew's mind was to hand him the killer along with a signed confession.

After supper that evening Jack Eddy told me he had been tied up on other matters all day, but now he wanted to talk with Bus Bauer. After a six-hour shift in Goodyear's vulcanizing pit, Bus usually wanted to be left alone, left to sit by his radio and relax. After a little arm-twisting by Jack, he reluctantly agreed to accompany us to the Lenox for a beer.

Jack Eddy was never one to waste time on amenities so before Bus could take a sip from his Carling's Black Label bottle he said, "What's going on at your union that had Red Spivey shook up?"

Bus scowled and said, "What goes on with the union is our business, nobody else's."

"Look, Bus, this is murder we're talking about. Red was your friend so if something was going on that got him killed it was more than union business, right?"

Bus had to think that one over for a minute. "Yeah, I suppose you're right, but if Red knew somethin' wasn't right, I sure don't know what in hell it was."

"The union doesn't have any money, does it?"

"Sure we have money. We pay dues, you know, and some other unions have pitched in to help us in our fight to get organized."

"So who handles this money?"

"I don't pay no attention to the inner workings. Why should I? I ain't an officer, you know. Nick Bicanic, he's the head man but he ain't the treasurer. That's Arnie DePaolo, if I

161

remember correctly. They're both straight shooters so if you're thinkin' one uh them was up to somethin' you're crazy."

Jack knew he wasn't going to learn anything more from Bus. He wasn't happy, but we had another beer and talked a little baseball before leaving for home. Bus went inside to his radio while Jack and I sat on the porch swing for a while. He was frustrated and not good company. After ten minutes or so he got up, then before going inside said, "Tomorrow we talk to this DePaolo, buddy."

"Look, Jack, I have –" but he was gone.

Artie came wandering home from somewhere, probably from getting up to mischief with his pal Hawkeye. He paused long enough to say, "Hello, Bram. How are you?"

I nearly fell off the swing. Artie Bauer being polite? And speaking understandable English? Had my talk with him done some good? Surely not.


It was raining the next day when Jack Eddy stopped by the newsroom shortly after deadline so my enthusiasm for going back outside was at zero level. I did, of course, but only after Jack agreed to stop at a diner on Exchange Street before going on to union headquarters. In my opinion, eating took precedent over investigating any day.

Nick Bicanic greeted us politely, if not warmly. Who wants to have a private eye and a reporter coming around? He cooled a little more when Jack mentioned money. "That's Arnie DePaolo's department," he said. "When we take any in, it goes straight to him."

"Does this guy from Pittsburgh ever get his hands on it?"

"Minardi? Naw, 'course not. I don't know what you're after, mister, but our records are not open to the public. DePaolo or anyone else will tell you the same thing, but if you want to talk to him, that's him over at the desk in the corner."

Whenever I heard the name Arnie I thought of a gangster in the book and movie *Little Caesar*. This particular Arnie was not a tough guy by any stretch of the imagination. He was short and too skinny, had bulging eyes that seemed magnified by thick glasses and an Adam's apple that extended out almost as far as his chin, which wasn't far at all. DePaolo was not the sort of man you would expect to find in a union hall. He was a bookkeeper, of course, so there was no reason to believe he should look like a tire builder.

As usual, Jack Eddy was a far cry from being diplomatic in his approach. After introducing himself without bothering to do the same for me he said, "So all the money comes to you, right?"

"Well, uh, it does after Mr. Bicanic receives it. What I, uh, mean is it doesn't come to me directly. It ends up with me … uh, what I mean is –"

"Yeah, yeah, I get the picture. So who all gets to look at your books?"

"Uh, nobody. Well, that is everybody. The union officers, I mean. They, uh, can, but hardly any of them bother. I read a report at the meetings so they, uh, know where things stand. I mean, uh, financially."

"How about Red Spivey? Did he look at 'em?"

"I, uh, don't know. He's an officer, uh, I mean he *was* an officer but, well, uh, I can't say if –"

"Okay, pal, I understand. You keep the books but beyond that you don't know from nothin', right?"

"Well, uh, I …" but Jack was already halfway to the door so I nodded at the ill-at-ease little man and followed along behind.

When we were back in the car I said, "So what do you think? Did you learn anything?"

"The same thing you did, friend. Mike Bicanic has first crack at the dough and then he passes it on to that pathetic excuse for a man who keeps the books."

"There you go, Jack, making another snap judgment about a man after talking to him for two minutes. As far as I can see we didn't learn much of anything. A lot of people could have taken a look at DePaolo's books and there's not much reason to think any of this was connected to Spivey's murder."

"Not much reason? There's *every* reason. The killer took that tin box with him when he left so no one would make the connection. Even you should be able to see that."

"Maybe you're right. It does seem funny, him spending so much time going over those papers and then having the box they were in disappear after he was killed. One thing, though, there's no way to know just when it did disappear. For that matter, maybe he put it somewhere else and it'll turn up one of these days."

"It won't happen."

"Another thing, Jack. Esther Spivey isn't in the clear. She could have disposed of the box herself."

"Then why tell us about it?"

"Yeah, there is that, but … oh, the hell with it."

When Jack Eddy arrived home just before supper that evening I could tell he was excited about something. Before he could say what it was, Mrs. Bauer called us to the table and she brooked no delay when the food was ready for the hungry horde to descend upon it. I was disappointed, though, to find she had prepared liver and onions. I kept my mouth shut, but agreed with Artie when he said, "How can anybody eat this stuff? I'd just as soon eat worms or maggots."

Miss Ferrabee gagged, Mabel Klosterman turned pale, and Artie's mother cried, "That's enough, young man! Leave the table and go to your room!"

"Aw, Ma –"

"Move!" shouted Bus Bauer, and Artie moved.

Jack Eddy covered his mouth with his napkin and pretended to be choking to hide his laughter. Artie's older brother, Paul, got up and said, "I'm going to my room, too." I was tempted to join the parade, then was thankful I hadn't when Mrs. Bauer brought out cherry cobbler for dessert. With two chairs vacant at the table, I was able to have seconds.

The temperature had dropped steadily during the afternoon so it was too cool to sit on the porch, but Jack Eddy pushed me out the door and toward the swing. Before I could utter a protest he said, "I think I've got it figured, buddy. It's too late now so we'll have to wait until morning to go back to the union hall."

"I work in the morning, Jack, remember? So exactly what have you figured out?"

"It had to have been Nick Bicanic. He took in money and then held onto some of it instead of handing it over to that wimpy little guy. Spivey figured it out and confronted him, so Bicanic went to the house and knocked him off."

"That's guesswork on your part. You haven't figured out anything that wasn't as plain as the nose on your face. You haven't got a shred of evidence to back you up and one of these days going off half-cocked will get you in big trouble. Not me, though. I want no part of it."

"Suppose I told you Bicanic just bought a big new house on West Hill?"

"So what? Lots of people buy houses."

"I'm talking a fifteen thousand dollar house, sport. Where would a guy like Bicanic come up with dough like that unless he had his hand in the union's till?"

"I don't know, but you can count on one thing: I won't be there when you ask him."


I was surprised the next day when Jack Eddy didn't come charging into the newsroom right after deadline with some scheme he'd concocted to get me to go along when he talked to Bicanic. When I still hadn't heard from him by the time I finished my afternoon rounds I walked down the hill from Central Police Station to Main Street and on north to the Metropolitan Building. After getting off the elevator on the fifth floor and saying hello to the new Wellington receptionist, a swell looking girl I could have gone for, I walked down the hall to Jack's private office and said, "So how'd it go?"

He looked up from the stack of papers on his desk, ran his fingers through what was left of his sandy brown hair and said, "How'd what go?"

"Come off it, Jack. Your showdown with Bicanic."

"There wasn't one, friend. I made a few inquiries this morning and found out he married money. His old lady paid for the house. Cash on the barrelhead."

I grinned at that. "So you're back at the starting gate, right?"

"Not at all. I made a few other inquiries."

"And?"

"Arnie DePaolo has a wife and kid, a daughter about ten. She had something wrong, I forget what, and had an expensive operation at Children's Hospital a couple of months ago." An unpleasant leer came over his face. "Also paid for in cash."

"Maybe he married money too."

"Not a chance. He lives in a dump out on Miles Street and drives an old clunker, a Wills-St. Clair ten years old or better."

"That was a make of car? Never heard of it."

"There's a lot you've never heard of, buddy. Sure it was a car. A big one built like an army tank, but you're getting away from the subject, which is a habit of yours."

"That's your opinion. So what're you going to do now, confront DePaolo?"

"Right. I'd rather talk to him at home instead of the union hall so we'll go by his place tonight after supper."

"Now look, Jack, I've told you I want no part of this."

"I figured you'd want to be in on the kill. Want me to call Tom Kennedy at the *Beacon Journal*?"

"That's it, isn't it? Publicity, that's all you really care about, isn't it, Jack? Admit it."

"Sure, I'll admit it's important, but that's not all I care about, sport. So do I call Kennedy or not?"

I had to bite my tongue to keep from saying the things I really wanted to say. I was angry, as angry as I'd ever been in my life, but I had no choice other than to say, "Okay, I'll go along," before storming out and slamming the door behind me. I would never know whether or not he had been serious about calling Tom Kennedy. I couldn't take the chance, knowing that if Jack's latest brainstorm amounted to anything and the *Beacon Journal* was first with the story I'd be in big trouble with Ben Goldsmith.

DePaolo's house on Miles Street was like others in the neighborhood, a modest but well-maintained working-class home with a neatly kept yard. More than an hour of daylight remained when Jack pulled his Auburn to the curb, but dark clouds were low in the sky and moving swiftly eastward. Thunder rumbled behind them, a sound that in recent months had made me think of war, of the Japanese invading China, of

Hitler and his goose-stepping Germans marching into one country after another. The prospect of having to don a uniform and pick up a rifle held no appeal, yet seemed more likely with every passing day.

As bad luck would have it, DePaolo's little girl answered Jack's pounding on the door. She was a pretty girl about Artie's age, eleven or twelve, with dark hair, a shy smile and gracious manner as she asked us to step inside while, "I go get daddy."

"I hate this, Jack," I said. "If you're right it'll break her heart."

"That's the way the cookie crumbles, friend."

"You know something, Jack? You're a cold-hearted bastard. Don't you have any feeling at all for a kid like that? Doesn't trying to tear her life apart bother you even a little?"

"Look, ace, if I'm right it will prevent tearing Andy Butler's life apart, and his family's life, so don't put on your pious, sanctimonious act for me."

He was right, of course. But that didn't make thinking about the little girl any easier. She was cured of whatever her problem had been and was happy now, content with her small role in life and the pleasant home her father had provided. Jack Eddy had to do what he did, it was his job, but at times having to witness it could be gut-wrenching. DePaolo had been working at something in the basement and was wiping his hands on a rag as he came toward us along a hallway, a stunned expression on his face as he saw who his visitors were. "Mr. Eddy, what, uh, is it? Is something wrong?"

With his customary tact Jack replied, "Yeah, DePaolo, plenty's wrong. We know the story so why don't you make it easy for everyone and fill in the details."

The man had turned pale and perspiration glistened on his forehead as he said, "I have, uh, no idea what you're talking about."

"Cut it out, DePaolo. Just come clean, get it off your chest. For starters, how much did you steal from the union?"

He slumped down in a chair, head droopy low. "I didn't steal, I borrowed. I've been paying a little back every week.

167

What would you have done if your little girl had to have an operation to save her life?" He looked up defiantly and had suddenly regained his confidence, had lost his stammer and his need to break every sentence with an uh.

Jack nodded, turning sympathetic. Not really; it was merely part of his routine. "I understand, DePaolo. Then when Red Spivey discovered what was going on you had no choice but to silence him, right?"

"Found out? Silence him? There was nothing for him to find out. I mean nothing that he *could* have found out. There was nothing on paper, nothing at all."

"You expect me to believe that?"

"I can't control what you believe, but it's the truth. Bicanic gave me ten thousand in cash at the same time a number of other big contributions came in. I just held it out, paid for the operation and then put back what was left and entered it on the books. As I said, I've been paying the rest back as fast as I can. I had no more to do with Red's death than you did."

I believed him and could see that Jack was wavering himself. Then he surprised me by saying, "Okay, I'm beginning to think you're telling the truth."

"Are you going to report what happened to Mr. Bicanic?"

"Not unless something new turns up. It's no affair of mine."

When Jack had driven to the end of the block and turned onto Ackley Street I said, "You have no idea what's going on, do you? All you're doing is going from one possible suspect to another hoping that sooner or later you'll get lucky. You're a detective in name, a player of hunches in reality."

I expected him to snap my head off, but he didn't answer. Instead of going home he pulled into the lot behind the Lenox Café, opened the door on his side and walked toward the entrance. I followed, of course, thinking I had finally gotten through to him, had really hurt him. We drank from bottles of Burkhardt's beer in silence for several minutes, then he turned to me and said, "You're right, buddy. Come to think of it, you are a lot of times and maybe I don't give you enough credit."

I was taken aback. This was not the Jack Eddy I had come to know so I was at a loss for words. But the lapse was only momentary and then his supreme confidence came rushing back. "I know where I went wrong, friend. I took someone's word for something and it sent me off on a wrong track. Come to think of it, you played a part in it yourself."

"That's it, blame me for your wrong guesses."

"I'm not blaming you, just said you fell for the same line and it threw me. I should have known better."

"I don't suppose you'd care to tell me what you're talking about?"

He gulped down the last of his beer and said, "Polish off that brew and I'll let you in on the kill."

As he stood up to leave, I said, "Not again, Jack. I've had all I can take for one night."

I could just as well have been talking to my empty bottle because when we were back in the car he drove down the street to the Spivey house. "Esther came to the door with an expectant look. "Have you learned something? Is Andy going to be set free?"

"Yes to both questions," Jack said when we were seated in the living room. "How far were you going to go with it, Esther? You weren't going to let them ship him down to Columbus, were you?"

She looked shocked, but it may have been an act. "What do you mean?"

"Come on, kiddo, let's quit playing games. Your dad wasn't studying union records, there wasn't any tin box. You did a good job, really had me looking in all the wrong places and we might have nailed an innocent man to the cross. You wouldn't have wanted that, Esther. Maybe you thought you wouldn't care as long as Andy was free, but you would have. It would have haunted you the rest of your life, so now let's get it over with. They'll go easy on you, you know that. You'll get plenty of sympathy for finally having more than you could take from an abusive father. Your mother couldn't stand any more of it and left, but you stuck it out because you were in love and wouldn't leave town. How many times did your old man beat you, how often did he slap you around?"

She buried her face in her hands and broke down completely, sobbing and gasping for air. It was all but unintelligible when she murmured, "I never thought they'd arrest Andy. I'm sorry, so sorry."

Jack went over and sat down beside her on the couch, putting his arm around her shoulders. "You picked up the gun as soon as Andy left, didn't you?"

She nodded, and then they sat quietly for a moment before Jack said, "Who can blame you? They'll go easy on you, kid, you'll see."

From beginning to end everything about the case was disturbing, with one exception. Seeing Ed Mayhew scowl and then turn away when we ran into each other at Central Police Station the next morning was gratifying. I added to his discomfort by loudly saying, "Good morning, Ed." He didn't answer, of course. It would have spoiled it if he had.

Jack Eddy was in a somber mood when I stopped by his office in the afternoon. He was shuffling papers around on his desk until he saw me in the doorway, then he leaned back in his chair, chewed on a pencil for a second or two, tossed it aside and said, "Got a cigarette, buddy?"

I took a crumpled pack of Spuds from my shirt pocket and tossed them down on his desk. "Have you ever thought of buying a pack of your own, Jack?"

He lit a Spud, ignoring the question, blew a smoke ring in my direction and said, "I hate these menthol fags. Why don't you smoke the regular kind?"

"Because hardly anyone but you bums these off me, that's why. When I carried Old Golds I got to smoke half a pack and the moochers got the rest."

Jack grinned and said, "Cheapskate." He picked up a pile of assignment sheets, threw them down again with a look of disgust, saying, "Dull stuff, friend. Boring. Nothing coming in but insurance jobs, things like that."

"I'd think you'd be glad for something dull and boring for a change."

He motioned with his head toward a Philco table model radio on a file cabinet. "It's not just that, old friend. I was listening to the news before you got here. That Hitler bird is

170

determined to have a war. If not over this current mess in Czechoslovakia, then the next thing that comes along. We'll be in it, buddy. You told me that once and I said you were crazy. Now I'm a believer. It's going to happen and before it's over we'll be in it. You and I'll be in it right up to our necks."

"I hope you're wrong."

"Don't place any bets on it. You know what's the worst thing about war?"

"Everything, but I've an idea you have something specific in mind."

"Right. The worst thing about war is that they hand you a gun and tell you to go kill people. Not some guys you hate and know deserve it, but people you've never seen before. If you're good at it they'll give you a medal. Then when you're home again the rules change and if you kill some really rotten bastard they'll throw you in prison or strap you in the chair."

"You're thinking about the Spivey case again, aren't you?"

"Right again. Any guy who beats on women deserves to be shot. There's no excuse for it, none at all.

"Well, Esther did the job."

"And where will she end up? Prison, and some people call it justice. So where were those people when Red was dishing out his brand of justice with his fists?"

"Don't look to me for any answers, Jack."

"Everything about that Spivey business was rotten. One guy loves his daughter so much that he turned thief for her, the other guy slapped his around and had no regard for her at all, so he ends up dead. Got what was coming to him, thinking he could handle every situation by beating on someone."

"Are you going to do anything about DePaolo?"

"Turn him in, you mean? Why should I? It's none of my business unless the union hires the agency to find where its money's going, and that's not going to happen."

"Good. I'd hate to see him in trouble."

"No you wouldn't. You'd hate to see his little girl unhappy. The problem with you is you're too sentimental when it comes to girls, little or otherwise. I'd think your job would have toughened you up a little."

"If that means not caring about kids, I don't want to be tough"

"You need to get married and have a bunch of your own."

That was enough for me. When I reached the door I turned and said, "Maybe that's what you need, Jack. You might turn halfway human."

Sue Baney and I took in a movie that evening. Afterwards we stopped at Kesselring's on Triplett Boulevard for ice cream, a sundae for her, a banana split for me. While we were eating I said, "Jack Eddy thinks I should get married and have a bunch of kids."

Sue choked on her ice cream, wiped her mouth and dried her eyes, then said, "I hope that's not a proposal. If it is, it qualifies as the world's worst."

I could feel my face turning red. "Don't get me wrong, Sue. I just meant that's what Jack said."

"Why did he say it?"

"He thinks I'm too soft on kids so I should have some of my own." A thought leaped to mind and I laughed. "If I ever did, with my luck they'd probably turn out to be like Artie Bauer."

That made Sue laugh. "And I suppose you wouldn't like that? Be honest, Bram, you think the world of that brat."

"That's not true. Well, maybe he's okay."

On that note, I drove Sue to her apartment and then went on home by way of Market Street. Along the way I was wondering how many years Esther Spivey would have to serve in the prison for women at Marysville. Not too many, I hoped. Would Andy Butler be waiting for her when she got out? Who could know?

Aside from a scuffle outside a tavern, all was quiet on Market Street until I passed Goodyear's Plant One and could hear the hum of machinery. It was satisfying to find it that way. It was a pleasant May evening, life was back to normal, all was well with my world again.

# SWITCHBACK

The man on the next stool in the seedy diner turned and said, "You a reporter from Wheeling in town about the murder?"

He was partially right. I was a reporter, but from Akron, not the nearby city in West Virginia, and I wasn't even aware of a murder. I pretended otherwise, nodded my head and said, "What can you tell me about it?"

"Ben St. Clair knocked off Anse Rodin last night. Pumped two bullets in him whilst he was sleepin.' We all seen it comin' and figur' Ben oughta get a medal, not throw'd in a cell up in Cammackville."

"Sounds like this Rodin wasn't too popular around town."

A harsh laugh and then, "Rodin the rodent, that's what we called him. Mean as a timber rattler since he took to drink 'bout five years back."

My new acquaintance had muscular arms but the sallow complexion of a man who spent his days far from the sun. Among the hills and hollows of East Central Ohio that meant underground in a coal mine. He was one of the lucky ones who had a job, something most miners did not in June of 1938. The Great Depression had put too many factories out of business, caused too many others to cut production, forced too many families to heat only one or two rooms of a house. The demand for coal was at low ebb.

"So why did St. Clair kill him?" I asked.

"Rodin was married to Ben's ex-wife."

"A love triangle?"

"Naw, nothin' like that. Ben had no use for her, never did, but they had a daughter and not long ago Ben found out Rodin took a razor strop to her sometimes since he got to drinkin'. Just t'other day Ben whupped the daylights outta him on the street out front here. Said he'd chop him up and feed him to

173

the hogs iffen he ever laid a hand on her again. A buncha people was watchin' and heard him say it."

"Is that all they have to go on? Doesn't sound like a very strong case."

"Naw, the county cops found his gun there. Had his initials stamped right on it. Anyway, he confessed."

"This St. Clair, does he live in a big house on Maple Street?"

"Yeah, it's his maw's place. How'd yuh know?"

So that was why I was in the miserable little town of Switchback. Before I could reply the man eased himself off his stool and said, "Gotta get to work. Name's Joe Blair."

"Bram Geary," I said as he extended his right hand. When I took it in mine it seemed like my bones were splintering. Along with the savage grip he gave me a wild-animal grin as he said, "Iffen yuh need to know more yuh can always find me here mornin's and suppertime."

With Blair's unwashed body no longer beside me I became aware of the heady aroma of congealed grease and frying bacon that permeated the long and narrow room. A waitress who looked forty but might have been fifteen years younger poured more coffee into my cracked mug. "One refill," she snarled, "then it's another nickel." An elderly gentleman on the stool next to the one vacated by Blair hopefully pushed his mug forward. "No more for you, Pete," the waitress told him, then went on to pour refills for several other customers.

When her back was turned I slid my mug down to the old fellow and said, "Take mine, I've had enough." He gave me a suspicious look and said, "Didn't put nothin' in it, did yuh?" I shook my head, wondering when I'd wise up and stop playing Mr. Nice Guy. He pushed the mug back toward me, saying, "Wouldn't dare. Lucinda'd skin me alive."

Someone had put a nickel in the jukebox at the rear and, ironically, a female vocalist with the Russ Morgan band came on singing, *I Double Dare You.* I glanced around the rest of the dingy establishment. A flyspecked portrait of Franklin Roosevelt, the only artwork other than four girly calendars, smiled cheerily down on the scene that offered little cause for cheer. Why wasn't I on the highway leading back to Akron instead of drinking rancid coffee in such a place? And because I wasn't, what was I going to do next?

It had begun four hours earlier when Mrs. Bauer, my landlady at the boardinghouse on Dudley Street, had shaken me awake to say, "Tomorrow's your day off, isn't it, Bram?"

A reporter covering the police beat was accustomed to being routed from a warm bed in the hours before dawn because of a murder, a fatality on some lonely road, a house fire with people trapped inside, but not to be asked if his day off was coming up. Before my sleep-drugged mind could comprehend what was going on, Ivy Bauer said, "Mr. Reimer has to get to Switchback and his car won't start."

"Switchback? That town somewhere west of Wheeling? Why?"

"He had a phone call from an old friend. It's an emergency."

I got dressed, tiptoed along the hallway to the bathroom, splashed cold water on my face, brushed my teeth and then went downstairs to where Mr. Reimer and Mrs. Bauer stood waiting. The elderly man, a retired druggist, was smiling apologetically, twisting the brim of his gray fedora nervously in his hands. As always, even at breakfast on a Sunday morning, he was wearing a suit and tie.

"I'm terribly sorry, Abraham. I didn't know what to do until Mrs. Bauer suggested asking you to drive me." He was the only person who called me by my proper name. Oddly enough, coming from him I rather liked it. Not from others, though. It was odd, too, that I had never heard Mr. Reimer's first name.

As we started for the front door, Mrs. Bauer handed me a brown paper sack. "I made some sandwiches in case you get hungry. Wait a minute, I've got a Thermos of coffee ready in the kitchen." Trust Mrs. Bauer not to let two of her "boys" set off into the night without something to see them through a hunger pang or a moment of thirst.

So we headed south past Soap Box Derby Downs and the ghostly outline of the Goodyear Zeppelin hanger where the giant dirigibles *Akron* and *Macon* had been built. I thought of the great silver airships, so stately and graceful, but now resting in watery Atlantic and Pacific graves.

We rode in silence, my 1934 Hupmobile cruising at a steady sixty-five along deserted highways, only occasionally passing an oncoming car. We were engulfed in an inky blackness broken only now and then by a lone light over the door of a barn, revealing the structure's outline and that of a dark and silent house close by. I slowed down on the empty streets of Massillon, Dover and New Philadelphia, then speeded up again. Passing through Cadiz reminded me that despite being hit harder than most by the Depression, its residents were proud of the town's favorite son, actor Clark Gable.

Now we were on the final leg of the journey so I glanced at Mr. Reimer and said, "This friend, is he in trouble?"

"It's a she. Her only son is the one in trouble."

"She was your girlfriend?"

"Oh, no. Just friends. We grew up together."

"In Switchback?"

"Until my junior year in high school, then my father's mine shut down and we moved to Benwood on the West Virginia side of the Ohio River."

I had known Mr. Reimer for five years, but realized that I knew almost nothing about him. I had just accepted his presence without thinking that he had a past. I knew he had owned a drugstore on Fourth Street in the suburb of Cuyahoga Falls and never missed a Cleveland Indians baseball game on radio, that was all. He was so sedate, so dignified, that it was hard to visualize him as a youth in a rough and dreary coalmining town. "How long ago was that?" I asked.

"Since we left Switchback? Fifty-two years."

"But you've kept in touch?"

"Not until two years ago when I heard her husband died and I sent my condolences."

I couldn't get a handle on the situation, but didn't want to ask more questions. Fifty-two years, that would have made it

1886.   Before automobiles, before airplanes, before radio, before just about everything we now took for granted.   Who would have been president in 1886?   I couldn't remember.

Mr. Reimer dozed off then, breathing heavily.   I wondered if he felt old, or in his mind was he the same as he had been all those years ago?   I remembered reading somewhere that the biggest shock in a man's life came when he awoke one morning and found he was an old man.   Had that day arrived for him?

Asleep, Mr. Reimer seemed even older than he had. Smaller, too.   Old and small and alone, vulnerable in the dark of night in Appalachian hill country, unfriendly country.

The first light of dawn found few people up and about on the streets of Switchback.   We entered town on a hairpin curve, a switchback.   A steep hill rose just to the west and towered above the grassless yards and dilapidated houses we passed. Nodding toward the wooded hill, Mr. Reimer said, "Even in summer we didn't see the sun after three in the afternoon."

Following his directions, I drove south through the business district to Maple Street, then turned left.   "Pull up, here, Abraham," he said, so I drew to the curb in front of a large Victorian era house set well back from the street.   It had gables, a turret, heaps of gingerbread and a massive front door with an oval, cut-glass window.   The door opened and a portly woman stepped onto the porch while Mr. Reimer was retrieving his small suitcase from the back seat.   "I can never thank you enough, Abraham," he said.   "Be careful on the way back, and don't forget Mrs. Bauer's sandwiches and coffee."

"Want me to stick around and make sure everything's okay?"

"Oh, no, that won't be necessary.   You should be home in time to enjoy most of your day off work."

I watched as he walked up the sidewalk and climbed the stairs, then turned and waved when he was beside the woman. A feeling of guilt came over me.   It didn't seem right, leaving him alone without even knowing why he was there.   I drove back to the center of town, uneasy of mind, uncertain of what I should do.   I pulled to the curb when I saw an "EATS" sign and went inside the only place in town that seemed to be open, needing to collect my thoughts.

By the time I left the unsavory place my mind was made up, I was sticking around for a day or two. I walked to a phone booth on the corner, dialed the *Times-Press* number and told city editor Ben Goldsmith where I was and that I might be onto a good story and needed a couple of days to check it out.

"Nobody in Akron gives a damn about a murder in Switchback," he barked at me. "Half the population never heard of the place and the rest aren't interested."

"There may be an Akron connection, Ben. Along with that I figure on doing a story on the effect of the Depression in coalmining country. There are people in Akron who came up there from around here and from across the river in West Virginia."

He laughed skeptically. "You do a think piece? I can just see it happening. But okay, Geary, I'll trust you on this. Three days, that's it. Anything more and you'll be using vacation time."

A vacation in Switchback? A lovely thought, but three days was more than I had expected even though one of them was my day off.

I drove around a little, waiting for the town to come fully awake, if such a thing ever happened. I had seen the effect of the Depression on Akron and other cities of the Industrial Valley, but none of it had prepared me for Switchback. The business district was a shambles of vacant storefronts, some with boarded-up windows, some with shattered plate glass. The stores that remained open carried the bare necessities of life, which was why they had survived while those around them closed their doors forever.

It was the men, though, that opened a new door in my mind and left me shaken as few things ever had. Even at that early hour they were on the street. Small groups stood aimlessly on corners, others leaned against the fronts of buildings, the most downtrodden of all sat alone on curbs studying the pavement or looking straight ahead from glazed, unseeing eyes. They had lost their jobs, then their hope, then their pride. The mines had shut down through no fault of their own, but that didn't prevent guilt from creeping into their thoughts until in time it overwhelmed all else. They left home early and stayed away all day in a vain attempt to distance themselves from reality, from the awareness of wives lacking the resources to provide their families with even the basic necessities, of children who were ill-clothed and ill-fed and sometimes went to bed hungry.

If they could somehow manage to come up with even a quarter it would be enough to buy a pound of hamburger and a quart of milk, but where were they to find that quarter when so many others were looking for one? Had it been weeks or even months of such an existence they would not have hit rock bottom, but it had been years. Now only ashes remained of the hopes and dreams that had once inspired them.

I don't believe I had ever felt quite so depressed. It was contagious, this all-consuming despair that engulfed Switchback. In the best of times a coalmining town was a dreary place, yet energetic, a community where men worked at a dirty, dangerous job and felt a certain pride in being strong enough of mind and body to do so. Such towns were not for the weak of heart, but now nearly everyone had become just that. Yes, it was infectious, this malaise, even to an outsider.

Shortly after eight o'clock I did what most newspapermen do when in need of information in a strange town; I went to the newspaper office. While driving around I had seen a faded *Exponent* sign above a doorway in a ramshackle brick building just off Switchback's main street. The windows were boarded up so I wondered if it was still publishing, but when I tried the door it opened and I was greeted by the familiar smell of ink, newsprint and dust.

I introduced myself to the lone occupant and explained why I was in town, or, because I wasn't certain myself, did the best job possible under the circumstances. The *Exponent,* a weekly paper, proved to be a one-man operation with the editor, Stan Mendelbaum, also serving as reporter, makeup man, printer, pressman, advertising salesman and circulation manager. Mendelbaum, lean and sparse of hair, was pushing sixty so the ninety-hour workweek would have been a challenge for him.

"Ben St. Clair." he said, leaning back in a wooden swivel chair beside a cluttered roll-top desk. "Not a man who'd shoot

179

another in the back, you can be sure of that. If Ben were of a mind to shoot someone, it would be face to face. Know anything about him?"

"Nothing."

Mendelbaum wiped his glasses with a handkerchief, squinting at me as he began, "Back in 1920 or thereabouts he was the star athlete at Switchback High. Did it all, but football was his best sport. Ran like a deer and hit like a battering ram. They called him The Blaster, and that's how the school's teams got their nickname, the Switchback Blasters. Some people think it was because of blasting in the mines, but Ben was responsible. Had a scholarship to play football at Ohio State, but a week after high school graduation he got married and went to work out at the Little Sally. Ever heard of it?"

I shook my head. "It's a mine?"

"Used to be the biggest in these parts. Then in 1928 the methane gas let go. The men had been saying they could smell it, but an inspector the state sent down from Columbus said there was nothing to worry about. It was a rainy October morning when it went up. Forty-seven men died and more were left crippled. Ben was a hero again that day. The Little Sally had a circular metal staircase near one portal. They rode an elevator or followed sloping tunnels to get in and out so I'm not sure what that staircase was for. Anyway, a miner named Rostoff, Ivan Rostoff, was badly injured. Ben picked him up and carried him to the surface on those slippery metal stairs. No one could understand how he managed to do it."

I was beginning to agree that St. Clair didn't sound like a back-shooter. I said, "Why would he turn down a chance to play at Ohio State to get married?"

"Had to. Or he thought he did because it was the honorable thing to do." Mendelbaum filled and lit an old pipe, then through a cloud of white smoke said, "You see, he and a girl named Nancy Holliday were sweethearts all through school and were planning to get married after Ben graduated from college. But there was another girl named Margo Rexstead, an easy mark for any young fellow in town. Ben was no different than the rest, and surely no smarter, so one night after he'd had a few beers with the boys he ended up in the back seat of a

Buick with Margo. Next thing she claimed she was pregnant and Ben was the father. Could have been any one of a dozen or more men, but Ben accepted what she said and married her."

"Was she pregnant?'

"Oh, yes. The one good thing to come out of the shabby business was their daughter, Brenda."

"Then she's the one this Rodin was supposed to have slapped around?"

"Right. Ben and Margo were divorced when Brenda was about ten, then a few months later Margo married Anse Rodin and she and the girl went to live at his place about three miles east of town. It seemed all right, I guess, until Rodin turned into a mean drunk. A few weeks back Margo left him for another man, another lowdown bum in my opinion, and Brenda, who had just turned eighteen, moved in with her grandmother. Ben lived there, too."

"Whatever happened to the other girl?"

"Go up to the library and you'll find her. Nancy Holliday's the librarian."

"I've been wondering about your windows being boarded up."

"Couldn't afford to replace the glass after the Nazi thugs broke them out. They'd have just done it again, anyway."

"Nazis? Here in Switchback?"

"You'd better believe it. Nazis, Communists, Socialists, Mussolini-style Fascists, we've got 'em all. When men sink down far enough, when their bellies are empty, they're easy marks for any fanatic with a good line of bull."

"Why'd they pick on you?"

"With a name like Mendelbaum, you have to ask?"


The police station, my next stop, was in the rear of Switchback's City Hall, a forbidding structure of dark red brick with soot-blackened stone trim and battlements that would have been more at home on a fortress. The cop at the desk was overweight and unshaven, but my initial impression of having encountered an incompetent slob was wrong. After telling him who I was and why I was there, he proved to be well informed

181

and cooperative. Cap Warner was his name, but the Cap had nothing to do with rank.

He had been on duty all night. The murder had been out in the county in the jurisdiction of the sheriff's department, so what he knew of the case came from monitoring the radio. He said, "It was comical, listening to them, then it got irritating. "The only way any of those deputies got badges was by being one of the sheriff's cronies, either old friends or members of that scumbag Nazi bunch that parade around in their fancy outfits looking for trouble. Not one of them could find a snake in a woodpile unless it bit him so that's why they took the easy route and picked up Ben St. Clair."

"I heard he beat up Rodin and threatened to do worse. And that his gun was used and he's confessed."

"That's the puzzling part of it. I played ball with Ben in high school and we ran around together. He's the last man on earth who'd shoot a sleeping man in the back, so why in hell did he say he's guilty?"

"Don't ask me, I don't know the man."

"And there's one more thing. Ben's gun has his initials engraved on it. Would a man with iron nerves get panicky and drop it there and run? Not a chance."

We talked a little more, then I asked if there was a good hotel in town.

"The Belmont. A block west of Main Street across from the railroad depot." When I got to the door he chuckled and said, "It's the *only* hotel in town."


The Belmont was like most hotels in a small town, four-story red brick with a large sign on the roof. To my surprise it was clean, had a nice lobby, a bar, a restaurant and even a coffee shop that was open from five in the morning until midnight. I chose a two-dollar room with a bath rather than the one-dollar variety with communal facilities at the end of the hall. The *Times-Press* would pay my expenses, or so I hoped.

A row of phone booths lined one wall of a hallway connecting the lobby with a drugstore and newsstand. The first in line was out of order so I used the next to call Mrs. Bauer and say I was staying in Switchback for a few days. She had a dozen questions regarding Mr. Reimer's well being. Without really knowing I assured her that everything was okay. In the end, though, I was forced to tell her the reason he was in Switchback was because of the murder. That was enough to make her extract a promise from me to call her every day.

I bought toilet articles at the drugstore and two shirts, socks and a few boxer shorts at a haberdashery on Main Street, all of which set me back nearly five dollars. I needed them anyway, but was glad I had twenty dollars in my wallet when I had started out. There were times when I had nothing but change in my pocket until payday.

After gathering my necessities and getting settled in my room, I drove out to Maple Street. Mrs. St. Clair answered my knocking at the door, but when I began explaining who I was, Mr. Reimer called out, "Abraham, is that you? Is something wrong? You didn't have an accident, did you?"

As he hurried to join Mrs. St. Clair in the doorway I assured him that everything was fine and I had decided to stick around a few days to do a little research for a story on coalmining. I followed them to a spacious living room furnished with overstuffed chairs, a matching davenport, ornate tables and lamps with stained-glass shades that fit the Victorian exterior. There I was introduced to a young man of about eighteen, a shy and introverted friend of Brenda's named Clarence Kohl. Brenda was expected soon so he was waiting for her. He retreated to a chair in a dark corner to do so.

Mr. Reimer was too wise to fall for the tale I had told him, of course. "You've heard about what happened, haven't you?" he said.

When I admitted that I had, Mr. Reimer said he appreciated it but didn't believe there was anything I could do to help. I agreed, but didn't tell him so. Instead I said, "Maybe I've heard things that you haven't, Mr. Reimer. No one who knew him believes Ben St. Clair is guilty. What I can't figure out is why he confessed."

Before he could reply, Mary St. Clair came in from the kitchen carrying a tray with coffee and oatmeal cookies. Once we were settled with our cups she looked at me and said, "I can't begin to tell you how much it means to have Wolf here for moral support."

I looked around, expecting to see a large dog, but found only the three of us plus the young man who seemed to have been swallowed up by the massive chair in which he was seated. Puzzled, I said, "Wolf?"

Mr. Reimer smiled sheepishly. "I'm Wolf," he said. "My first name is Wolfgang so when we were kids everyone called me Wolf."

Hoping to hide my laughter, I pretended to choke on my last bite of cookie, an act that fooled no one. I wasn't alone; from his dark corner Clarence giggled a little. Now I understood why Mr. Reimer's first name had remained a dark secret. As for Wolf, if there ever was anyone ill-fitted for the name, he was it.

Brenda arrived just in time to keep me from making some inane remark to cover my embarrassment. Unlike her friend Clarence, whom she proceeded to ignore, Brenda was self-assured to the point of being brash. She was a petite young woman, and pretty, but she needed to tone down her voice a few notches and, I came to learn, treat her elders with a bit more respect. At twenty-four, I seemed to be one of those elders in her eyes.

After the introductions, she turned to her grandmother and said, "Any word about dad?" When told that there was nothing new she said, "Those cops are so stupid. I can't believe they really arrested him."

It wasn't my place to do so, but I couldn't help saying, "He did confess, you know."

She gave me a what-rock-did-you-crawl-out-from-under look. "You know why, don't you, mister? Because he's lonely and unhappy and doesn't care what happens to him."

Put in my place, I swallowed the rest of my coffee and told them I had to go.

"If you're going to be staying awhile," said Mrs. St. Clair, "we have plenty of room so bring in your things."

"Uh, thanks, but I took a room at the Belmont. I come and go at odd hours and wouldn't want to put you out."

"I'd give you a key so you wouldn't bother anyone."

Mr. Reimer sensed my discomfort. "I think he'd be happier on his own, Mary. He's accustomed to living that way."

"Well, all right," she said, "but at least take your meals here. We eat at noon and six."

I told her I'd let her know in advance anytime that was possible, then made my escape. They were nice people, but the atmosphere was tense and constrained so I inhaled a deep and appreciative breath of warm June air when I was outside again.

After a hotdog and glass of milk at the hotel's coffee shop I drove around in search of the library. It proved to be a handsome stone structure with a red-tile roof and "Carnegie Library" carved over the front door. The librarian, an attractive woman somewhere shy of forty, was helping an elderly lady pick out a book from a shelf labeled "Mysteries." The brown-haired younger woman was recommending Dashiell Hammett's "The Glass Key." After picking up the cane she had let fall, the other began shaking her head. I was close enough by then to say, "It's very good. I'm sure you'd like it."

The old woman, eighty if she was a day, turned to glare at me, but then said, "Well, if you say so, all right."

After the librarian, whom I felt certain was Nancy Holliday, had used the little rubber stamp on the end of her pencil to complete the checking out process the octogenarian hobbled off muttering, "It had better be good." When she was out of hearing range I was given a wry smile and a, "Thank you. We had been at it for fifteen minutes before you came in, but it's always that way with Mrs. Mikterian. Now, can I help you?"

I hesitated, wanting to ask if she indeed was Nancy Holliday, then losing my nerve and saying, "Do you have clipping files on local history? Something on the coalmine disaster?"

"Which one?"

"There's been more than one? I was thinking of the Little, uh . . ."

"Sally. The Little Sally. That was ten years ago this fall, and yes, I have a folder with clips from the *Exponent* and the Wheeling and Martins Ferry papers."

"You seem to remember it well."

"It was a terrible thing, a horrible tragedy. Worse even than the one a few years earlier at Dawson Number One or those back before the war."

"I can't understand how men go on working in those places. The conditions are so miserable even without the danger."

"It's their job. It's what they do. Without the mines there isn't much work to be had around here. That's why things are so bad today."

"I've heard that the man they arrested for murder was a hero at the Little Sally explosion."

An expression I interpreted as wistful came over her face. "Ben was never short of courage. Ben St. Clair, that's the man you're talking about. Courage and a sense of honor, those have always been his strong points. Sometimes, though, they've been his downfall."

"Do you think he's guilty?"

"Don't be ridiculous. Of course not."

"He's confessed, you know."

"As I said before, that misplaced sense of honor can be his downfall."

She went to get the folder then, and as she walked away I had to admire the fit of her tight brown skirt, the slight sway of her hips and the firm stride of her shapely legs. Ben St. Clair was a loser in more ways than one.

I spent an hour poring over the clippings, reliving that terrible day in the history of the depressing little town. I finished reading the last one with the feeling that I had a better understanding of Switchback and the grim fascination that such places have for a certain breed of hardy men.

When I returned the folder to the desk I worked up the courage to say, "You're Nancy Holliday, aren't you?"

"How do you know?" she asked suspiciously.

"Stan Mendelbaum told me about you and Ben."

Her face reddened as she said, "Did he also tell you about the only cowardly thing Ben St. Clair ever did? When he broke our engagement by marrying another woman he didn't have the nerve to tell me himself. I heard it from some catty girls who thought the whole thing was hilarious."

I left feeling abashed, wishing I had kept my mouth shut.

I was at a loss for anything more to do. After walking aimlessly for a while I returned to the miserable lunchroom where I'd had breakfast. The same waitress was on duty and the passing of time had done nothing to improve her disposition. After slapping a mug down in front of me so that the coffee splashed over the sides and puddled on the counter she reminded me, "One refill and that's it."

It was swill, barely fit for human consumption, but thoughts of the men on the streets outside who would have eagerly gulped it down led me to fill my pipe with pungent Bond Street tobacco so that the smoke would dilute the taste as I sipped away until it was gone. Then with my foolish sense of guilt over having a little money in my pocket assuaged, I went back to the hotel. It had been a tiring day so I stretched out on the bed, knowing I needed to rest but believing I wouldn't be able to sleep.

The whistle of a train lumbering its way through town with a load of coal from some mine that was still working jarred me awake. I looked at my watch and was amazed to see that I had slept for more than two hours. After freshening up a little I went down to the lobby and again used the phone in the second booth to call the St. Clair house.

When he came on the line, Mr. Reimer sounded dispirited. "Abraham, they won't allow his mother or anyone else to visit Ben. Isn't that unusual?"

"It depends on a number of things, Mr. Reimer. Sometimes in a murder case they do it that way."

"They told her Ben doesn't want to see anyone or even talk to anyone on the phone. Did you ever hear of such a thing?"

"I can't recall, but it may happen without me knowing about it. I just don't know, Mr. Reimer."

"The oddest thing of all, Abraham, is he refuses to see a lawyer. He says he's guilty and doesn't need one. That's what they told Mary, but it's hard to believe it's true."

"It could be. From the things people have said about him he's strong-willed, the sort of man who makes up his own mind and doesn't want anyone telling him what to do."

Poor Mr. Reimer was caught up in events completely unfamiliar to him. The same was true of Ben St. Clair's mother, of course. They were bewildered by it all, unsure of what they should do and frightened by the thought of doing the wrong thing, or doing nothing at all. I wanted to help someway, but like them I was uncertain of how to proceed. If we were in Akron I might have been of some use, but here among strangers I was lost.

Of one thing I was certain, I needed to hear a cheerful voice. After getting change from the desk clerk I used more of my dwindling funds on another long distance call, this one to Sue Baney. Our once great relationship had been a little strained of late, but talking to her usually was good for my morale. She answered on the second ring and her first words came as a shock: "Is that you, Bram? Whatever are you doing in a place like Switchback?"

"You know where it is?"

"Of course. Have you forgotten that I'm from not far away in West Virginia?"

I hadn't forgotten, it just hadn't come to mind. I explained the situation, although doing so wasn't easy, then said, "How did you know I was here?"

"Jack Eddy called me a little while ago. He said about the same thing you just did and he doesn't understand what you're doing any more than I do."

"I'm surprised he called you." And with good reason; my across-the-hall neighbor at the boardinghouse on Akron's industrial east side rarely went out of his way to be considerate of anyone other than himself. When he did, I always suspected an ulterior motive.

"He felt I should know where you are," Sue replied. Then without realizing it she seconded my opinion by adding, "It was thoughtful of him and to me that's what's surprising."

"He's not a bad guy, Sue. Not as bad as you think, anyway."

"That's probably true. He couldn't be."

"Come on, Sue, give the guy a break. I wish you'd get to like him better."

"*Better*? I don't like him at all, so let's change the subject. When will you be home?"

"A couple of days, I think. Maybe we can have dinner and go to a show."

"You know my number. Now get off the line and quit wasting your money."

It had been good to hear her voice, but I wasn't too sure she had been glad to hear mine. I decided she was, though, so I went into the dining room and splurged on the fifty cent dinner: swiss steak, mashed potatoes and gravy, green beans, a salad, cherry pie and my choice of wine or beer. I chose the beer. I had a couple of more in the bar, nickel mugs of Iron City on tap, but only after I had gone out and wandered around for a while.

The streets of Switchback were even drearier as the approaching night hid what little color there had been in the light of day. My opinion of the town didn't improve when I passed half a dozen Nazis fitted out in all their finery and regalia. One of them was Joe Blair, my acquaintance from breakfast. He let out a whoop when he saw me and stopped long enough to say they were going to a meeting with a guest speaker from the German American Bund in New York. He invited me to come along, but I escaped by saying I had an appointment.

Learning that Blair was a Nazi seemed to explain why he had a job in a mine when so very few men did. But being confronted by storm troopers on the street of a town in the United States was an unsettling experience. Was the whole world going mad? Sometimes it seemed that way. Communist Party headquarters at the main intersection in Akron, Nazis marching down the streets of Switchback, what would be next?

After returning to the hotel and going into the bar, I added a few more items to my list of depressing facts. Like most bartenders, the one at the Belmont was the garrulous type and knew everything that was going on around town. When I mentioned my encounter with the Nazis he told me what he knew about them, including the fact that they'd had a run-in with Anse Rodin, the murder victim. They had wanted to use part of his land and that of a neighbor for training purposes. The neighbor, a man named Jed Claiborne, had agreed but Rodin had refused. That squelched the deal and left both the Nazis and Claiborne furious, the latter because the Nazis were going to pay a large sum of money for use of the land.

"But the one who was really het-up," said the bartender named Tony, "was Margo Rodin, Anse's wife. She wanted that money in the worst way because the old boy sure wasn't bringing in much of it the past few years. When she left Anse a while back she moved in next door with Claiborne."

"Didn't anybody like the man? I haven't heard a good word for him since I hit town."

"Not much good to say about the old devil. He even had enemies in Bellaire and Bridgeport and Martins Ferry and a few other towns close by. Back during Prohibition, Anse brewed the best beer and moonshine around. Even after it ended and the speakeasies went back to being regular bars again he kept at it for a few years. What some barkeeps down along the river would do was serve a bottle of Corby's or some other cheap whiskey, then fill the empty with Anse's hooch, which set them back a lot less. The guys who'd drink that kind of rotgut never knew the difference. Some of the boys cleaned up pretty good that way so Anse made some enemies when he got to liking his own product too much and quit selling it to them."

I finished off my second beer and went up to my room, worn out more by the things I had heard than any work I had done. What a sad thing it was that a man could spend a lifetime of forty-five years in the same little Appalachian hill town and then die without having a single friend to say a good word for him.


When I looked out the window in the morning, dark clouds scudded low over the ramshackle buildings of downtown

Switchback. A drenching rain, that's just what I needed to make my day, but it never arrived. By the time I had shaved and showered the sun was managing to make a few brief appearances through the overcast.

I was still in the spending mood so I ordered the twenty-five cent breakfast in the hotel coffee shop: scrambled eggs, bacon, hash browns, toast, orange juice and coffee. A cute waitress about my age even smiled, and when she poured more coffee into my cup didn't caution me that one refill was the limit without plunking down more cash. Strange, though, that the only other customer was a traveling salesman mapping out his day's itinerary. Apparently the locals preferred the greasy food and snarling waitress at the place that as far as I could tell went by the name of the sign over the door, EATS.

Unlike the salesman a few stools down the counter, I had no itinerary to map out. I sat with my third cup of coffee, enjoying a pipeful of tobacco, wondering what I was going to do and why I was hanging around town. When the salesman left to start out on his rounds the pert little waitress with a turned up nose and a twinkle in her brown eyes leaned on the counter across from me and we chatted about nothing in particular for a few minutes. Her name was Sally, so I asked if she was named after the mine and she laughed and said no.

We were exchanging meaningless banter like that when I felt a firm grip on my right shoulder and heard, "Figured I'd find you cosying up to a pretty girl, buddy."

I spun around on my stool and found Jack Eddy standing there. "What . . ." I said, then stammered a few seconds and started over: "Jack, what are you doing here?"

"Hoping to get a little chow." He winked at the waitress, who now had eyes only for him, and said, "How about it, kiddo, think you can scrape up a little grub for me?" After she took his order and went back to the kitchen, he turned to me again. "You know how to pick the cuties, friend. What do they call her?"

"Sally, but you haven't answered my question. What are you doing in Switchback?"

"Never been here before, buddy, and figured a place with a name like Switchback was worth seeing."

"Get serious, will you?"

"Well, the truth is there's nothing at all going on back home, nothing coming in but boring insurance jobs, stuff like that. I had some time off coming to me so I took a few days of it to drive down and check up on you, keep you out of mischief."

I wasn't going to admit it, but I was glad to see him. Jack Eddy was a first-rate private eye, an assistant manager at the Akron branch of Wellington's National Detective Agency. He had a way of cutting through things that to me were a bewildering mishmash and going right to the heart of the matter. He was arrogant, overly ambitious and at times downright annoying, but he knew how to get things done. One thing was certain, Switchback had not seen the likes of Jack Eddy so before he left there would be people who'd be pleased he had come, others who would wish they had never heard his name. It was that way wherever he went.

As for me, along with being pleased to see him I was flattered that he had sought out my company. Jack was a loner who kept people at a distance, but a real friend to those he liked. Showing up in Switchback made it seem that I was one of the few he cared about.

One of those annoying things, however, was that whenever Jack Eddy was around I could just as well have been part of the wallpaper for all the attention paid me by the girls. It didn't matter that Jack was hard of eye and thin of lip or that at twenty-six his sandy hair was growing sparse. At five-eleven he stood four inches shorter than me, and that should have counted for something, but it didn't.

Sally was like all the rest. As she placed his food on the counter she giggled and blushed when he said, "That looks great, sweetheart, almost as good as you. I knew you'd come across."

I could never have used a double entendre like that, or if I had it would have resulted in a slap on the face. Jack Eddy got away with it all the time. I turned aside in disgust.

While he ate breakfast I filled him in on the happenings in Switchback. When his plate was empty he leaned back with his second cup of coffee, bummed a cigarette off me even though I could see a pack of Camels in his shirt pocket, and then, satisfied, said, "So what's on your agenda for today?"

"Nothing. There's not a thing to do that I can see."

He emitted a scornful, "Humph!" and sat shaking his head. "No imagination, that's your trouble, friend. Everything neatly laid out in front of you and you couldn't see it even if it jumped up and hit you in the kisser. First of all, who had access to St. Clair's gun? Aside from himself, of course, and from what you say he didn't do it. Next question, why did the guy confess?"

After taking a sip of coffee and blowing a smoke ring in my direction he said, "It floors me that you haven't been out to the scene of the crime, buddy. That's our first move, then we'll pay a visit to the St. Clair house and after that we should have a good idea of what our next step will be."

I might not have been out to Anse Rodin's place, but at least I knew where it was and that was more than could be said for Jack Eddy. I was a little steamed by what he had said. Maybe more than a little. We were going out the revolving door to the street when something occurred to me. "If you're going to spend the night here, Jack, you'd better check-in."

"I'm way ahead of you, buddy. I took care of that as soon as I got here."

Of course he had. Anyone that perfect would have done so, and that steamed me up even more.

"We'll take my car," I said.

"No we won't, mine's more comfortable. Anyway, I like to have my hands on the wheel." Control, he always had to be in control. Fine, I'd save on gas.

The road was winding and narrow and Jack drove too fast until I cried, "Stop!" He slammed on the brakes and pulled over in front of a sign that arched above the entrance to a side road. The faded lettering read: Little Sally Mine. I said, "There it is, the Little Sally."

"I can see that for myself, sport. So what?"

There was an explosion there ten years ago. Forty-seven men were killed and it's been closed ever since. Ben St. Clair was one of the heroes that day."

Jack gave a low whistle. "Forty-seven. Wow. A man has to be nuts to work down in one of those places. So how did St. Clair come out a hero?"

I filled him in as we drove on. We didn't go far before seeing a mailbox with "Rodin" painted on its side in crude black letters. Some prankster had added a T after the name. Jack turned in and followed a rutted driveway to a dilapidated house set well back from the road. Never having been painted, its clapboard siding was a dirty gray. The chimney leaned at a precarious angle and the porch steps sagged in the middle. Untended bushes and a bumper crop of weeds gave it the look of a shack somewhere in a Congo jungle. "Great place," said Jack. As he opened his door he added, "Watch out for snakes."

With that cheery thought in mind I followed along behind him. Before we reached the steps a woman walked out on the porch, a cigarette drooping from a corner of her mouth, a shotgun cradled in her arms. "Hold it right there, boys," she said in a voice with the texture of sandpaper. "Who are you and wha'da you want here?"

She was about forty, maybe a little younger, and she could have stepped right out of a scene from the Hatfields and the McCoys. Her slitted eyes and set jaw stopped me in my tracks, but Jack ventured a little closer, removing his gray fedora and saying, "Good morning, my dear. We're with the Norka Insurance Company and need to see the crime scene before authorizing payment on the policy. Just routine, you know."

"Anse had a policy? It's news to me. Who gets the money?"

"Why you do, assuming you're Mrs. Rodin."

"That's me. How much?"

"I left the papers at the hotel." He turned and said, "I believe it's three thousand, isn't that right, Mr. Ellsworth?"

When it dawned on me that I was Mr. Ellsworth I mumbled, "Uh…yes, that's right."

"So may we come in and look around for a minute or two?"

"You sure can, boys, be my guest. Come right ahead. When'll I get my money?"

"Shouldn't take long for the home office to finish up the paperwork."

The house was filthy and smelled like a sewer. The bloody sheets were still on the bed where Rodin had died. I couldn't wait to get back outside and inhale some clean country air. When we were in the car again I said, "The Norka Insurance Company? Akron spelled backward, but where did you dream that one up?"

"Out of the blue, buddy, out of the blue. Dangle the possibility of money in front of somebody like that and they'll melt like butter every time. A real doll, wasn't she?"

"I just hope I never see her again, especially if she's toting that shotgun."

"She won't remember you, just me, so quit worrying."

Knowing he was right was just one more irritation to add to the others of the day. It was late morning when we pulled to the curb in front of the St. Clair house. Mr. Reimer was taken aback at seeing Jack Eddy, but he was aware of Jack's talents so his surprise quickly turned to elation. Like a man who suddenly found hope in what had been a hopeless situation, he told Mrs. St. Clair of Jack's background and capabilities. She, too, became excited.

Jack wasted no time in starting to ask questions. Where had Ben kept his gun? Who knew about it and had access to it? The answers didn't clarify the situation, at least in my mind. Ben had been awarded the gun as first prize in some amateur athletic event in Zanesville a month before he graduated from high school. It bore his initials and came in a presentation case that was kept on the fireplace mantel in the room in which we sat, although Mrs. St. Clair couldn't explain why. She was a clubby woman – garden, bridge, and even bowling – and was active in a variety of civic affairs so it seemed that half the people in town had been in the house during the past week or so.

"How about Ben's ex-wife, the charming Mrs. Rodin?" asked Jack.

Mrs. St. Clair smiled at Jack's choice of words. "Yes, Margo came by to visit Brenda a few times, but not while Ben was here. They didn't get along too well, you know."

Jack turned to me and said, "That librarian you told me about, what's her name?"

Before I could reply, Mrs. St. Clair said, "Nancy Holliday, a lovely young woman. We talk about books and authors and when I can't get to the library – I don't drive, you know – she drops them off to me. I mean books, of course." Everyone smiled at that and she blushed a little before going on, "Nancy also comes when Ben isn't here. They were engaged, you see, but haven't even spoken since Ben's unfortunate marriage."

"Everybody says Ben is a swell guy, but it sounds like a lot of people make a point of avoiding him. Has a temper, does he? Argumentative?"

"Oh, no. On the contrary, he's withdrawn, pays very little attention to anyone and doesn't seem to care about much of anything. It breaks my heart because he was so energetic as a boy, so enthused about everything and so interested in everything. Now he just sits alone staring off in space most of the time, seldom has two words to say."

"This big change, it dates back to his marriage?"

The talk was depressing to Mrs. St. Clair. She nodded and said, "Yes, that just seemed to take all the starch out of him. Brenda was the only good thing to come from it. He loves her dearly, but never has been able to really get close to her." She gave a despairing sigh and shake of her head. "I don't know if you understand what I mean. I can't seem to put their relationship into words."

As if on cue, Brenda walked in the front door. With her was a brassy, cocky youth her age who did his best to project himself as a tough, worldly-wise guy. It was laughable, the act put on by the fellow we were told was Bob Thornton. Obviously he would have much preferred being introduced as Humphrey Bogart. Almost as an afterthought, Clarence Kohl followed them into the room. He got as much attention from Brenda as I did from the girls when Jack Eddy was around.

There was no way to escape having lunch at an oversized table in the dining room. An elderly woman served us a salad of dandelion greens and a heaping portion of spaghetti, which wasn't bad, but not as good as could be had at a dozen Akron restaurants. When Jack Eddy asked, Mrs. St. Clair said the woman came in six days a week to help with the cleaning and cooking. She lived in a poorer section of town – they all were, in my opinion – and needed the money because her husband had been crippled in a mine accident years earlier. Jack didn't appear satisfied until told that the man, whose name was Ivan Rostoff, had been bed-ridden for ten years.

Mealtime at the St. Clair home was somewhat of a social occasion with anyone who happened to be around at the time just casually taking a seat at the table. It looked to me like Mrs. St. Clair held perpetual open house. Strange, in view of Ben's taciturn nature. Then again, he may not have cared one way or the other. Jack Eddy asked a few questions while we ate, none of which were probing or upsetting to anyone, and aside from that the conversation was desultory at best. After having chocolate pudding for dessert, we took Mr. Reimer aside and talked a few minutes, then made our excuses and left.

"What a weird setup," I said when we were back in Jack's car. "People coming and going, that Kohl kid practically living there, that Thornton trying to act like the heavy in a second-rate movie. Do you think he might be the killer?"

"*Him*?" Jack's laugh was curt and scornful. "That guy never did a thing in his life for anyone else, or anything that might make him live up to his phony image. He's just a meatless bone."

"Maybe, maybe not. So now what do we do? We've run up against a brick wall, Jack."

"You think so? We'll see." He took a battered Hi-Speed gasoline map of Ohio from the glove compartment. "How do we get to Cammackville? We're going to pay a visit to Ben St. Clair."

"No visitors allowed yet."

"We'll see about that, too."

We stopped at the hotel and Jack went up to his room while I sat in the lobby watching the comings and goings. A Rotary meeting had just ended in a room opening off the restaurant so some of Switchback's self-styled leading citizens were milling around before going back to wherever they spent their working hours. Observing people like that interested me. They were always the same wherever you went.

I had picked up a Wheeling paper at the newsstand and skimmed over it when the crowd thinned out. The usual

197

stories, something else that was always the same wherever you went: armed robbery, a house fire, the Japanese capturing another previously unheard of city in their invasion of China, Hitler mouthing off about having no further territorial demands in Europe if only a large portion of Czechoslovakia was handed over to him. Poland and Russia wanted a bit of it, too. Good stuff like that, so I tossed the paper aside after checking to make sure that Little Orphan Annie, Dick Tracy and Tailspin Tommy were getting along okay.

When Jack Eddy stepped out of the elevator, I did a double-take before I knew it was him. He had changed into an expensive blue serge suit I hadn't known he possessed, was wearing wire-rimmed spectacles and carrying a leather briefcase. What really shocked me, though, was that the hair visible below an expensive homburg hat was gray and he had grown a salt-and-pepper mustache during the half hour he had been gone. He had aged twenty years, and I was speechless.

"Let's get moving, buddy," he said, so I followed out to his car.

When the shock had worn off I said, "What in hell is going on? That fake mustache, those glasses, I thought guys like you only wore disguises in the movies."

"I'm a lawyer from Pittsburgh, if anyone asks. You're my law clerk."

"I don't like the sound of this. You're going to do something illegal, aren't you? If I'm with you, I will be too, so where's my disguise?"

"You don't need one. Nobody pays attention to a law clerk. You'll be forgotten before we're out the door."

"Now look, Jack, I don't even want to go in that door."

"Then you can sit out in the car and miss the fun."

We made most of the ten-mile trip to Cammackville in silence, aside from the times I pleaded with him to slow down. It was a harrowing ride, up and down hills, through wooded hollows, around one hairpin curve after another, past crudely lettered signs on rocks high above the road, signs with encouraging messages like, PREPARE TO MEET THY MAKER. I wasn't prepared, but it seemed as though I should have been whenever we met an oncoming car or speeding truck

198

and when Jack ignored signs warning of dangerous curves ahead.

Cammackville proved to be more prosperous than Switchback, thanks to the elaborate stone courthouse and the people it drew to town. At one side of the courthouse square was a red brick house, the sheriff's living quarters, and attached to it at the rear a rectangular structure with barred windows and a forbidding air about it.

I followed Jack Eddy inside, of course, and watched in admiration as he played his role to the hilt, the dignified and expensive big-city lawyer who didn't have time to waste on hick-town jailers and cops. It worked, and in no time we were seated in a small room waiting for Ben St. Clair to be escorted to us. Jack winked at me when we were alone. I stared at him, shaking my head.

Every bone in Ben St. Clair's body was resentful and every movement he made expressed the fact when he was ushered inside and found two strangers waiting. "Who the hell are you guys?" he said. "I made it clear I don't want a lawyer. I don't need one because I'm pleading guilty at the arraignment tomorrow."

Jack bristled at the arrogant attitude of the man. "Look, smart guy, we're here because of a friend and because of your mother, not because of you. As far as I'm concerned they can fry you tomorrow, but that would make some good people unhappy."

On that cordial note we got down to business. Jack discarded his pretext, told Ben who we really were and why we were there. "Maybe you don't give a hoot about your own skin," he said, "but how about showing a little consideration for your mother and daughter. Think Brenda would be proud the day they strapped her old man in the chair?"

Ben's face flushed in anger. "You leave Brenda out of this, mister. She's got nothing to do with it."

The truth suddenly hit me, although it should have much sooner. Ben St. Clair was all too willing to take the fall because he believed his daughter was the murderer. Why had it taken me so long to see the light when it was so obvious?

I listened as the two of them exchanged barbed remarks the way men who take an instant dislike to each other are prone to do. It was accomplishing nothing that I could see, not that it mattered now that the truth had dawned, but to ease the charged atmosphere I said, "I talked to Nancy Holliday yesterday."

He whirled on me like a bull that had just been hit on the snout. "Leave her out of this too, fella! Who the hell do you think you are butting into my business?"

That made my blood pressure shoot up as only a few things ever had. "*Your* business? Why you self-centered, egotistical, self righteous bastard! She ceased to be your business the day you decided to marry someone who had slept with half the men in town and you didn't even have the guts to tell Nancy to her face, just let her hear it from so-called friends who were laughing themselves silly behind her back. What really gets me is that she's still carrying a torch for you after all these years. You're not worth it. You don't even come close."

Rather than retaliating as he had with Jack Eddy, he stared at me in shocked silence for a moment. Then he shook his head and said, "She quit caring long ago."

"She should have, but she didn't. Too bad, she deserves more than she got out of life." I turned away, stood up and walked over to the window and looked at the world beyond the iron bars. What little passed between the two of them after that didn't make it past my ears.

A few minutes later we were back on the street. As soon as we were out of hearing range Jack Eddy started laughing. "Wow! I didn't know you had it in you, buddy. You really let him have it, and I loved every word of it."

"He got to me, Jack, he really did. I can't stand those self-righteous types."

"Well, friend, I don't think we saw him at his best. Under different circumstances we might have thought he was a swell guy and had a couple of beers with him."

"Maybe, but I doubt it. Things don't usually rile me up that way. So what's next, now that we know Brenda's the one he's trying to protect?"

"We knew that from the start. At least I did and you should have. But just because he's willing to take the rap for her doesn't mean he's right and she's guilty."

It was the next morning before we were able to make contact with Brenda, who had gone to a dance in Wheeling with Bob Thornton. Apparently she wasn't so broken up over her father being in jail that she'd let it interfere with her social life. Jack and I had dinner in the restaurant at the Belmont. The food was excellent and I wouldn't have minded a second helping of pork chops. Even so, only half a dozen other tables were occupied. The Depression, its effect could be seen everywhere. After that we spent an hour in the bar listening to Tony's views on world affairs, then took a little walk to get some fresh air. We were in bed before ten o'clock, or at least I was.

Brenda, her grandmother and Mr. Reimer were dawdling over their breakfast coffee when we arrived at the St. Clair house. I looked around and said, "Where's Clarence?" Without him it seemed like a piece of furniture was missing.

In a bored tone Brenda said, "This is one of the days he works at Bonner's Grocery. He's a stock boy or something."

We talked a while and Jack told Brenda about our visit to see her dad, which she had already heard second-hand. He didn't mention how acrimonious the meeting had been, of course. When all the questions had been answered he posed two of his own: "Why were you out at Anse Rodin's place the day he gave you the latest beating, and how many people knew about it?"

"I still had things out there that I wanted to get. Some clothes and records and my little radio." She thought for a minute before answering the second half of the question. "I don't think anybody knew about it except the people who were here two days later when I forgot and came downstairs wearing a short-sleeved blouse and they could see the marks."

"And who would that be?"

"Let's see, there was dad and grandma. Oh, and Clarence and Bobby Thornton."

"Did your mother know?"

Brenda shook her head, but Mrs. St. Clair said, "Yes she did. I told her."

We left soon after that. This time we had taken my car, so when I was behind the wheel and ready to step on the starter I said, "Now what? You think you have it figured out, don't you? Are you ready to tell me what's going on in that mind of yours?"

He gave me one of his favorite one-knuckle punches on the arm. It stung like fire and made tears well up in my eyes. "What," he said, "and spoil the surprise? You're not one of those people who tell the ending when a movie's only half over, are you?"

As I pulled away from the curb he said, "Let's find that grocery store."

"Bonner's? I've seen it. It's only a couple of blocks away."

When we pulled up in front of the small frame building on a corner just south of downtown, Jack said, "Wait here, friend," and got out and went inside. A few minutes later he returned with Clarence Kohl in tow and had him get in the back seat. Jack climbed in front again, then turned halfway and sat with one arm over the seat. I moved a little, too, so that I could see what was going on. As most introverted young fellows would be when confronted by a pair of older men under such circumstances, Clarence was pale and shaken.

"Let me tell you a story," said Jack. I couldn't see him playing the role of "The Singing Lady" on the network radio show for children, so I grinned until he cast an unfriendly glance in my direction. He went on, "There was this young fellow who was crazy about a girl, had been since they were kids in grade school. She didn't pay him much attention, but he never stopped hoping that she might start feeling differently about him. There was nothing in the world he wouldn't have done for her, so when he found out a man had mistreated her he picked up a gun and killed him. Sound familiar, Clarence?"

He didn't get an answer; Clarence just stared at him from eyes wide and round.

"But this was a good kid," Jack continued, "so his mind was in turmoil when the girl's father was arrested for the deed. He didn't know how to handle it, but knew he would have to come forward before the father was put on trial and sent to prison."

There was an interlude of silence that dragged on for a minute or more, then Jack said, "How about it, Clarence? Isn't it time to come clean, get it over and done with?"

The youth suddenly found his voice, and it was surprisingly forceful. "What did you expect me to do, sit around and let that bastard go on beating her? I'm glad I did it and I'd do it again." His voice trailed off, though, as he added, "I never thought they'd arrest Mr. St. Clair."


The murder had been committed out in the county so it was the sheriff's case, but from what he had heard Jack felt it would be better to turn Clarence over to the police in Switchback. Cap Warner was pulling desk duty again and that was fortunate, far better than having it be some young hotshot.

I didn't feel like hanging around while the processing took place so I left and drove back to the St. Clair house. They were stunned by the news, could hardly believe it was true. I heard, "Not Clarence, surely not Clarence," a dozen times before heading back downtown again. Jack was ready to leave when I got to the jail. Clarence was back in a holding cell until the sheriff's men arrived to take him to Cammackville so I didn't see him again, and was glad of it. The poor, misguided kid faced a lifetime of misery because of a hopeless love for a girl who didn't care.

Jack and I had coffee in a booth at the greasy diner with the "EATS" sign and received the usual admonition about refills from the surly waitress. When she had returned to the counter I said, "How did you know, Jack?"

"One thing was obvious from the time I got here. There were only two reasons why the killer would have dropped the gun and left it for the cops to find, either it was someone trying to frame Ben or someone who panicked. There were several possibilities – the ex-wife, Brenda, the kid. The only one Ben

St. Clair would have tried to protect was his daughter, but she didn't fit the picture. Clarence did."

"I guess you're right, but it still isn't clear in my mind."

Jack Eddy laughed, leaned across the booth and gave me another one-knuckle punch on the arm. "It doesn't have to be, buddy."


I made my final trip to the St. Clair house in early afternoon. The shock had worn off; preparations were underway for Ben's homecoming. Mr. Reimer told me he was going to stick around a few days and not to worry about how he'd get home.

When I returned to the hotel Jack Eddy had already checked out and was gone. I lingered in the lobby a little, trying to gather my thoughts, then went upstairs and stuffed my things in a paper sack, went down again and checked out myself.

The *Times-Press* was my first stop when I arrived in Akron at five o'clock, but before writing my story I called Mrs. Bauer to say I wouldn't be home for supper. She clucked her tongue when told that Mr. Reimer was staying on in Switchback for a while.

The phone rang just as I laid my story on Ben Goldsmith's desk. I barely had time to say hello before Goldsmith shouted, "Who's there with you?"

I glanced around the newsroom that had been bustling a few minutes earlier and found it deserted. "No one, but I'll look around and –"

"There's no time for that. Shirley Temple's having dinner at the Mayflower so get down there fast."

"What for?"

"For once just try using your head for something beside a place to hang your hat," he said, and hung up.

I ran the few blocks to the hotel, having no idea what I'd do when I got there. My press card got me past the brute guarding the door to the dining room and from there I had only to hurry over to the crowd hovering nearby as the young actress and her parents ate supper. Having her in Akron was a major event, and a surprising one even though the Saalfield Publishing Company on the south side had sold more than 50 million copies of various Shirley Temple books. She was America's darling, a little curly-top who had cast a bright light on a country mired in gloom and darkness, had made people smile and leave theaters feeling better than they had when they arrived.

That didn't help me know how a police reporter should cover the story of a 10-year-old girl eating pork chops and asparagus. Hope reared its head when I saw the *Beacon Journal's* leading writer of feature stories scribbling notes. With three Temple bodyguards giving me the fish eye, I elbowed my way over to where I was standing behind her. When she wrote something down, I wrote something down. It may have been cheating, but it saved my day, perhaps my job.

From a pay phone in the lobby I called Sue Baney and said, "It's me, I'm –"

"I knew you were back."

"How did you know?"

"Jack Eddy called and said you'd be coming."

"Seems like he's calling you a lot lately. Have you had supper?"

"Come over here, I'll fix something and we can listen to the fight."

Things had been happening too fast for me. The Joe Louis rematch with Hitler's pride and joy, Max Schmeling, had been the major topic of conversation for weeks and I had forgotten about it.

We had hamburgers and home fries as we listened to the preliminaries. With the fight about to begin Sue said, "There's a couple of beers in the ice box, if you'll get them." I hurried to the kitchen, not wanting to miss a second of the bout I had been anticipating for so long. The bottles were behind everything else, I had to open three cupboard doors before finding glasses, and I had to hunt around for an opener.

"Has it started yet?" I called as I hustled along the hallway to the living room.

"It's over," said Sue, and it was hard for me to forgive the grin on her face. In ninety seconds of the first round Joe Louis had knocked out the only man who had ever beaten him. I had missed it.

Switchback, Shirley Temple, the fight that began and ended without me. I would never look back on the week as a high point of my life.

Ben Goldsmith liked my Shirley Temple story, ran it in page one, but there was a sneer both on his face and in his voice as he said, "Damn similar to the one in the *Beacon Journal*. Guess a guy like you has to get his ideas wherever he can." He cut the Switchback story to the bone and ran it with the state news on page thirty-seven. He was right, though, nobody in Akron cared about the murder of a shiftless man a hundred miles away. As for the story on the effect of the Great Depression on a coalmining town in Appalachia, it never got written. Goldsmith was right about that, too.


Mr. Reimer returned home by bus a few days later. He didn't have much to say and I didn't want to pry. I had the feeling that any idea he had about starting a new life in Switchback with his old flame was dampened by the hectic comings and goings at the St. Clair house. After seventy years of bachelorhood it would take some doing to adjust, to take the part of an old dog having to learn new tricks.

I often thought of driving down to Switchback for a day, nosing around a bit to see what had developed in the lives of the people I had met. Above all I wondered if Ben St. Clair had come to his senses and made up for all the lost years with Nancy Holliday. And Brenda, had she also wised up and dumped the phony Thornton kid? Did she and her father develop a closer relationship? What about Joe Blair and his wannabe Nazis? The *Exponent,* was Stan Mendelbaum still managing to keep it going? And Clarence Kohl, how was he making out in prison, assuming he went there?

I didn't learn the answers because the trip to Switchback turned out to be like so many things people intend to do, but always tomorrow or someday soon. It never happened.

206

# THE SURVIVOR OF THE STORMS

After Roman Stankowski had hobbled off to the restroom I turned to the little man seated beside me and said, "What do you make of it, Ernie? Do you believe his story?"

"I can't make up my mind. It's a wild one, that's for sure, but I can't see why he would be telling it if it isn't true."

"Unless he's a nut case. Say it is true, then he doesn't need a newspaper reporter, he needs a detective. I know the best in the business if he wants to talk to him."

"Ask him when he comes back."

So I did, and he did. I went to a phone booth and called home, the boardinghouse on Dudley Street. Mrs. Bauer grumbled when I asked her to get Jack Eddy, but she climbed the stairs to his room and a couple of minutes later he was on the line. Twenty minutes after that he came striding .into the restaurant at the Mayflower, Akron's finest hotel, gave the glad hand to a couple of people he recognized, then sat down at our table in that cocky way of his that made it seem that the chairman of the board had arrived and now we could get down to business.

After being introduced, Jack shook Roman Stankowski's hand but gave me a raised-eyebrow look that clearly asked if I had summoned him to meet some bum off the street. His manner was more cordial when he turned to the fourth man at the table and said, "So you're Ernie Pyle, the guy with that cream-puff job. I read your stuff sometimes. Not bad."

It had begun nine hours earlier when I walked into the *Times-Press* newsroom after completing my morning rounds on the police beat. I pulled up short because every desk was deserted. Instead of banging out copy with deadline approaching, everyone was gathered in a tight little circle near the managing editor's office. I walked over to see what was going on, then stopped halfway and went back to my desk. Ernie Pyle, the star of the Scripps-Howard syndicate, was to be in Akron for a couple of days, and it was obvious that he had arrived. He was the envy of nearly every reporter in the land because of his assignment: driving around the country, stopping for a day or week or month wherever he pleased, and then writing a daily column on anything of interest to him. Even the best of us had to admit one thing, though: He had the plush assignment because he could write the socks off every other Scripps-Howard employee.

Pyle had a way of putting words together that painted a picture, brought his columns to life in your mind so you could see the scenes he described and, when he wrote about people, you could feel their pain or share their joy. Any reporter worth his salt could do it on occasion; Ernie Pyle did it five days a week. People loved his stuff. Woe to the copy editor who trimmed his column to fit a space if readers were able to tell something was missing.

With someone like that you expect a bigger-than-life character, so I was stunned when the crowd parted and there he was, Ernie Pyle in the flesh. He was a shrimp, a skinny little guy with a nearly bald head, a tortured expression on his face, and the biggest Borsalino hat I had ever seen in his hands. It was brand new, fresh from the carton, but wouldn't be that way for long if he continued to twist the brim as he was doing. It took about five seconds to realize that this was not someone who basked in the glory of his notoriety but instead was a mild-mannered little guy who hated being the center of attention. But then he smiled at something someone said, and it lit up the room.

The brass hats were taking him to lunch. Even city editor Ben Goldsmith was going along, so his assistant had taken over his desk. A couple of hours later Goldsmith laughed as he told a few of us what had happened during their stay at Puffy and Louie's, one of those restaurants that were popular in the 1930s, the kind where the waiters made a game of insulting the customers and people couldn't get enough of it. Certain people, that is, and I knew Ernie Pyle was not one of them. Pyle had been set up in advance. When asked what he wanted, he hesitated a second or two, so the waiter yelled, "Hey, this rube won't order!" Other waiters came running, picked up the chair with Pyle on it, carried it outside, and set it down on the sidewalk, then went back to their duties. They polished his bald spot, and when the group was ready to leave and Pyle had retrieved his decrepit old raincoat from a hook, the waiters came running again and started pulling silverware and salt and pepper shakers from the pockets, making quite a spectacle of it. The big shots from the paper thought it was hilarious. Poor Ernie . . . well, I guess he managed a weak grin.

In late afternoon I was dawdling around the office, thinking it was too early to go home, too late to do anything else, when Ernie Pyle came in, saw I was the only one there, said, "Hi," and turned to leave again. He was almost to the door when he stopped, took a few steps back toward me, and said, "Is there a quiet place close by where a man can get a drink?"

"Stone's Grille at this time of day. It's a few blocks north on Main Street."

"Care to join me?"

Do zebras have stripes? I was on my feet before he had time to change his mind. When he asked my name and what I did at the paper I said, "Bram Geary. I cover the police beat."

"A lot of the best men in the business started that way."

As we walked up High Street he said he wasn't drinking at the time, but I knew his reputation for hitting the bottle and decided that to him a couple of drinks didn't constitute drinking. He also told me his wife, Jerry, was going to join him in Akron late that evening. Pyle didn't say so, but I had heard via the grapevine that she had been drying out in a sanitarium somewhere. Word had it that the pair of them kept a distillery or two in business.

An hour later and Stone's would be busy with men lined up at the bar and early diners on the other side of the barrier, but at four o'clock there were only a couple of others in the place. When we were seated on barstools, Pyle repeated the strange story told to him the previous evening by a man he had met at the Mayflower. After winding it up he said, "It's interesting, but it's not something I can use. If you think you might, I'll be talking to him again about seven thirty at the hotel."

After a grand dinner of Mrs. Bauer's meat loaf and mashed potatoes with apple pie for dessert, I drove back downtown, was introduced to Roman Stankowski, heard his story firsthand, then phoned Jack Eddy. An assistant manager at the Akron office of Wellington's National Detective Agency, Jack had the room across from mine at the boardinghouse.

Stankowski was a husky man of about forty with a round Slavic face tanned and creased by hard years spent in the sun and wind. He walked with a pronounced limp and a tic kept his right eyelid in motion. He wore a cheap brown suit and a red-and-blue-striped necktie decorated with a few stains from meals long eaten. As he repeated his story a third time, skepticism was written all over Jack Eddy's face.

In as few words as possible it went like this: Stankowski was a sailor on a Great Lakes ore boat, the kind longer than a football field, or even two. It was one of many plying the waters between the west end of Lake Superior and the ports on Lake Erie. From Duluth it carried iron ore from the Misabi Range to Cleveland, Ashtabula, Conneaut, and Erie, then made the return trip loaded with coal from the bituminous fields in Pennsylvania, West Virginia, and Southeast Ohio. The season began with the Blessing of the Fleet in April, ended in late November or early December when the lake waters began to freeze over. The Great Lakes are plagued by deadly and, in some years, frequent storms that in an hour's time can turn placid blue water into towering waves twenty feet high. On Erie, the shallowest of the lakes, the storm-driven waves hit in rapid succession, so there is no time to recover from one before the next hits. They say that six thousand ore boats and other craft have gone to the bottom on the Great Lakes, taking thirty thousand people with them. It's a dangerous way to earn a living.

I recalled an early December day when I had stood in a light rain on an embankment overlooking the harbor at Conneaut. An ore boat, probably the last of the season, was trying to fight its way past the breakwater into the open sea beyond but was making only slight progress. I watched, cold and wet but too fascinated by the battle between man and nature to leave. At last it made it through the breakwater, so after a few more minutes I turned and headed for my car, thankful that I was on shore and not on that long, wave-battered ore boat.

Roman Stankowski was born in 1900 and had grown up near the lake in Lorain. He married an Akron girl named Marie Strabic the day after Christmas in 1922. She was pregnant when he returned to his boat, the *John W. Morgan,* in early April 1923. On the first trip of the season, Stankowski had a run-in with the captain of the *Morgan* and left the ship at Duluth. Another, the *Carty-Jamison No. 2,* was ready to head out and was short a man, so Stankowski signed on at the last minute. While heading east on Lake Erie the boat was caught in a vicious storm a dozen miles east of Cedar Point. Stankowski had just gone off duty and was ready to climb onto his bunk when there was a terrific crash. He made his way on deck and found the boat had broken in two. The last thing he recalled was being hurled across the deck, then inky blackness.

That was in April 1923. He awoke in a hospital bed, his head swathed in bandages. Semiconscious, he was aware of people coming into his room every now and then, looking at him and shaking their heads, then leaving. He was lucid the following day and was told he had been picked up by a small lumber-hauling boat out of Saginaw. That didn't make sense to him because his ore boat had been on Lake Erie, not Huron. Late in the day he was given a newspaper by an orderly. Some of the stories on the front page also didn't make sense, so he looked at the date. He let the paper fall and for a few minutes sat there stunned, thinking his head was hurt more than he realized and his mind was playing weird tricks on him. He managed to get out of bed, stumble unsteadily to the bathroom and look in a mirror. Instead of seeing the reflection of a twenty-three-year old, he saw the grizzled face of a middle-aged man.

The date on the Saginaw paper was correct, it was May 27, 1938, not an April day in 1923. He was totally bewildered. According to the story, the ore boat he had been on when it went under was the *Lewis J. Russell,* not the *Carty-*

*Jamison No. 2,* and he had never heard of the *Lewis J. Russell.* Nor had he heard the name the nurses were calling him, Mr. Cermak—Joseph Cermak. Doctors examined him, one after another, and he gradually came to accept the fact that he was the victim of some form of amnesia that had blotted out fifteen years of his life.

At a library after being released from the hospital he read the story of the earlier sinking of the *Carty-Jamison No. 2* on a day when several boats were lost. Two men from his boat had been rescued by the Coast Guard. One was hospitalized, the other disappeared before anyone had an opportunity to talk to him. That, he decided, could have been him.

As Joseph Cermak he had received a check for a goodly sum from the owners of the *Lewis J. Russell.* He knew that wasn't his real name and so wondered if there really was a Joseph Cermak who had gone down with the ore boat. Or, difficult as it was to believe, had he been Joseph Cermak for fifteen years?

He traveled to Akron by train, wondering what he would find when he arrived. It turned out some things were just as he remembered, others far different. There was no trace of Marie Stankowski after all those years, and he was bewildered as to what to do next. He had been hanging around for weeks doing odd jobs to augment the check he had received.

Jack Eddy wasn't buying it. "So you want to find your wife," he said, "and you want to know what this Joseph Cermak was doing during the missing fifteen years, right?"

"That's it. Can you help me?"

"I'll think about it." Jack handed Stankowski a Wellington's National Detective Agency business card and said, "If you're still interested in the morning, come to the office and we'll talk some more about it."

We left then and Ernie Pyle headed to the depot to meet his wife. When we were back at the boardinghouse I followed Jack Eddy to his room. "You don't believe him, do you?" I said.

"I don't know, buddy. I don't place much stock in this amnesia business. Hell, even the medics don't know much about it."

"If he's not on the level, why come up with the story?"

"How do I know? Look, friend, maybe he's off his rocker, or maybe he's concocted some sort of alibi for a crime he committed during those years he claims are a blank. I don't have much truck with this kind of stuff, but if he shows in the morning I'll give it some thought. Provided he's got a fistful of cash for a retainer. I'm not tying the agency up on a thing like this without it."


After finishing my afternoon rounds the next day, I decided to stop by City Hospital to see my sister Catharine. We were young kids when our parents died in a car crash, so we had grown up at the Children's Home. Catharine had recently graduated from nurses' training and now worked in the emergency room. I didn't see her as often as a big brother should. This was made clear when she saw me after I had been standing around for a few minutes and said, "What are you doing here, Bram?"

"Just wanted to say hello, see how you're doing."

"I'm doing fine. So what do you really want?"

"Well, I did want to ask what you know about amnesia. Is there really such a thing?"

"Of course."

"Could a man have it for fifteen years and not remember anything about those years?"

"Of course."

"Can it be faked?"

"Of course."

"Will you quit saying that? Tell me what you know about it."

"Not much, really. There are differing opinions about what is genuine and what isn't. In some cases there's no doubt, in others the doctors don't always agree. There's a lot about amnesia that is still unknown."

"For Pete's sake, Catharine, this is 1938, not the Civil War era. I thought you people knew all about such things."

"You're wrong. Now I have to get back to work."

I turned to leave, then said, "That poor guy they helped in here while I was parking the car, the one that could hardly

213

breathe with asthma or something. How is he?"

"Dead," she replied, then walked away.

I left shaking my head. She could stand a little work on her bedside manner.


Jack Eddy pulled his 1932 Auburn sedan up in front of the boardinghouse shortly before supper time. I stepped out on the porch to meet him. "Did you take Stankowski's case?"

"Yeah. After he gave me a thousand dollar retainer."

"A thousand bucks? Wow! That's a lot of money."

"We'll earn it, buddy, and probably more than that."

"I've been thinking, Jack. Would Stankowski be better off forgetting the whole thing?"

"Not if he's on the level, friend. What's worse, finding out the truth, good or bad, or spending the rest of his days moping around barrooms with those questions in his head? That could drive a man haywire. Or make a souse of him."

"So now what?"

"Our Detroit office is checking out his story in Saginaw. I've got Cliff Austin and a new man, Mac McKelvey, chasing down the long-lost wife, and Cal Andres is up at the lake seeing what he can find out about the sinking of the *Carty-Jamison No. 2* in 1923."

"You still don't believe his story, do you?"

"I don't know, buddy. I'm keeping an open mind."

"Think it's time for me to write a story on it?"

He walked on into the house with a shrug of his shoulders. "That's your department. I don't care one way or the other."

So I went back downtown after supper and wrote up what I knew, although making sense of it wasn't easy. When I walked in the newsroom the next morning Ben Goldsmith was all excited. He loved the story and wanted to know when there would be a follow-up. That made me begin to regret ever hearing of Roman Stankowski.


Sue Baney was full of questions about my story when I picked her up that evening for a ride around town and maybe an ice cream soda someplace. She kept calling Stankowski "that poor lost soul" and nearly bit my head off when I suggested he might be a con man. "Con men don't pay a detective a thousand dollars," she said. I admitted she had a point.

Her reaction was like that of many people, and it puzzled me. Not once had I ever heard her express concern that the world seemed headed for another big war, but mention some down-on-his-luck slob and she got all choked up and teary eyed. I just couldn't understand people. At Sue's insistence we took in a movie, Mickey Rooney in *Love Finds Andy Hardy,* but my mind was on things more important than the escapades of a precocious, puffed-up kid.

I hadn't seen Jack Eddy for a few days before he came swaggering into the newsroom, perched himself on a corner of my desk, and, as if he were announcing some world-shaking piece of news, said, "We found Marie Stankowski."

"I assume that was an editorial 'we' and it really was one of your operatives that found her. So where was she?"

"Here in town. And don't get flippant with me if you want to hear about it. Anyway, Cliff Austin found she had Stankowski declared legally dead years ago. After that she remarried and is living up in Cuyahoga Falls with her second husband and Stankowski's fifteen-year-old son. She got hitched to a Myron Bullington up in Ravenna, which is why Cliff didn't track her down the first day. He says Marie is a shriveled-up harpy and the kid is a totally obnoxious pain in the butt."

"Then she isn't living here in town but up in the Falls."

"So who can tell the difference? You're really in a mood today, aren't you, buddy? Combative, I'd call it."

"Does Stankowski know yet?"

"Two days ago. And an hour ago he gave me another five hundred bucks to check out the new husband. He nosed around a little and thinks there's something fishy about the guy."

"Like what's so fishy?"

"I said it was an hour ago. Sorry I don't have it all wrapped up yet, but do you think you could give me the rest of the day to work on it?" He jumped up off the desk and headed for the door. "You're really something today, pal. Better take an aspirin or a good-humor pill."

Artie Bauer, twelve-year-old son of my landlady, was sitting on the front porch steps when I arrived home in late afternoon. In passing I said, "How's it going, Artie?"

"What's it to yuh?"

I pulled up short. "What's your problem, kid? Forget how to act civil?"

"Aw, hell. Maw wants to know why I ain't goin' to the Boy Scout meetin' tonight."

I sat down beside him. "And why aren't you?"

" 'Cause me'n Hawkeye got throwed out last week."

"For what, not being able to speak a recognizable form of the English language?" I laughed a little. Artie didn't.

"Nothin' like that. The scoutmaster said some kids just ain't cut out to be Scouts."

"What in the world did you do, Artie? What brought this on?"

"Nothin'. Well, yuh know that Camporee out at Camp Manatoc two weeks ago? Me'n Hawkeye won the fire buildin' contest."

"And for that they threw you out of the Scouts?" He grinned, then started laughing. "Well, yuh see Hawkeye brung along a little can uh lighter fluid and I had these matches. You shoulda seen it, Bram. Them other kids was rubbin' sticks together and me'n Hawkeye had flames shootin' ten feet in the air. They give us first prize, then took it away again."

I got up and went on inside the house. That scoutmaster was right.

Sue Baney and I had hamburgers at the Spotless Spot drive-in a few evenings later, then went back to her place and danced to some numbers on the radio. Visions that I didn't tell her about flashed through my mind when Larry Clinton's band played the big hit of the day, "I Married an Angel." Before going to bed I tapped lightly on Jack Eddy's door, opened it when he called, "Come in." He was sitting in his easy chair—something I didn't have in my smaller room— wearing just his shorts and undershirt and reading the latest issue of *Liberty* magazine. He said, "Come to pick another fight, buddy?"

I ignored that. "I've been wondering what it was that Stankowski thinks smells bad about Marie's new husband. Have you found anything out yet?"

"Not much, but we're working on it. This Myron Bullington impressed our man who checked him out as a weakling that has the idea he's a big shot. A phony who doesn't realize he is one. He works at an old two-story building on Orleans Avenue, but nobody seems to know what kind of an operation it is. No sign on the place, the front door is always locked, a dozen or more employees that have to knock to get in every morning. If somebody knocks on the door during the day, no one answers. When they get a delivery at a loading dock at the side, a few employees come out and do the work so the driver never goes inside. Stankowski saw a truck load up with merchandise and drive off a couple of times. No lettering on the truck, no identifying marks."

"How big a truck?"

"Good size. Not a tractor-trailer rig, but big."

"Doesn't sound like much to me."

Jack Eddy laughed. "Why doesn't that surprise me, buddy?"


A few days went by before I heard anything more. In the meantime I had driven down Orleans Avenue, a dreary street in the shadow of the Goodrich plant at the south end of downtown just a couple of blocks from the *Times-Press*. Calling it an avenue was someone's idea of a joke because it ran for only a single block south off Exchange Street. The buildings that lined both sides were a hodgepodge of dilapidated one- and two-story structures that at some point in the distant past might have been halfway respectable. Now they were a display of failed enterprises that brought

217

to mind the song "Boulevard of Broken Dreams." Except, of course, that boulevard was an even bigger misnomer than avenue.

What Jack Eddy had to tell me after supper at the boarding-house wasn't exactly earthshaking. "Cal Andres got a job at that dump on Orleans Avenue today, buddy."

"No kidding. What did he find out?"

"Not much so far. They had him unloading and then unpacking crates from a truck all day. From what little he saw, most of the people were just packing up other boxes for shipment. He should know more in a day or two."

"If it's some kind of shady operation couldn't he be in danger?"

Jack gave me a one-knuckle punch on the arm that stung like fire. "That's what our line of work is all about, buddy. Cal can take care of himself. He didn't go in and start asking questions and stand gawking around, you know."

"How did he ever get a job there?"

"Watched the place one afternoon until the employees started leaving, then followed a couple of them to a bar on Main Street. Once there he struck up a conversation and one thing led to another with Cal kind of steering things. Cal was back at the bar the next day, and one of the guys told him to meet him the next morning because the plant manager agreed to talk to him about a job. The manager, by the way, turned out to be Myron Bullington."

I thought about it before turning in that night. It took a real adventurer to have a job like Jack Eddy's or Cal Andres's. I could see where the excitement, the living on the edge of danger, could be appealing to a certain breed of man. I decided I wasn't one of them.

I was sitting alone on the front porch swing listening to Kenny Baker sing "Love Walked In" on someone's radio across the street when Jack Eddy parked his Auburn sedan in front of the boardinghouse late in the afternoon a couple of days later. Jack came bounding up the steps, excitement written all over his face. Before I could open my mouth, he said, "It's a record counterfeiting operation, buddy."

"A what?"

"They're counterfeiting phonograph records down there on Orleans Avenue. A first-class operation with top-grade equipment, a press for printing labels, the whole shebang."

"I don't get it. You mean to sell?"

"What else would you expect?"

"Come on, Jack. A record only costs thirty-five cents."

*"Only* thirty-five cents. To a kid that's big money, but that's not the point. Look, let me explain it to you. They pick up legitimate records the day they're released, or maybe have connections to get them before they hit the market. From that they make their own masters on the best equipment available and run off as many copies as they want. A real expert—a Tommy Dorsey or a Benny Goodman—might tell the difference in quality, but not one person in ten thousand could. A machine applies the labels they printed, then they box them up and they're ready to ship."

"Ship to where? Record stores have their own wholesalers they buy from, don't they?"

"They don't go after the really big stores, but in the territory they cover there are hundreds of mom-and-pop dealers plus other businesses that sell records as a sideline. One day a couple of tough guys with bulges under their suit coats walk in, tell them they represent a new wholesale company and from now on they'll be getting their merchandise from them. The implication being 'or else.'"

"So Bullington runs the operation in Akron, but the outfit in Cleveland is behind it, right?"

"You called it, friend. The Murray Hill Mob's name is written all over it, but no one could ever prove it in court. They've got a couple of strong-arm boys in the plant at all times, of course."

"There must be money in it, Jack, but it doesn't seem like enough to interest that bunch."

"Believe me there is. The initial setup costs some dough, sure, but not as much as it would cost you or me to do the same thing. Then the material they use for the records is cheap stuff, not the quality that RCA, Columbia, or any big company uses. After a dozen plays a record may start getting scratchy, but so what? Let's say they clear a nickel on every record they peddle. One by a top band or someone like Crosby might sell fifty thousand copies in their territory. A lot wouldn't sell that many, but multiply that nickel by all the records sold and it adds up to real money. And you can bet they don't take returns on records that don't sell. Mom and Pop take the hit, not them."

"It's a pretty sleazy way to do business."

Jack laughed at that. "You're expecting ethics from those boys? Get real, buddy."

"How big a territory do they cover?"

"I don't know exactly yet, but it's big. Very, very big. And it's a safe bet that the Akron plant isn't the only one they have."

"So now what? What's Wellington's going to do about it?"

"That's still in the planning stage. You can be sure of one thing, we're going to bust up the operation. That may not put them out of business, but it'll sure hit them where it hurts. I'll make certain you get first crack at the story when it breaks, so keep it under your hat for now."

Jack Eddy was a secretive person. I knew next to nothing about his background other than that he had lived in Indianapolis and graduated from Shortridge High School. And that he was transferred to Akron from the Indianapolis branch of Wellington's National Detective Agency, of course. Aside from that his past was a blank as far as I was concerned.

I had been checking on some of my Irish ancestors and discovered there had been Eddys in Ireland. So I said, "Jack, did your ancestors come over from Ireland?"

He shook his head.

"There were people named Eddy there, you know."

"My ancestors stayed where they were in Cork. The city, I mean. My parents came over and so did I."

I was taken aback. "You mean you were born in Ireland? You don't talk like an Irishman."

"Sure and now didn't I leave when I was five?"

"Now you *are* talking like an Irishman. Are you saying you grew up here and learned to speak American?"

"And isn't that the truth of it, lad? My parents never lost their accents, but I did."

"Do you speak Irish?"

"Gaelic? Yes, a little, although not in everyday conversation. And you, did your ancestors come from Ireland? Geary sounds Irish."

"They did. My paternal grandparents did, that is. In 1849 at the time of the famine. Why did your parents leave?"

"No choice. The Easter uprising in 1916. My father was one of the boys with Michael Collins and the others. He wasn't caught at the time like so many were, but he had to flee. He managed to get back to Cork and, with the help of friends, was able to get on a ship leaving for America. My mother and I followed a month later."

"It's amazing, Jack. My grandmother was from Clare, but my grandfather was from Cork."

He put his head back and laughed. "And that, my friend, is probably the only thing we have in common."


I was thinking about going to bed the next night when the hallway phone rang. Ivy Bauer was starting to get up from her chair, until I said, "I'll get it." A good thing as it turned out because it was the night desk at the *Times-Press.* "There's been a murder on 18th Street in the Falls, Bram. You'd better get up there."

So much for bed. I cranked up my Hupmobile and headed north. Once across the High Level Bridge and in Cuyahoga Falls I followed 18th Street until I came to a couple of police cars and a crowd gathered in front of a two-story house a little north of Broad Boulevard. By then instinct told me who the victim would be, so I wasn't surprised when a detective told me it was Myron Bullington. He had been shot in the back of the head while on his knees just after parking his car in the driveway. Gangland execution style, with the killer waiting for him to come home after a late night at the plant or, more likely, a couple of hours at a tavern.

I didn't hang around long, knowing that an arrest was a rarity in a professional murder and that small town police were ill-prepared to conduct a real investigation. I was certain that when the Falls detectives learned about Roman Stankowski he would head the list of suspects even though everything about the killing pointed to the mob. When I woke Jack Eddy after returning home, he echoed my thoughts. "And the worst thing about it, buddy, is that Stankowski dropped out of sight a couple of days ago."

My morale was at a low ebb the next few days. Even seeing Sue Baney a couple of times couldn't shake my depression. Where was Stankowski and why had he pulled a disappearing act? Worst of all was the world news. Hitler was demanding a big chunk of Czechoslovakia, and now even Poland wanted some Czech territory. All of Europe was in an uproar, and in Germany, life had become intolerable for the Jews. Now those with Aryan first names had to change them to Israel or Sarah. No matter that Heinrich or Franz had been World War heroes, they now were Israel.

A delegation representing German Jews had gone to a conference of nations in Evian, France, to seek a place for them to emigrate, something Hitler approved of, but it seemed that no one wanted them. Even the United States said only the normal quota of immigrants from Germany and Austria, 27,370, would be admitted, and most countries wouldn't go that far. Australia declared, "As we have no real racial problem, we are not desirous of importing one." Intellectuals were especially unwelcome everywhere. Only Holland and Denmark agreed to take all Jews that wanted to come.

What a wonderful world it was. The only good news was that the Japanese army had tried to take over a piece of Soviet territory and the Russians had kicked the daylights out of them and sent them running for home. It was their first major setback in an attempt to take over the entire Far East. But we were all sitting on a powder keg, and with each passing day I had a clearer vision of myself in uniform with a rifle in my hand. I hated the thought.

I decided a hot bath might cheer me up. The pleasurable aroma of Lifebuoy soap was medicinal. It would be my third in a week, but so far Mrs. Bauer hadn't complained. She was waiting outside the bathroom door, though, when I started back to my room. "You've been using too much hot water, Bram. If you keep it up I'll have to raise your rent."

"It won't happen again," I told her, but wanted to ask why the same rule didn't apply to Jack Eddy. I had counted and he had taken four baths the previous week.

I had joined most of the boarders and three members of the Bauer family in the living room listening to the *Jack Benny Show* on radio one evening when Jack Eddy came in the front door, paused long enough to give me a nod, and then went on upstairs. I followed him to his room when a commercial came on.

"It's set for nine o'clock tomorrow morning, buddy. Join us at the office about half past eight."

"What's set? What's it all about, Jack?"

"We're going to raid the plant on Orleans Avenue, what else?"

"Now wait a minute, Jack. It sounds to me like there might be gunplay."

He shrugged as if to say it didn't matter. To me it did.

"The Akron cops know about it," he said. "I talked to Plato Largis, and he'll be there with some of his boys in blue."

"Any word yet on Roman Stankowski? Will he be there?"

"Not likely. We haven't a clue as to where he is. Neither do the Cuyahoga Falls cops, and like we thought, he's their chief suspect in Bullington's murder."

"Do you think the mob got wise to him hanging around and picked him up? Maybe they're holding him in the recording plant."

"Not a chance. They don't hold on to people, they dispose of them like they did Bullington. I would bet, though, that it was Stankowski's poking into their business that somehow made them decide Bullington was a dangerously weak link in the operation."

"Who's running the plant now?"

"One of the strong-arm boys from Cleveland."

"I don't much care for the sound of this, Jack. If you think I want to be in on a reenactment of the gunfight at the O.K. Corral, you're badly mistaken."

Again he shrugged his shoulders. "Doesn't matter to me, friend. Sorry we didn't take your personal safety into account when the plans were drawn up. It'll be a big story, though, but if you want to miss out on it, it's up to you."

He knew I couldn't. That was one of the infuriating things about Jack Eddy. He knew how I felt about being around when bullets started flying, but he didn't care. On the other hand, he knew I had a job to do and was good enough to tip me off with inside information. Personally, though, I would have preferred to rush down there after the shooting ended and get the story that way. But knowing about it ahead of time meant I had to be there from start to finish. If I wasn't and Ben Goldsmith heard about it, I'd be out of a job. I shuddered to think what Sue Baney would say when it was all over. Provided that I was still around to tell her about it. One thing for sure, I wouldn't get much sleep that night.


It began quietly enough on a sunny morning when it was good to be alive but might be difficult to stay that way. I was in Jack's Auburn along with Cliff Austin and Mac McKelvey. We drove to the end of Orleans Avenue and parked around the corner on Cedar, another short street that ended at Orleans. I figured Jack didn't want his car in the line of fire. Cal Andres was at work inside the plant, and another car of Wellington operatives stopped at the far end of Orleans. That group was to work their way around behind the plant.

Foot traffic on Orleans was next to nonexistent, so I knew we would stand out like the proverbial sore thumb. I brought up the rear as we spread out, rounded the corner, and started toward God only knew what. Then, with me already thinking there were too many people on the street for it to look normal, two cars filled with Akron cops careened around the corner off Exchange Street and pulled to the curb with brakes squealing.

Cops poured out onto the street like clowns leaving one of those funny cars at a circus. Some ran around to the loading dock at the side of the plant. Plato Largis was with a group that pulled a battering ram from the first car. I watched open mouthed as Jack Eddy ran to join them just as the ram hit the front door with the sound of a Mack truck plowing into a concrete wall at sixty miles an hour. Then the fun began.

Shots rang out as Akron cops and Wellington ops scurried through the doorway. I followed, hesitated outside the door, then went ahead and stepped inside just in time to take a bullet through my hat. Fortunately, the old brown fedora sat high on my head. Even more fortunate was the fact that I stood six three and not six five.

The shooting continued for a minute or so, then an eerie silence fell over the place. Two burly characters in civilian clothes were led past me on the way to a short ride to police headquarters. One clutched his left arm where blood seeped from a bullet wound. Jack Eddy and Plato Largis followed behind but stopped when they saw me examining my hat. Jack pointed to it and said, "Is that a bullet hole?" and then began laughing.

Cliff Austin joined the group in time to say, "Look, an entry wound and an exit wound." They were all laughing as if my narrow escape were some big joke that everyone got except me.

To change the subject I said, "All that shooting and one thug took a bullet in his arm, that was it? I don't think there's going to be any marksmanship awards handed out."

But I was wrong. When we were back on the street we learned that the mobster who had taken over running the plant had bolted out a door onto the loading dock, gun in hand, and was shot dead by an Akron policeman.

Jack Eddy's head was shaking. "It's the worst thing that could have happened. He was our best bet for tracing this setup back to the mob in Cleveland."

I didn't say so, but I didn't think it came close to being the worst thing that could have happened. I made a few notes, went back inside where cops were starting to haul recording equipment out to the street, made a few more notes, then hurried off on foot to the *Times-Press* building.

The trip took only a couple of minutes, and when I arrived with my bullet-riddled hat on my head, I quickly became a hero. Even Ben Goldsmith was impressed. So much so in fact that he summoned a photographer to take a shot of me with a finger sticking through the entry hole. Then he broke his own rule that a reporter should not be a part of the story by having another man write a short sidebar to go with the front page photo and my banner story on the raid.

In mid afternoon I had a phone call from Sue Baney. "Someone just showed me the paper, Bram. You were in on another shootout, weren't you? You know what I told you, you know how I feel about dating a man who is constantly involved in such things. And this time you were shot in the head."

"Not the head, Sue. The hat."

"That's it, Bram. We're finished, through, all washed up. Don't call me again . . . ever." It sounded like another shot when she banged the phone down. It didn't worry me too much because I was sure she would change her mind. Besides, people from other departments were still coming to the newsroom to see the hole in my hat, and I was basking in the glory of it all.

Despite her orders I called Sue Baney that night. As soon as she heard my voice she banged the receiver down again. I felt bad but not too bad because I was the center of attention at the boarding-house. Pretty Kitty Bauer was nowhere to be found, but pudgy Mabel Klosterman broke out in a sweat when she examined the hole in my hat. "Oh, Bram," she said, "you were almost killed." Prim and proper Nora Ferrabee shook her heard while saying, "To think that such things go on right here in town." Mr. Reimer, the retired druggist, said, "My, my, Abraham, you really should be more careful."

Ivy Bauer and her husband, Bus, didn't seem as impressed as the others, and the brat Artie looked at the bullet hole and said, "Aw, that's nothin'. Didn't even draw blood." But it was Jack Eddy who really got under my skin as he stood by watching with a laconic smirk on his face.

Later I followed him up to his room. I said, "No word on Stankowski yet? I thought sure we'd find him locked up somewhere in that plant."

"I can't figure why you'd think that. I don't believe for a minute that the mob has anything to do with his disappearing act. But just for the sake of argument let's say they did. Then why would they have him stashed away down there? If they grab somebody off the street it's the last anybody sees of them, you know that, buddy. They're not in the business of running a jail."

He was right, of course. I had just been trying to look on the bright side. I just didn't get it. Why would Stankowski give Wellington's money to check out the Orleans Avenue plant and then just wander off without waiting to learn the result?

There was good news a couple of days later when Jack Eddy stopped by the newsroom to tell me the gun used to kill Myron Bullington was the one carried by the mobster killed on the loading dock during the raid. "He must have loved that gun, buddy. The procedure called for him to ditch it after shooting Bullington, but he didn't. A stupid jerk, but it gets Stankowski off the hook."

It was pleasantly cool a week later, so after finishing my afternoon rounds I walked north on Main Street to the Wellington Agency's office in the Metropolitan Building, along the way inhaling the blended aromas of diesel fumes from city buses, rubber from the Goodrich complex, and cereal from the Quaker Oats plant a block west. I arrived just as Jack Eddy was convening a meeting of the operatives. Before he got started I poked my head in the door of his office and said, "Any word yet on Stankowski?"

"Come on in and join the party," he said, winking at the new man, Mac McKelvey. "Nothing on Stankowski, but Mac found Joseph Cermak up in Duluth."

"What?" I said, stunned by the news, then repeated, "What? What are you talking about?"

McKelvey, a thin man as tall as my own six three with a shock of unruly dark hair and a sardonic twist to his mouth for someone only twenty-one-years old, said, "He decided he didn't care for Stankowski's life, but figured Cermak's was okay."

"And that's it? He just walked away? And what about those missing fifteen years?"

"Not missing anymore, at least most of them," McKelvey continued. "From the start of the 1925 shipping season Cermak was working on ore boats right up until the *Lewis J. Russell* went down this spring. Never married again, never did much of anything but work, and then during the off season hang around a couple of waterfront bars that were speakeasies back during Prohibition."

It was a tremendous letdown. I had visualized all kinds of scenarios, some involving a life of crime, a few on the romantic side. This was so ... so routine, so commonplace.

McKelvey was still talking. "... but no one would hire him on an ore boat because of his gimpy leg, so he's working for a ship's chandler."

"Then his memory came back? For both lives?"

"Not really," said Jack Eddy. "Or so he says. He's okay on the Stankowski end of it, and Mac kind of rebuilt a memory on the Cermak side for him."

I took a chair in the corner and sat through their bull session, not really paying attention until Cal Andres said, "Jack, did I ever tell you about a couple of boaters I talked to up at Lorain who swear that on foggy nights they saw the *Carty-Jamison No. 2?* Came too close for comfort, both said, and they could read the name clear as a bell."

Oh no, I thought, a ghost ship. As if there weren't enough unanswered questions. The others were laughing, making remarks about people with overactive imaginations. Maybe, but I wasn't as sure as they were. It was Lorain where Roman Stankowski had been born. I could see it in my mind, a ghost ship taking one of its sailors home.

When the others had left I turned to Jack and said, "I don't know what to make of it. When you think about it the whole story is kind of crazy. It seemed like such a mystery at first.

You know, who he really was, what had happened to his wife and kid, what he had been doing during those years missing from his memory. And now it seems like nothing."

"Come on, buddy, do a little *real* thinking. This survivor of the storms, a not-too-brilliant sailor who somehow managed to live when two ore boats split asunder with him on board comes to town and breaks up a huge record counterfeiting operation, decides the woman he was once married to is a grouchy old shrew with a fifteen-year-old kid who is a foul-mouthed punk, then quietly slips away and goes back to a life he enjoys. You call that nothing?

"You know, friend, I didn't realize you were such a dreamer. You wanted it to turn out that Stankowski was one of the triggermen in the Saint Valentine's Day Massacre, then hooked up with the Dillinger gang to rob a few banks, and all the while was secretly married to Greta Garbo. Now when you find out the truth, which actually is pretty exciting stuff, you find it anticlimactic."

I didn't want to laugh but couldn't help myself. "Put that way, maybe you're right. I can't imagine what Sue Baney's going to say when I tell her about this final development."

"I thought she wasn't having anything more to do with you."

"Oh, she'll come around."

"You think so, huh? If you're right she'll say the same thing she said before. She'll cluck her tongue a few times and say 'that poor lost soul.'"

I laughed again and headed for the door, turned there, and said, "She's right, you know. Stankowski really is a poor lost soul. And now we're never going to know what he really does and doesn't remember about those years."

"The human mind is a funny thing, buddy."

"You can say that again. After all this I don't think mine will ever be the same. But I wonder what Stankowski or Cermak, whatever you want to call him, was doing from the spring of 1923 until the spring of 1925? And what about that ghost ship?"

He grabbed a pencil from his desk and threw it at me. "Get out of here, troublemaker. I've got work to do.

I wrote a letter to Ernie Pyle briefly outlining the end of the Roman Stankowski story. And every night or two I called Sue Baney, said, "Hello" and then moved the phone a foot from my ear because without fail she slammed the receiver down when she heard my voice. It sounded like someone slapping two boards together.

Was our year-long romance finished? I didn't know the answer any more than I knew what was going to happen with Europe seemingly on the brink of war. And that ghost ship—had those men really seen it, or were they the types that enjoyed stirring the pot just to get a rise out of people? Irishmen like Jack Eddy, maybe. I didn't really believe in such things, and ghost stories didn't do a thing for me. And yet . . .

I took some late evening walks on the gritty streets of East Akron, a little lost, a little lonely. Why, I wondered, did life have to be so complicated?

# PANIC ON PORTAGE PATH

The ransom note was delivered to the mansion on Portage Path on the postman's Monday morning round, the first of two on his schedule for the day. The crudely printed address did not contain a name, just the house number, street, and "city." After opening it along with the rest of the mail that had accumulated during their month at Bar Harbor, the residents, Quentin and Roberta Makepiece, were perplexed. The text consisted of letters cut from a magazine and newspaper. The message was concise: "If you pay $50,000 yor sun will be returned safely."

The Makepieces were in their seventies and their children, two daughters, were grown, married, and living far from Akron. Both had sons who were in their teens. After a hasty but concerned conference, Roberta Makepiece phoned their eldest daughter in Baltimore and then the other in California, forgetting the three hour difference in time. The latter, awakened from a sound sleep, grumpily agreed to check, then returned to the phone to say the two boys were safely in the bedroom they shared. The report from Baltimore had also been reassuring.

"Do you think it's someone's idea of a joke?" Mrs. Makepiece asked her husband.

"Not hardly. I think we had better notify the police."

Having arrived home late Sunday evening, the Makepieces were unaware of the excitement in the affluent neighborhood the previous Friday. On Saturday it had changed to panic, and by Sunday, to despair. Unknowing and unprepared, the response to Quentin's phone call left the elderly couple bewildered and more than a little frightened. Four Akron detectives were at their door within minutes, and close behind were two FBI agents. All doubt was removed that the letter might have been a poor joke.

I was making my rounds at Central Police Station when the call came in. After phoning *Times-Press* city editor Ben Goldsmith to say I was on my way to the west side and someone else would have to finish my routine checking of police reports, I hurried to where I had parked my 1934 Hupmobile. It was a fine car, an olive green sedan with black fenders and just a little more than fifty-five thousand miles on the odometer. It received rough treatment, though, in my haste to get to Portage Path, where I had spent much of the past three days. Sweat had soaked through my shirt by the time I arrived, and I was hoping that the remainder of August of 1938 would be cooler and less humid than the past week or two.

It had begun with a mass search of the neighborhood for the two-year-old son of a rubber company executive, Frederick Stauffer, and his wife, Joanne. The blond youngster called Bobby had been playing on the front lawn of a sprawling redbrick home directly across from the unoccupied residence of the Makepieces'. His nanny, a large woman in her forties named Prudence Longfellow, said she had a sudden and urgent need to use the bathroom and felt it would be perfectly safe to leave her charge alone for a few minutes. When she returned he was gone.

More than a dozen policemen were soon on the scene and the fruitless search was underway.

Portage Path was part of the route that Indians had followed while portaging their canoes between the Cuyahoga and Tuscarawas rivers. It was a street of stately homes occupied by those who had hit it big in the rubber industry and other lucrative businesses. I couldn't help but wonder if the response would have been the same had it been a child in Kenmore, East Akron, or some other working-class neighborhood.

There had been a possible witness to the kidnapping. The maid at the house to the south of the Stauffers' said she had been looking out a first-floor window when the nanny made her hurried trip inside. Within seconds, the maid said, a brown panel truck had pulled into the Stauffer's driveway, blocking her view of the child. Again, within seconds, the truck had backed out onto the street. The child was nowhere to be seen.

The maid had not noticed the number of the truck's license plate. In a short time she appeared less certain of the truck's color and a little unsure of herself in telling the police that crude white lettering on the panel read JOE'S RADIO SHOP. The wording, she said, was not the work of a professional sign painter and might even have been cut from some sort of material and applied with adhesive.

Although the area within a hundred miles of Akron was canvassed by police, they failed to find a Joe's Radio Shop. The closest was a Joe's Radio Shack in a small town near Mansfield, but the proprietor did not own a truck and had an airtight alibi for the day of the kidnapping.

A second letter arrived at the Makepiece house the following day. It said the nanny, unaccompanied by the police or anyone else, was to deliver the ransom money in well-circulated, small-denomination bills. She was to walk south along Seiberling Street in East Akron the following night with the money in a satchel. When the contact was made and the money handed over, the child would be given to her. If there was any sign of police in the area the boy would be killed. This note was handwritten by someone more literate than the writer of the first.

The police and FBI agents insisted on a presence in the neighborhood, one which offered little opportunity for concealment. The Stauffers were adamant in their refusal. Their only interest, they insisted, was the return of their son, not the apprehension of the kidnappers. They were emphatic in warning that if their wishes were not respected and anything went wrong they would make sure the resulting publicity reflected poorly on both the Akron police department and the FBI.

And so it was done their way, although the nanny appeared reluctant until reminded that it was her negligence that was responsible for the boy's abduction. An hour after she set out, walking south from East Market Street, a passing motorist saw the nanny lying beside the road. She had been hit on the head, but the wound was superficial. She said a car had pulled up beside her, a man had jumped out, grabbed the satchel, and struck her. It all happened so fast, she said, that she couldn't identify either the man or make, model, or color of the car. Nothing had been seen of the missing child. No one doubted her word.

Then the story died. Slowly at first, then day by day, less mention was made, until finally, two months later, there had been nothing at all for some time. The FBI pulled out, then the Akron police, although both swore the case was on the front burner and would remain so. There had been no new developments, though, and few people expected any would come.

For me it had been a quiet couple of months. The girl of my dreams, Sue Baney, said she was through with me, so there had been no dates with her or anyone else. My social life, if it could be called that, consisted of two Saturday afternoons spent by myself at Old Forge Field watching East High's football team beat Maple Heights 53-0 and Buchtel 52-0. At least life was moving smoothly for the Orientals, although their remaining games might change all that.

Even the police beat had been rather routine, and nothing much was happening in the lives of the other tenants at Mrs. Bauer's boardinghouse on Dudley Street, the place I called home. Jack Eddy was complaining that the private eye business was too slow for his liking, pudgy Mabel Klosterman had a couple of unmemorable dates with her sometimes boyfriend, the burly and slow-witted Joe Kurtz, and pretty Kitty Bauer seemed to have lost interest in Jack Eddy and now was dating a poor man's imitation of Rudolph Valentine in his role of the sheik.

After three weeks had passed with no mention of the kidnapping in any area newspaper, I drove to Portage Path and talked with Joanne Stauffer. She was low in spirit, discouraged by the lack of results and apparent lack of attention the kidnapping of her son was receiving from law enforcement agencies. That's when I told her about Jack Eddy. For more than a year the assistant manager of the Akron branch of Wellington's National Detective Agency had occupied the room across the hall from mine at the east side boardinghouse.

234

She was interested. In her opinion there was nothing to lose by hiring a private agency to look into the case, and the Stauffers certainly could afford the cost, whatever it might be. While I was still there she called Jack Eddy and set up an appointment with him at her home for that afternoon.

October had turned suddenly cool and you could feel the creeping up of winter, but I put on a warm sweater and was waiting on the porch when Jack Eddy arrived home half an hour before supper time. As he parked his sleek 1932 Auburn sedan behind my car I went down the steps to meet him. "Are you on the Stauffer case?" I asked.

I wasn't surprised, of course, when he nodded his head before saying, "Thanks for the recommendation, buddy. Guess I owe you a favor." He made it sound like owing me a favor was tantamount to having root-canal surgery.

I knew he had followed the story at the time it was hot news. He never commented on it, at least not to me, but I had seen him shake his head on several occasions after reading one of my stories in the *Times-Press.*

"Think you can do any good?"

"How the hell would I know at this point? The agency certainly can't do any worse than the police and those clowns from the Federal Bureau of Incompetency. It's too bad that Plato Largis was off on vacation in Greece or someplace at the time or the Akron cops might have figured it out."

"He's their best man, granted, but what could he have done that the other detectives didn't?"

"For starters he probably would have seen right away that the whole setup was phony. Those letters to the house across the street – what a joke they were. Do you honestly think that even the dumbest kidnappers wouldn't have known the right address for the Stauffers? Then there was the time they spent looking for that truck. All they had was the word of the next-door maid that it even existed. She was a loser from the word go, came across as either a complete idiot or a lousy liar. And they checked out the Stauffers' own maid and their cook to see if either had doctored the nanny's lunch to make her have that sudden need to rush to the bathroom. But tell me, what else did they do?"

"They checked out all the delivery people and other workers who came to the house. The yard man, for instance. The gas man, the mailman, those kinds of people."

"You're right, friend, they did all the routine things. The easy, obvious things. When something developed they hurried to investigate, but they were just putting out fires. Nobody was using any imagination."

"Well, the FBI agents—"

"Played like they were Melvin Purvis chasing Dillinger or Pretty Boy Floyd. They tapped a couple of phones and waited for informants to give them a tip. That's what the FBI does best, but when it comes to knocking on doors and doing the legwork, they aren't too enthusiastic. The police should have put Plato Largis in charge as soon as he was back in town. He would have brought a little imagination to the job."

"Taking others off the case and giving it to him wouldn't have been following protocol."

Jack Eddy laughed, repeated "protocol" like it was a four letter word, and gave me a one-knuckle punch that left my right arm feeling paralyzed. After blinking back a few tears, I said, "So what are your plans?"

"Plans? Do you think we're waiting for Christmas or something? We started working on it as soon as I got back to the agency. I've got Cal Andres doing a background check on the maid next door and Cliff Austin doing the same on the nanny."

"The cops have done that, Jack."

"Yeah, sure they did. We look at things from a little different angle, buddy."

He could have said that again and been correct, but I didn't say so. The police were bound by a lot of rules that the Wellington Agency ignored. Sometimes their unorthodox methods produced results because they seldom worried about building a case to take to court. As a result, they were held in respect by citizens, scorned by less efficient cops and feared by criminals who knew the agency could get rough when someone like Jack Eddy felt it was a good idea.

Jack was a complex man, one I had never been able to figure out. He was excessively ambitious, determined to work his way to the top of Wellington's hierarchy, and he didn't much care how he did it or who got hurt along the way. On the other hand, I had seen him down on a dirty basement floor helping a kid with his Soap Box Derby car. Then, too, a couple of times when he thought I might be in over my head he had showed up unannounced and without a client to foot the bill. And thanks to Jack I had enjoyed the inside track on some good stories. But he could be ruthless when the need arose, as I had witnessed a few times. He stood only five eleven compared to my own six three, and his sandy brown hair was growing thin on top. That and his round Irish face could easily have led someone to think he might be a pushover. The truth was that Jack Eddy was hard as nails. I was always thankful to be on his good side and not someone he was hunting down.

I tapped on the door of his room late the next night. He had missed supper and only arrived home fifteen minutes earlier, obviously weary. "Where do things stand?" I asked.

"On the Stauffer case? Have you ever really looked over the layout there, buddy? The house to the north is quite a distance away and shielded by trees. On the other side of Portage Path the only house or yard with a view of the Stauffers is the Makepiece place, and they were away on vacation. That leaves those in the house to the south or someone in a car on the street as the only possible witnesses to the kidnapping. Traffic is light along there, the man in the next house was at work, and the woman was at a club meeting. The only one there was the maid, and her version of what happened leaves me cold. Cal Andres has found out a few interesting things about her, so maybe by tomorrow I'll have something' concrete to tell you. Right now I'm going to hit the hay, so you can hit the road."

At the police station the next morning I sought out Plato Largis. When I walked in the door of his office, he grinned and said, "Bram Geary, ace reporter. What's on your mind, kid?" I was expecting him to explode when he heard that Jack Eddy was poking around in the Stauffer kidnapping. Instead, he sat at his desk, nodding his head as I filled him in. When I was through he said, "He may be right. I'll have your head in a basket if you mention this to anyone else, but I don't think the investigation was handled too well. What he said about imagination, I kind of agree."

I was anxious to find out what progress was being made, so after completing my afternoon rounds I walked north on Main Street to the Wellington office in the Metropolitan Building. I was there so often the cute, blond elevator operator didn't ask what floor I wanted, just took me up to the fifth. Apparently she thought I was another Wellington operative. I didn't mind, even played the role a little.

I had arrived, it turned out, shortly after Cal Andres had ushered the next-door maid into Jack Eddy's office. Jack came out to tell me so and asked if I wanted to sit in on their interrogation. I did, of course, although it turned out to be a little upsetting.

From the first, I had sized up the maid, Gertrude Slade, as somewhat of a dim bulb. She was a stocky woman in her mid twenties, about five three, with oily-looking black hair and eyes set too close together. She was scared out of her wits, what little she had, and neither Jack nor Cal was doing anything to put her at ease.

Before going back into his office Jack had told me that she had an older sister, Florence. The two had shared a cheap apartment above a store on South Arlington Street, although Gertrude spent most of her nights at the house where she worked on Portage Path. Florence was looked upon as reclusive and aloof in the neighborhood. The interesting part, however, was that she had left the day of the kidnapping and hadn't been seen since.

"The police found that out, Jack. I heard about it before."

"Sure. Of course they did, but they let it drop when Gertrude said her sister just happened to leave on vacation that day. Guess they never got around to checking to see if she came back again. She still hasn't."

Once we were in the office, Jack and Cal gave Gertrude a real grilling. "Where's Florence?" was repeated again and again. After hearing "I don't know" a dozen times, Jack said, "You know taking part in a kidnapping is a capital offense. It's called the Lindbergh Law because it was enacted after the Lindbergh baby was kidnapped, and it can get you strapped in the hot seat down at

Columbus. You want to risk that, Gert, or do you want to cooperate?"

The woman was at the point of incoherence, totally confused and unsure of what to do. It was obvious that she knew more than she had ever let on, but just as obvious that she was equally afraid of something or someone else, perhaps sister Florence. When it seemed they weren't going to get anywhere with her, Cal said, "Where are you from, Gertie?"

"Gharkeyville/[1] she replied, then immediately seemed to regret it. "But I haven't been there in years." After thinking about it for a moment more she added, "Neither has Florence."

"How do you know that?" asked Jack Eddy. "You said you didn't know where she is since she left back in August. Why not Gharkeyville?"

Gertrude was extremely agitated. "No, no, no. She'd never go there. She has to be somewhere else."

"Why wouldn't she go there, Gert? Seems to me like the very place she would go."

She was befuddled, desperate as to what to say next. Finally she croaked, "No, no, no," again. "She can't be in Gharkeyville, so please forget that idea."

Cal Andres looked at Jack and said, "That's where she is, Gharkeyville. No doubt about it, Jack."

Gertrude screamed, "No! No, she isn't! Please, please forget that!"

Even I could tell that Florence was in Gharkeyville. But why did it upset her sister that way? "Because," said Jack Eddy when I asked him later, "she's got the Stauffer kid there."

"You really think so?"

"I'd bet my last dollar on it."

"Where the heck is Gharkeyville?"

"In southwest West Virginia, just a couple of miles from the Kentucky state line. We knew that, by the way, before Cal asked her. Remember that miserable little town of Switchback you went to last spring?"

"How could I forget?"

"Well, from what we've learned, Gharkeyville makes Switchback seem like the Garden of Eden. It's another coal mining town down in Hatfield and McCoy territory. Cal knows

239

a little about it because he grew up in a place like it on the other side of the state line."

"Cal doesn't seem the type. He's so suave and well spoken I'd never have taken him for a hillbilly."

"That's your problem, friend. One of them. You stereotype people, try to fit them into a little niche. Cal has worked hard to become the way he is. Maybe you've never noticed, but he's one hell of an actor. He can play any role you could name, and that's one of the reasons why he's so good at his job. So anyway, have you got any vacation time coming?"

"About five days. Why?" Then the light dawned. "Now wait a minute, Jack . . ."

So we talked about it for a while. "It could be a big story, buddy." Jack said, then a minute later said it again. "Maybe the biggest of your career."

"Not to mention yours. Look, if you think I'm going to spend my vacation time in a place like Gharkeyville—"

"It's up to you, pal. I hear Tom Kennedy at the *Beacon Journal* is fed up with being scooped on the police beat, so he'd probably jump at the chance to go along."

"You know what you are, Jack? You're an extortionist, an . . . an arm twister. You have the mind of a criminal."

He laughed and punched me on the chest. "Of course I do. How else could I be so good at my job?"

"It takes one to know one, isn't that what they say?"

"Know your enemy, buddy. Always know your enemy."

"Dammit, Jack, you've got me over a barrel. So when do you leave?"

"First thing tomorrow morning."

I did my best to work it to my advantage. "Look, Ben," I said to my city editor, "it could break the Stauffer kidnapping wide open. You want me to get first crack at the story, don't you?"

Ben Goldsmith leaned back in his chair, either smirking or sneering, I wasn't sure which. "From what little you've told me, it sounds like another one of your wild-goose chases. But I'll tell you what I'll do. If it turns out you're right, then you've been on company time. Only eight hours a day, though, no overtime. If you're wrong, well, you've been on vacation."

It sounded reasonable. Except that bit about one of my wild-goose chases. Just what was he talking about? I wondered.

It didn't make me happy when Jack said we'd go in my car. "The Auburn would draw too much attention in a place like Gharkeyville," he said. "Chances are the people there have never seen one, but they won't notice another old clunker."

He knew that would get under my skin. The Hupmobile was a far cry from an old clunker. One good thing about taking it, though, was that I'd be behind the wheel. I packed a small suitcase in the morning and was out at the car a few seconds ahead of Jack. After tossing his bag on the backseat, he said, "I'll drive."

We headed due south and made good time to Marietta. We ate lunch there at a downtown diner. When we were settled in a booth where no one could overhear, I said, "You've been holding out on me, Jack. There's more to it than you've told me, isn't there? There has to be, or you wouldn't be driving all the way down to Gharkeyville."

He lifted one eyebrow, then gave a careless shrug, as if to say I was wasting his time. "Nothing important, buddy. Cal Andres found a store that sells secondhand stuff near the sisters' apartment. One day the owner had a little yellow sunsuit in the window. Something for a kid about two. He had seen Florence around the neighborhood, but never with a kid, so he was surprised when she came in and bought it. He showed her a few other things he had for someone that size, and she seemed to enjoy looking over the stuff. Then she suddenly got nervous and hurried out of the place.

"On top of that, Cal saw a woman pushing one of those— what do they call them? Taylor Tots?—with a boy about two in it. He talked to her a while, mentioned Florence, and the woman said she was glad Florence was gone because she scared her."

"Scared her? How?"

"Every time she saw her, Florence made a big fuss over the boy. It got so it was happening so regularly the woman got the idea Florence was lying in wait for her. She felt there was something unnatural about it, and it frightened her."

"Sounds like Florence may have been around the bend."

"You called it for once, buddy. There are women like that, you know. Get obsessed with someone else's kid because they don't have one of their own. There's one more thing. Cal checked the county records and found that Florence had a baby at City Hospital six months after she came to Akron a few years back. It was a boy, stillborn."

And Jack Eddy had said all that was nothing important. Our food arrived and we didn't talk anymore until we finished eating. I thought about what he had told me, of course. I had to agree with that mother, it was kind of scary.


Marietta is a pretty little town on the north bank of the Ohio River, so I wouldn't have minded hanging around for a while. That was out of the question, and we soon were back on the road. Or to be more accurate, a series of them that got progressively worse as we went up, down, and around the precipitous hills that West Virginians call mountains. They might not be the Alps or the Rockies, but driving through them was just as difficult, maybe more so.

After what seemed an eternity we came to a sign telling us we had arrived at Gharkeyville. Like others we had seen along the way, the sign was riddled with bullet holes. I was totally spent, as worn out as if it had been the longest ride of my life. Actually, when I thought about it, it *had* been the longest ride of my life. I had been to Fort Wayne once and Pittsburgh a couple of times, but fell far short of being a world traveler. I had an ominous feeling that that would change in the next few years, thanks to Adolph Hitler. He claimed that after being handed a large chunk of Czechoslovakia he had no further territorial demands in Europe. The amazing thing was that some people actually believed him.

As promised, Gharkeyville was a dismal little town. Tired as I was, though, it looked okay to me. Best of all was finding that it possessed a hotel, or something that passed for one. I was eager to flop down on a bed and was almost, but not quite, ready to pass up Jack Eddy's offer to buy dinner. The diner a couple of doors down the street was as bad, if not worse than the one in Switchback, where the waitress snarled at customers and the main offering on the menu was a greaseburger. I settled for pork chops, which were a little on the thin side but not too bad, and home fries that had been cremated and were ready for a well-deserved burial.

I awoke refreshed in the morning. For breakfast we found another diner that was a slight cut above the one where we had eaten the previous night. The waitress gave me a quick smile before starting to flirt with Jack. For the umpteenth time I wondered what it was about Jack Eddy that attracted females like flypaper attracts flies. I was taller, better looking, and had a far more pleasing personality, and yet they completely ignored me when Jack was around.

I was eager to hear what he had planned for us to do but wasn't too thrilled when he gave me my orders. I was to drive to the nearby county seat and check various records at the courthouse, a boring assignment. He was just going to nose around a little to see what he could learn. I had a sneaking suspicion that while I would be poring over musty old records, Jack Eddy would be spending time learning more about that waitress.

Most of the things I found in the records seemed of little importance to me. Florence wasn't married when she left home, or at least hadn't been in that county. She was thirty and her sister Gertrude was twenty-six. The elder Slades also had two sons, Anse, who was thirty-two and R. B., twenty-eight. It appeared that the parents and even a couple of grandparents were still alive and living at the family homestead. Aside from the father and one male grandparent, the only one with a criminal record was Anse. His sheet was as long as my arm.

The tax maps were of some interest. The Slades owned a large tract back in the hills a couple of miles from Gharkeyville. If the map was accurate, the land was on a county road, probably dirt, that ended at their property. Isolated as could be.

Jack Eddy was having lunch at the place where we had eaten breakfast when I arrived back in Gharkeyville. A different waitress was on duty, which made me wonder when the other had clocked out and where Jack had been at the time. I showed him the notes I had made, then asked what he had found out.

"Nothing," he said in a disgusted tone. "These people won't talk to an outsider. I didn't want to come right out and ask about the Slades, but subtlety gets you nowhere down here."

I smirked a little and couldn't help saying, "The great Jack Eddy swaggered to the plate and was called out on three pitches."

I thought he was going to slug me, but he managed to contain himself. After a pause that allowed him to regain his equilibrium, he said, "Cal Andres is on his way. Should be here before midnight. Cliff Austin is with him. If you see either one don't act like you recognize them, just walk on by."

"Both of them coming? You must be expecting a war."

"Cal knows how to talk to people around here, we don't. Cliff is just for backup."

We sat quietly for a few minutes. If we needed backup it did indeed sound like Jack was expecting serious trouble. I had a disquieting thought. "Jack, Anse Slade shot some guy about the time Florence headed up to Akron. Maybe it was the one that got her pregnant. Anyway, the fellow didn't die, so Anse got six months, suspended."

"I'm not sure that shooting someone is a serious offense in these parts."

"Another thing, Jack. A while back I read a book called *Battle Cry* that was set somewhere around here, and it had a couple of characters named Anse. One was Bad Anse. Did you ever hear of anyone named Anse before we came down here?"

Jack leaned his head back and laughed. "God, but you have a way of hitting on the trivial, friend."

I was bored out of my mind until the middle of the next morning when I saw Cal Andres. He was wearing a worn pair of bib overalls, a tattered flannel shirt, and was leaning up against a post on Main Street whittling a stick of wood with a nasty-looking knife. Several other men were nearby doing pretty much the same thing. It seemed to be a major pastime in Gharkeyville. How could people stand to live that way? I wondered. I would have been willing to bet that not a single one of them, Cal excluded, had ever heard of Hitler, let alone Czechoslovakia.

There was a weekly newspaper, though. It ran obits on the front page along with admissions to the hospital at the county seat. Releases, too, of those who hadn't moved over to the obituary column. There were the expected chicken dinner reports from the various towns and villages in the vicinity so you could keep up to date on who visited whom the past week. If you checked closely you could find that some people ate at the expense of their friends five or six nights a week. Also which single males and single females seemed to always show up at the same house at suppertime.

So social activity in the county appeared brisk. Privacy, at least with a large segment of the population, was not sought after, especially at mealtime. The *Gharkeyville Gazette* contained some church news, a few stories concerning coal mines or a store opening or closing, but not a word on national or world events.

I searched in vain for a paper from a larger city. The man behind the counter at a variety store said they received the paper from Charleston but were sold out. "How many copies do you get?"

"Two. One of 'em's reserved for Doc Singletary."

"Then you actually sell one copy?"

"Yup." That ended the conversation.

The news on the radio station at the county seat was more of the same, obits and hospital admissions and releases. Closed in by the surrounding hills, cut off from the outside world, it could have been medieval times rather than 1938. Aside from the decrepit cars and trucks on the street, of course.

Flat caps were part of the uniform for the males of Gharkeyville, although a few broke ranks by wearing battered fedoras that made my old one look pretty good. The youths that weren't wearing flat caps wore those little beanies made from the crown of an old fedora with the bottom turned up and scalloped. The women were nearly all clad in shapeless print housedresses, and most of the young girls wore dresses made from patterned flour sacks, also shapeless. Occasionally I saw an overweight woman, but most of them, like the men, were thin and had drawn, pinched faces. Depression faces, a sign of the times seen everywhere, but more pronounced in Gharkeyville.

It was late evening before we had a council of war in Jack's room at the hotel. Cal Andres did most of the talking. He had wormed his way into the trust of a few people that took him for one of their own. Cal was an enigma. In a suit and tie he could pass for a successful businessman or a rubber company junior executive and was able to mingle at will with those types. In bib overalls and a flat cap he was perfectly at home on the streets of Gharkeyville. He wasn't a big man, no more than five nine, but he worked out at a gym almost daily, so he was wiry and strong as a bull. Before coming to Gharkeyville he had shaved off the slim, Clark Gable-style mustache and mussed up the slicked-back dark hair that gave him the appearance of a Latin romancer. He could stand out in a crowd or lose himself completely in one, whatever suited the occasion. In a sense, he was a human chameleon, an ideal private eye.

"The Slades could be dangerous, Jack," he said. "They run a big still on their property, and the sheriff and the revenuers leave them alone. They peddle their moonshine over a large area, but from what I heard, most of the buyers pick the stuff up themselves. Nobody came right out and said he was afraid of the Slades, but I could tell that people give them a wide berth, especially Anse. He doesn't run the moonshine business, the father does that, but he's the strongman of the operation. Back home we'd call him an enforcer for the mob. Oh, and one more thing, Anse has a brown panel truck.

"The other son, R. B., is regarded as a pretty nice fellow. As for Florence, she's looked on as a little 'tetched' as they say down here. Now here's the interesting part: She showed up a couple of months ago with a kid, a boy about two she claims she had while up north. The husband she had married up there had died, or so she told everybody. We know that was a lie. For a week or two she was showing the kid off around town. Since then she hasn't been seen."

Jack Eddy shook his head for a moment, then gave a curt laugh. "I think I get the whole picture now. It's about like we figured, this Florence was nuts to have a kid. One day she was visiting her sister Gertrude on Portage Path and got a look at the Stauffer boy. He was the one, none other would do. It was easy to talk Gertrude into going along with her plan, and she managed to recruit Anse for the job. From the sound of him that wasn't too difficult.

"It worked to perfection until it was Gertrude's time to play her role. She's incredibly stupid, so when she talked to the police about seeing the panel truck she got all flustered, and when asked to describe it she could only remember her brother's truck. It was probably supposed to be black or red, but she said brown. Then she managed to recover enough to tell about the fake lettering. Next she had the job of mailing the ransom letters. I never would have believed it possible, but she was dumb enough to get the wrong address on the envelopes. Florence must have written the second letter and left it with Gertrude to mail later.

"In the meantime, Anse, Florence, and the kid were either back in Gharkeyville or well on their way. None of them are what you would call heavy on the gray matter, and yet they managed to pull off a pretty decent snatch, one they almost got away with. They let Florence run loose with the kid for a couple of weeks, but something happened, and now they've got her tucked away at home. The question is how do we get the boy and Florence away from that mountain hideout and back to Akron. The cops can take care of picking up Anse. And I don't mean the local cops. Whatever, he's none of our concern except for dealing with him when we pick up Florence and the kid."

Cliff Austin said, "It won't be easy, Jack. I used Bram's little sketch and drove up there in Cal's car this afternoon. Man, talk about isolated. The way I see it, we'll have to approach on foot and by going through the woods. There's a Y in the road about half a mile away. We can have Bram park his car there because we'll need one and then give him a signal or a time when he should drive up to the house."

I didn't like the sound of that one bit.

"And we have to remember," said Cal Andres, "that these are hill people. The men will all have guns. That means four of them. Chances are that Anse is the only one that knows

Florence's story is phony, so the others will think that *we're* the kidnappers. Like Cliff said, it won't be easy."

Again, Jack Eddy's laugh was curt. "Since when did any of us look for easy jobs?"

If it hadn't been for foolish manly pride, not to mention embarrassment, I would have raised my hand and shouted, "Me!"


The next day was the shortest of my life. The hands on the clock just seemed to whirl around out of control, and all too soon it was evening. We checked out of the hotel, left Cal's car parked along the street leading out of town, then the four of us drove in my car to the dirt road leading to the Slade homestead. As planned, I was to wait at the point where the road forked off to the left; the other three took off on foot. The signal for me to pick them up would be gunfire. That was a comforting thought as I began my lonely vigil.

It was only later that I learned what transpired when they reached the house. Cal Andres did a bit of stealthy window peeping and found the entire family, including the Stauffer boy, gathered in the living room listening to a program on radio. Cal and Jack Eddy moved to the rear of the house, Cliff Austin to the front.

The fun began with Cliff firing two shots in the air. Anse Slade, who was carrying a pistol in his jacket, rushed out the front door as Jack and Cal charged in the back. Cliff leveled Anse Slade with a bullet in the leg. Cal stopped R.B. and the two older men from reaching the rack holding their rifles. Jack swooped up the kid in one arm and Florence in the other. All the women were screaming their heads off.

I came careening up the rutted drive within seconds after Cal and Jack came out of the front door. Everyone piled into my car. Florence was still screaming and trying to put up a fight. As we roared off back down the drive, someone at the house began firing. I gave the Hupmobile a little more gas when I heard a bullet ping off its back end.

Then we were in the clear. "They'll be after us, Jack," I yelled.

Jack, Cal, and Cliff laughed. "Not until they hike somewhere to get a vehicle," Jack said. "Cliff has the distributor caps off the two back there at the house."

We dropped off Cal and Cliff at the other car, then headed north as fast as the hills would allow. Cal's car, a souped-up 1935 Buick, was close behind. It was tricky enough driving those narrow, winding roads with daylight making the curves and other hazards visible. At night it was tortuous. Jack was in the backseat with Florence. Her right hand was cuffed to the armrest, her left to Jack Eddy. The child was asleep on the seat to his left.

At Jack's orders we didn't take the most direct route, the one we had followed on the way down. Florence began keening as soon as we were on the open road. It was the fearful cry of an agonized banshee. After fifteen minutes of it, Jack stuffed a handkerchief in her mouth.

I breathed a sigh of relief when a little before first light we crossed the Ohio River on the Silver Bridge at Gallipolis. We were still in hilly country, but it wasn't anything like that around Gharkeyville. Near Logan we pulled up at a roadside diner and parked well away from the other cars and pickup trucks. Cal Andres pulled his Buick up beside us, and he and Cliff went inside. A short time later they came back with food for the rest of us. Florence refused to eat, which didn't come as a shock.

In the meantime, I had checked the rear of my car and found a bullet hole in the left fender. Fortunately it was above the level of the tire or anything else of importance. Just seeing it, though, made me even more aware of how easily our adventure could have ended in disaster. With a disabled car, armed men in pursuit, and two miles from town, what would we have done? I didn't even want to think about it.

Jack Eddy made a call from a phone booth on the outskirts of Canton, and half an hour later we saw the Akron city limit sign. I did as ordered and stopped in front of the downtown police station. Cal parked right behind us. Jack and Cal got the handcuffs off Florence, and then Cliff Austin frog-marched her inside. The few people on the sidewalk stood gawking as over and over she screamed, "Give me back my baby!"

Fifteen minutes later we pulled into the Stauffers' driveway. Jack Eddy had called the house from the police station, so both of them were waiting outside for us. Joanne began crying as soon as she had the boy in her arms. Jack gave her husband a brief summary of what had happened, then we both got a kiss from Joanne before we headed back downtown.

The only way for the *Times-Press* to beat the *Beacon Journal* was to put out an extra. It was a big enough event to warrant one, and my story created a sensation throughout the city. Only it wasn't actually my story. Ben Goldsmith had a rewrite man handle it with me feeding him the details. I was mentioned only as "a *Times-Press* reporter." Goldsmith said, "We're not having another first-person story with you coming out the hero." I didn't really care but was a little put out that I didn't even get to share the byline. Uppermost in my mind was getting home to the boardinghouse and falling into a deep, well-earned sleep.

And thus it ended, or so I thought. Goldsmith had given me the next day off, as he should have, and I decided to spend it doing nothing but loafing around home. The weather had warmed up nicely, so I was relaxing on the front porch swing enjoying the escapades of Perry Mason in the latest Earle Stanley Gardner novel until Mrs. Bauer called me to the telephone. It was Jack Eddy on the line with a curt message, "Get down here, buddy, pronto."

I did, but reluctantly and grudgingly. Ben Goldsmith was my boss, so I didn't mind taking orders from him, but those coming from Jack Eddy were getting a little annoying. I lingered on the elevator at the Metropolitan Building, though, and made a date for the next night with the cute operator.

I was surprised to find Gertrude Slade coming out of Jack Eddy's office. Mac McKelvey was gripping her arm as he escorted her to another room down the hall. "We've had her stashed away next door at the Howe Hotel," Jack told me. "One of our female operatives was in the room with her, and Mac and another man rotated on keeping watch in the hall outside."

Before I could ask why, Cliff Austin came in prodding Prudence Longfellow, the Stauffers' nanny, toward us. She appeared angry, but it was just a facade. In reality you could see she was frightened half out of her mind. Jack wasn't gentle with her. After sitting her down in a chair, he said, "The jig's up, Prude, so let's not waste time. We know all about it, so come clean and have it over with."

She tried to brazen it out, but her voice was quivering as she said, "I don't know what you're talking about."

"Have it your way, kiddo." He picked up his phone. After a few seconds he said, "Bring her in."

When half a minute later Gertrude Slade was brought into the room, Prudence Longfellow blanched and gave a little gasp. "It's all over, Prude," said Jack, "so let's hear it in your own words."

Prudence knew he was right as soon as she saw Gertrude, the erstwhile next-door maid. She began crying. In a teary, choked-up voice she began, "I was coerced into going along with it by that horrible woman."

"Florence Slade?"

She nodded her head, wiped away the tears on her cheeks, blew her nose, and continued, "She found out about something in my past. I'm not going to tell you what it was, but she said if I didn't help them she would tell the Stauffers and then see that I never got another job."

The gist of the matter was that Prudence had just handed the boy to Gertrude and then hurried into the house, pretending she had to use the bathroom, making sure the Stauffers' maid saw her. Gertrude in turn said that she gave the child to Florence, who had been waiting. Anse Slade was there as well. He and Florence drove away in his car with the boy on Florence's lap. They headed straight for Gharkeyville.

"And it was Anse who took the money from you on Seiberling Street, then gave you a light tap on the head," Jack Eddy said to Prudence. "You were lucky he didn't kill you so they wouldn't have had to split the ransom with you."

Prudence nodded her head. "I only got a third of the ransom. How did you find out about it?"

"I did some checking on you," said Cliff Austin. "The first thing that seemed odd was that you moved into a more expensive apartment even though you were out of a job for the time being. When I found out you had bought a used car, that was the clincher in my book. I dug a little deeper and learned what it was that Florence held over your head to make you cooperate. It wasn't that big a deal, lady. You should have told her to get lost."

So now it really was all over. It gave me another good story, of course, but I was sick of the whole affair. The four participants were headed for lengthy stays in Federal prisons, but someone else could handle those stories.

My date with the elevator operator, Gail Robinson, didn't turn out too good. She was cute as could be, pleasant too, but she didn't have much upstairs except the blond curls on top of her head. To say the conversation lagged at times would be an understatement.

My heart, I had to admit to myself, belonged to my old girlfriend, Sue Baney. For months now she wouldn't talk to me, just banged down the phone as soon as she heard my voice until I quit even trying to call. It was Jack Eddy's fault, or so it seemed to me, because Sue had given up on me when I had tagged along on another of his cases that involved shooting. She didn't want a dead boyfriend, she said. I had to laugh ruefully when I thought of what she would say if she knew that my car now sported a bullet hole.

I wanted to forget the Stauffer-Slade case, but it kept popping up in my mind. So many lives ruined, so much worry and despair, all because a mentally unstable woman was fixated on having a child to replace her own that was stillborn. And not just any child, only the Stauffer boy would do. I took up my old habit of walking the streets of East Akron at night. I was looking for answers, I suppose, but didn't find any along the empty streets or by staring at the same old displays in the windows of locked stores. The world wasn't a pretty place, but it was foolish of me to think I could do anything to make it better. Even so I wanted to.

I was surprised when I walked into Kippy's at lunchtime one day and saw Sue Baney seated at the counter. I was even more surprised a few minutes later when she came over and stood by my stool. I looked around, opened my mouth, but found I was tongue-tied. Sue hesitated a moment, then cleared her throat before saying, "I just want to say that it was heroic of you to do what you did in rescuing that kidnapped little boy, Bram."

I cleared my throat, too, and croaked, "You read about it in the paper?"

"Yes, and Jack Eddy called me to elaborate on the part you played. He said you were the key to the success of the whole operation."

That was so like him. Jack Eddy didn't hesitate to involve me in something that might easily get me killed and then turn around and make it seem that I was the hero. And to phone my estranged girlfriend in hope of getting us back together.

Sue turned and walked toward the door, then looked back and said, "Call me sometime . . . if you feel like it."

My heart leaped up to my throat. I watched her walk away, admiring her trim little body and the swaying of her hips. When she was gone I checked my watch. It was going on one o'clock, so I would have to wait six more hours before picking up the phone.

# ALSO AVAILABLE BY DICK STODGHILL

**The Case Files of Jack Eddy – Volume 1**
The first eight stories in the series from Alfred Hitchcock Mystery Magazine: Blowup, The Old Squad, Seven Dollar Death, A Deceitful Way of Dying, Pictures in a Book, Deadly Money, Cast a Final Ballot, A Clinical Interest in Murder.

**The Rough Old Stuff**
Sixteen stories published from 1979 through 1985 in Mike Shayne Mystery Magazine.

**Midland Murders**
Eight stories from Alfred Hitchcock Mystery Magazine and one from Ellery Queen Mystery Magazine set in Midland, Indiana, a city easily recognizable as Muncie..

## NON-FICTION

**Normandy 1944 – A Young Rifleman's War**
The Battle of Normandy, neither glamorized nor sanitized as seen from ground level by an 18-year-old infantry rifleman.

**The Hoosier Hot Shots – And My Friend Gabe**
The story of three young musicians from the flatlands of Central Indiana who began performing without pay early in the Great Depression and went on to have their own coast-to-coast radio show, make 300 recordings and appear in 22 movies.

**From Devout Catholic to Communist Agitator – The Helen Lynch Story**
Details the strange life of a religious girl from Indiana who was expected to go on to a great literary career when she graduated from the University of Michigan in 1923. Instead she became a Communist working on behalf of the poor in New York City.

www.ingramcontent.com/pod-product-compliance
Lightning Source LLC
Chambersburg PA
CBHW050504260626
47157CB00004B/1179